"Here's a recipe for success: Start with a likeable, engaging sleuth determined to achieve her dream, despite everyone's objections, and add the complications of murder and kidnapping. Then stir in a large dose of family drama, a dishy lawyer, a difficult would-be fiancé, and lots of humor. Season with murder and kidnapping, then garnish with those sweet and savory biscuit bowls, and oh my, what a delicious mystery. Fast, fun, and so foodworthy!"

—Victoria Abbott, author of the Book Collector Mysteries

"Readers are treated to an eclectic cast of characters and a great new cozy heroine in Zoe Chase. J. J. Cook shows readers how it's done by giving them a well-thought-out mystery that will have them on the edge of their seats . . . A great new book." —Debbie's Book Bag

"Filled with colorful characters . . . I desperately wanted to try one of Zoe's deep-fried biscuit bowls! The descriptions of the various sweet and savory fillings had my mouth watering. This is a fantastic new culinary cozy series with a feisty, determined protagonist who I look forward to watching make her dreams come true." —Melissa's Mochas, Mysteries & Meows

"Witty, surprising, and sweet . . . I highly recommend this delightful cozy to anyone who enjoys cooking, mystery, and a touch of romance and whimsy . . . I, for one, am looking forward to the next book in the series. Zoe and Crème Brûlée are a hit." —Open Book Society

"Truly wonderful characters . . . [A] fantastic mystery . . . J. J. Cook has cooked up a real winner . . . I could not put it down." —Escape with Dollycas in a Good Book

continued . . .

"Lighthearted and funny . . . filled with delightfully eccentric and lovable characters . . . Sure to please fans who relish mysteries filled with recipes, pets, humor, and romance."

—*Kings River Life Magazine*

PRAISE FOR THE NATIONAL BESTSELLING SWEET PEPPER FIRE BRIGADE MYSTERIES

PLAYING WITH FIRE

"Engrossing . . . J. J. Cook is a master at cliffhangers."

—*Lesa's Book Critiques*

"I love the series and look forward to the next book. While I wait, I may just try a recipe or two from the back of the book."

—MyShelf.com

"The characters are a lot of fun [and] the town is a place you'd like to visit."

—*Kings River Life Magazine*

THAT OLD FLAME OF MINE

"Dark family secrets, a delicious mystery—and a ghost! What reader could ask for more?"

—Casey Daniels, author of the Pepper Martin Mysteries

"This book was so difficult for me to put down, and even more difficult for me to have it end. I could have continued reading this series forever."

—*Cozy Mystery Reviews*

"A fascinating, successful mystery. It's hard to go wrong with an intriguing mystery involving a ghost, a strong female character in a role normally reserved for men, and a spark of romance. J. J. Cook is kindling a sizzling good mystery series."

—*Lesa's Book Critiques*

FRY
Another
DAY

J. J. COOK

BERKLEY PRIME CRIME, NEW YORK

THE BERKLEY PUBLISHING GROUP
Published by the Penguin Group
Penguin Group (USA) LLC
375 Hudson Street, New York, New York 10014

USA • Canada • UK • Ireland • Australia • New Zealand • India • South Africa • China

penguin.com

A Penguin Random House Company

FRY ANOTHER DAY

A Berkley Prime Crime Book / published by arrangement with the authors

Berkley Prime Crime Books are published by The Berkley Publishing Group.
BERKLEY® PRIME CRIME and the PRIME CRIME logo
are trademarks of Penguin Group (USA) LLC.

For information, address: The Berkley Publishing Group,
a division of Penguin Group (USA) LLC,
375 Hudson Street, New York, New York 10014.

ISBN: 978-0-425-26346-4

PUBLISHING HISTORY
Berkley Prime Crime mass-market edition / February 2015

PRINTED IN THE UNITED STATES OF AMERICA

10 9 8 7 6 5 4 3 2 1

Cover illustration by Griesbach and Martucci.
Cover design by Jason Gill.
Interior text design by Laura K. Corless.

For foodies everywhere!

ONE

"Can you really make a biscuit out of sweet potatoes, Zoe?" Delia asked.

"I'm not sure," I replied. "I guess we'll find out."

It was four A.M. on the downtown streets of Charlotte, North Carolina. It was dark and quiet in the city. A line of food trucks with names like Stick It Here, Meggie's Mushrooms, and my food truck—the Biscuit Bowl—were in place as though they were waiting for the lunch crowd.

Only extra early.

It was the first morning of the Sweet Magnolia Food Truck Race. Ten food trucks from across the Southeast United States were competing for a fifty-thousand-dollar grand prize. Even if I didn't win the cash, the race was being shown on national food networks, which would be good publicity for the Biscuit Bowl.

How great was that?

The organizers had made it clear the day before the race started that there would be plenty of challenges, and even a few tricks, along the five stops beginning in Charlotte and ending in my hometown of Mobile, Alabama.

They weren't kidding.

We'd spent the night in Charlotte to be up early the first morning. Lucky for me, the race sponsors were footing the bill for the hotel and food. There was big money involved from businesses across the South, and for the charities that would receive donations from the race. The promotion was getting lots of media attention. I was happy to be part of it.

I hadn't been sure if my old Airstream RV, which had been converted to a food truck, was up for the long drive, but it came through like a champ. Lucky I had Uncle Saul with me to work on it as needed.

The challenge for today had been announced the night before once all the food truck teams were in Charlotte. We were starting off with each food truck making their specialty item with sweet potatoes replacing one ingredient. Once the item was made, we had to sell at least one hundred of them in the heart of the city, and get twenty people to say they were delicious.

I hoped my team was ready.

"Yeah, you can make 'em," Ollie said. "But what are they gonna taste like?"

"They're going to be great!" I enthused to make up for my team's lack of excitement. "You'll see. Get the flour."

My specialty was the biscuit bowl. A delicious, large biscuit made with an indentation in the middle, and deep-fried. My truck was named for it. My hopes and dreams were pinned on it.

I made my biscuit bowls fresh every day, filling the centers with either sweet or savory foods. It could be anything from chili to spicy apples. I tried to mix it up as much as possible.

Someday, I hoped to own a restaurant that brought people in from all over the world. I had the restaurant—*well*, a diner—but it needed about fifty thousand dollars' worth of renovation to bring it up to code.

That's why I'd started my food truck business. It was also a good reason to enter the food truck race.

"So you're gonna use the sweet potatoes with the flour, egg, and milk to make the biscuits?" Uncle Saul was struggling to understand what he'd come to call *food truck madness.*

His frequent rant was: *I owned a restaurant for years in Mobile. I had a standard menu. Customers ordered from it. I never went through crazy changes and looked for new kinds of food to make each day.*

I knew that to keep food truck customers—*my customers*—coming back each day, I had to have a good mix of old and new foods. If I didn't, they'd go somewhere else. There was a big jump in competition between when Uncle Saul had his restaurant and now.

"That's right." I pushed a curl out of my face. It had escaped the scarf I'd used to keep my curly black hair down. "My problem isn't *using* the sweet potatoes. It's baking one hundred biscuit bowls in this little oven."

Normally, I would've baked my biscuits at home in the diner where I lived. I tried not to spread that information around too much. It wasn't really *legal* to live in the diner. But I had to give up my apartment to afford the other payments.

You have to do what you have to do to find your dream, right?

I got up five mornings every week and made biscuits. I waited to deep-fry them in the Biscuit Bowl truck as I received orders for them. That way, they were as fresh as they could be when my customers ate them.

It wasn't an easy process, but it had worked for me. I was on the radar now. That meant a few food truck websites monitored where my truck was located each day, and a local radio station announced what my menu was. I had fans who followed me—at least thirty of them, by my last count.

For the race, however, the judges required that everything had to be done *in* the food truck. I had to purchase a small camping oven for the task. We'd tried it out a few times at home. It had worked fine—as long as there were no other electric appliances running in the truck.

You see my dilemma.

"I don't know how long it's going to take to bake so many biscuits," I explained. "It takes twenty minutes to warm up the deep fryer. We only have two hours before we start selling."

"It's gonna be fine." Uncle Saul grinned. His wild, curly black hair was like mine, but streaked with gray. He lived with an albino alligator named Alabaster in the swamp outside Mobile in a log cabin he'd built. He seemed to like it that way.

"That's why I brought you along." I mixed the orange biscuit dough. "You're the best cheerleader I have. And I appreciate you offering to leave the swamp for a few days. I know you hate being away."

He shrugged his bony shoulders. "I'd pretty much do anything for you, Zoe girl. Leaving Alabaster isn't easy, since she likes to sneak into the neighbor's chicken coop for a few free snacks. But I think Bonnie will keep a good eye on her."

"How's it going with Bonnie?" I asked about the wildlife officer who was sweet on him.

He grinned. "Don't worry about *my* personal affairs. I think you've got enough of your own to mind!"

"What about me?" Ollie towered above us in the food truck. He was a big man, an ex-marine, six-foot-six with a skull tattoo on the back of his bald head and neck. "Don't I count as a cheerleader? I think I'm always cheerful."

"Cheerful as a rock." Delia laughed at him. "If I had to get up every morning with *you* as my alarm clock, Ollie, I'd probably go jump in Mobile Bay."

Delia Vann had lost her job as a cocktail waitress in a sleazy dive back home. She'd been working with me in the food truck ever since. Not a big step up, but at least I respected *and* envied her.

She was as beautiful as any model or actress you see on TV—tall and thin, long legs, and gorgeous hair. I was short and on the plump side. Too much good food, I guess. It was hard not to taste when I cooked.

Ollie frowned. He had a secret crush on Delia and was trying to work out the details. The movement affected his whole face from forehead to chin. "I don't know why you'd say that. I work well with others and maintain my cool. What more is there?"

I saw him ogling Delia's long legs, now in tiny white shorts. Her cocoa-colored skin was flawless. The summer had put highlights into her long, dark hair.

Delia also had a way of handling things—mostly men— that I admired. She was so confident and poised. I was like Ollie—still trying to figure out the opposite sex.

I thought I knew what there was to know about relationships until I broke up with my boyfriend. I'd thought Tommy Lee and I were made for each other. Then I found out he was seeing someone else. It had dented my confidence a lot. If I couldn't figure out Tommy Lee, who could I figure out?

"There's a lot more to life, Ollie." Delia smiled as she took the tray out of the small oven for me. "Sometimes I think customers run away because they're scared when they see you."

I knew Ollie might be big and tough-looking, but he had a soft heart. Delia's words had to hurt. I felt bad for him.

Ollie had been homeless and living at the shelter a few doors down from the diner when I'd bought it. He'd led me to the diner accidentally after helping me and Uncle Saul fix up the Biscuit Bowl.

We'd clicked right away, and he'd stood faithfully by me after I got started. He was still homeless and living at the shelter. He seemed to like it that way.

I thought that could be a drawback for him with Delia. She knew a few wealthy men from the cocktail lounge and frequently dated them. I knew she didn't want to work in my food truck and sleep on a cot in the diner the rest of her life. I didn't blame her.

I had to keep everyone working together for the next five days while we almost lived together during the race. I couldn't let Delia hurt Ollie in case they had a future together. I had to keep Uncle Saul from becoming too depressed about the absurdity of the food truck world.

Hey! I was born for this. I was going to win that fifty thousand dollars—*or die trying.* The back door to the food truck opened. It was my sometimes attorney, Miguel Alexander. He was taller than me, but that wasn't hard since I was only five-foot-two and three-quarters. He was darkly handsome, a little sad, and had a wonderful, sexy voice that I could listen to all night.

I'd somehow managed to talk him into coming along for the race. I wasn't sure exactly *why* he'd agreed to be there. He'd helped me out of a jam once when I was getting started with my business. I still saw him from time to time. But food trucks really weren't his thing.

I hoped he was there for the same reason that I'd asked him to come—that there was something more between us. He could be aloof at times, and I didn't really know him well. He was older, worldlier than me. I knew he'd had personal problems in the past.

None of those things would have bothered me if I hadn't been already smarting from my boyfriend's betrayal. Sometimes I knew Miguel and I were meant to be together. Some days I thought the only thing I knew was biscuits.

But I'd been patient and cool. I was ready for the next step in our relationship—a *real* date. Just the two of us. Someplace nice.

"How's it going in here?" Miguel asked. "Alex Pardini, the host of the food truck show, is interviewing at the truck back from here. He should be by anytime now."

"It would be better if they'd given us bacon to work with

instead of sweet potatoes." Uncle Saul scowled as he monitored the biscuits that were in the little oven.

"You think you've got it bad, Pizza Papa has to use them
for *topping*." Miguel chuckled. "The Dog House either has
to put sweet potatoes in the buns instead of sausages—or
he has to put the sausages into the sweet potatoes."

"Thanks for the heads-up." I took a moment to smile at
him, hoping there wasn't flour on my face. I could feel our
gazes meet and cling. At least I thought I could. I *hoped* I
could.

I'd convinced Miguel to come along as our "outrider."
Every food truck team could have one outrider with another
vehicle. That person could pick up supplies or do other odd
jobs along the way.

"Do you need anything?" he asked.

"No. I think we're fine for right now. Thanks, Miguel."

"I hope everything is ready for the interview. I'll be outside if you need me."

"All right. Wish me luck."

"Good luck," he called out before he left the back of the
crowded food truck.

"Hats on," I told my team.

"Oh, Zoe," Ollie complained. "Do we *have* to?"

"Chef Art gave us a five-thousand-dollar stake so we
could participate in the food truck race. We're promoting
for him, and for ourselves. Put the hat on."

"You know, I got this tattoo for a reason," he continued
to grumble. "I don't want hair *or* a hat to mess with."

"At least you don't have my curly hair that you have to
try and stuff *under* the hat. I had to wear this scarf to hold
it down long enough to even try and put the hat on."

The hats were oversized white chef's hats with Chef Art
Arrington's name, face, and logo printed on them. They
were almost too big to fit in the food truck at one time, with
us and all the equipment jammed inside.

The oven chimed and Delia took out the first ten biscuits. "They look good."

"We have to try one," Uncle Saul said. "How are we gonna know what they taste like if we don't?"

I knew he was right. I hated to lose even one biscuit when we were trying to make a hundred. I usually didn't make that many for breakfast and lunch together on a busy Monday morning at home.

"Okay. Do it. I need some lipstick to talk to Alex Pardini. Delia, you saw the way I mixed that batch. Can you start another one? Ollie, get the next batch in the oven, please."

My lipstick was fresh and my team was humming when the TV host came to visit. He only peeked in for a moment before he disappeared and his assistant took his place.

"Alex only has five minutes for your pre-race interview." He looked at his clipboard. "*Joey*. You'll have to answer his questions as quickly and thoughtfully as you can. Don't forget to pour on the charm. Be as cute as possible, but don't look right at the camera. Got it?"

"That's *Zoe*," I corrected, but he was already gone. Hopefully Alex wouldn't make the same mistake.

I looked into the tiny mirror I'd put up near the door. A little racy red lipstick helped with my already pink face. There wasn't time for eye makeup. Lucky for me, my eyelashes were naturally dark.

"All right. I'm going out there. If I'm not back in five minutes, someone come and get me."

TWO

Alex Pardini's assistants had set up a little café table for two with an umbrella that boasted his network's affiliation.

I usually had a few small tables and chairs with me when I went out each morning. They were for my customers when I had to park where there weren't places to sit. I think people liked it when you gave them some extra consideration.

I'd had to leave them at home for the race. *No furniture outside the food truck.* There was a whole *book* of rules to follow. I had to keep reminding myself—*fifty thousand dollars.*

"Come on over and let's get started," Alex invited. He was a photogenic thirtyish man with thick blond hair and remarkable blue eyes. I'd noticed, watching him on TV, that he always wore blue to emphasize them.

"I'm Alex." He shook my hand. "It's nice to meet you, *Joey.*"

I smiled. The names *did* sound a lot alike. Just think how many names he had to remember, bless his heart.

"My name is *Zoe* Chase. Thanks for having me here." I sat down in the chair opposite him and crossed my legs.

"Fair enough, *Zoe*." He grinned; another man who realized how handsome he was. "Let's talk about your life as a food truck vendor, shall we?"

Before a word could come out of my mouth, my sponsor, Chef Art Arrington, came around the corner of the Biscuit Bowl.

His assistant, Lacie, a nervous little woman with huge glasses who wore her skirts too short, managed to make it to the table right before he did. She quickly put out a chair for him.

"All right! I love interviews, don't you?" Chef Art was famous in Mobile. He was like Colonel Sanders and Papa John rolled into one short, round body and white linen suit. He rubbed his hands together in anticipation.

"I'm sorry," Alex said. "I wasn't expecting a sponsor."

"That's quite all right, my boy. No harm done."

"I mean, this interview is *supposed* to be between me and the *vendor*."

"Not a problem. I'll sit back here and take it all in. Zoe, you give the man the answers he needs now, you hear?"

Chef Art had always been a larger-than-life figure in my hometown. He lived on an old estate called Woodlands outside Mobile where he entertained famous people from across the world in his mansion.

His wreath of white hair, bright blue eyes, and closely clipped gray beard were well known throughout the South. He'd once owned a famous restaurant back home. It was so famous that investors had asked him to open another one just like it in New York City.

That one had failed, but it hadn't tarnished his legend. Everyone knew him and admired him. Someday, I wanted to be just like him—except for the beard and the linen suit.

"Okay." Alex nodded to the cameraman who was to my left. "Let's get started."

There were several adjustments that had to be made because the light wasn't good for Alex. I tried to wait patiently.

The street behind us was starting to pick up traffic. I glanced at my watch. It was five A.M. If he was going to talk to me, he'd better do it. I wasn't losing the first challenge because my interview ran late. Staying on time was one of the rules.

"Zoe, how did you get started with your food truck?" Alex asked—*finally*.

"Well, Alex, I really wanted my own restaurant, but I couldn't afford to open one. I started the Biscuit Bowl for an investment in my future, and because I wanted to cook for people."

Chef Art cleared his throat. "She's my protégé, you know. I'm *very* proud of her."

Alex glared at him but continued the interview. "Tell us what a biscuit bowl is, Zoe."

I described, in detail, what a biscuit bowl was and what I could do with it. My speech should've been perfect—I'd been practicing for a week.

It went off without a hitch.

"That sounds really good," Alex encouraged me. "I'd like to have one, and I'm sure our audience at home would like to see me eat one."

Eat one? Take another biscuit out of my stash as we struggled to reach one hundred biscuits for the challenge?

It was the opportunity of a lifetime. What else could I do?

Delia had been watching from the open doorway. She removed her chef's hat so her long, silky dark hair fluttered around her shoulders in the early morning breeze.

"Here you are, Alex." She handed him a biscuit bowl, bending over to show a little cleavage.

The camera zoomed in that way because it was close to the biscuit, *of course.*

"Thanks." He couldn't take his eyes off her. The biscuit, orange with sweet potato in it, was in his hand. It stayed there for a full minute as he smiled at her.

The cameraman cleared his throat. Chef Art chuckled.

"Let's take a big bite." Alex studied the filling. "What's inside of here, Zoe?"

I couldn't think for a minute. *What are we filling the biscuits with today?*

Delia, now off camera, made a circle around her face with her hands and puffed out her cheeks.

"Apples. Spiced apples," I said as she nodded. *Smart girl.*

"Here we go." Alex took a *big* bite.

The biscuit bowl stayed together, one of my fears about adding sweet potato to it. He chewed and swallowed. He was looking at Delia. She blew him a kiss, but his words of praise were for my biscuit bowl. "Deelish!"

It was Alex's favorite way to express how much he liked a food when he ate it. I'd watched him say it on food TV for a year.

Chef Art was beaming. The interview was over. I was quickly shuttled away from the table and chairs so they could be moved to the next food truck.

Alex thanked me—and asked for Delia's cell phone number.

"I'll tell her you're interested."

He was okay with that and gave me his card. "Talk to you later, Zoe. Good job!"

I went back inside my food truck and gave Delia his card.

"You sounded great," she said. "I think he really liked the biscuit bowl."

"And the woman who brought it out to him." I grinned. "Thanks for rescuing me during my brain glitch."

"That was *my* idea," Uncle Saul said. "Ain't nothin' better than good food and a pretty woman."

"How do we stand on our biscuit count?"

"We're halfway there." Ollie yanked another tray of biscuits out of the oven.

"Great! Let's make sure all the fillings are ready. We need to be able to hit the ground running at six."

Uncle Saul stroked his jaw. "You know, I was thinking—two of us can sell while two of us stay here and keep making food."

"We could do that. There's nothing in the rules against it. Great idea! I don't know what to say about the filling. I'd planned for hot fillings, but we can't run the microwave and the oven at the same time."

"We could start with cold," Ollie added. "We've got apple and raisin filling that won't have to be warmed. They didn't say what had to go inside, right? Then we can move into the cheese and bacon filling."

"Absolutely." I smiled at my team. "You're the best!"

Chef Art joined us, the Airstream leaning a little lower with all five of us inside. "You did good out there, Zoe. Sounded like a pro. Make me proud this morning." He reached toward the pile of biscuits on the side shelf. "I'd like to have one of these."

"Get in line at six." Ollie slapped his hand.

Chef Art didn't look too pleased about that. "I oughta—"

I rushed in to keep that drama from happening. "We need one hundred biscuits. We're working *really* hard to get that right now. Every biscuit counts."

"What's the problem?" He shot an angry glance at Ollie but let it go.

I explained the situation to him. He offered to bake some of the biscuits in his RV, which was double the size of mine and had a huge kitchen in it. It was a nice idea, but we'd lose if we did it. "The rules say that all the food has to be made in the food truck."

"Crazy rules." He shook his head. "Where's Delia's hat?"

"She'll put it back on."

"Too bad she wasn't wearing it on camera. The audience would've gone wild."

When he was gone, Ollie laughed. "What's he talking about? The audience wanted to see *Delia*. They didn't care what she was wearing."

Delia smiled at him as she adjusted her chef's hat on her head again. "You always say the *nicest* things."

Ollie frowned. "You know what I mean. You'd look good if you were wearing a hat or not."

Uncle Saul laughed as he put in a new tray of biscuits.

I was about to rein in the banter before I lost Ollie and Delia when I heard a loud howling sound from the passenger seat at the front of the food truck.

Crème Brûlée!

I ran past everyone and outside to the passenger side door. Before getting the Biscuit Bowl set up for the race, I could walk between the driving and cooking areas. Because we had to add extra items, like the oven, and modify the back area to hold four people, the spot was closed now.

"I'm so sorry I forgot about you," I said to my very large white-and-tabby-colored Persian cat. He was lying on his back with his large paws up in the air. "I know. You're hungry. Let's come outside for a few minutes."

I strapped him into his harness—no mean feat since he kept rolling back and forth on the seat and batting at me with his paws.

"You know, you didn't want to stay with my mother. This is what happens when you go on an extended road trip. You have to get out of the RV and walk around a little in the soft grass and go potty."

It took both arms to carefully lift him out of the seat and put him in a nice patch of grass next to the Biscuit Bowl.

He'd given me grief all the way up here from Mobile, wanting his familiar litter box. So far, no accidents on the seat. I was hoping that wouldn't change.

I couldn't really walk him to the grassy spot. He hated

the harness and started meowing loudly and chewing on it. It was hard to imagine that he could bend his big body enough to reach the material with his mouth, but he could.

I was pretty sure there were lots of things he pretended he couldn't do so that I'd do them for him. He was devious that way.

I set him down in the grass and waited, holding his harness. I was worried that he might sneak off and get lost. Crème Brûlée never *ran* anywhere—I was safe from that problem.

He looked up at me from the grass and sweetly meowed.

He was so *cute*! But I had to be tough with him. "Just get it over with already. Then you can go back inside and eat your breakfast. Don't be so stubborn."

I heard shouting from inside the food truck parked in front of ours. Something slammed on the floor and broke. I grabbed Crème Brûlée, hoping he was done with his private business, and walked up to the Dog House.

The Dog House was the only other food truck from Mobile that had made the cut for the race. I thought it was probably the cuteness of the truck, which was made to actually look like a dog, with a face on the front and a tail sticking out the back. *Ingenious.*

I knew the owner, Reggie Johnson. He wasn't so cute. He was greasy with a lank ponytail sticking out of the back end of his baseball cap. He had bad acne scars, most of his teeth were missing, and his nose was twisted like he'd broken it a dozen times.

He wasn't a very nice person, either. There were several times back home that he'd zoomed in and cut me off for a prime location at the police station or down by the docks where the tourists disembarked from the cruise ships.

He'd come into the Biscuit Bowl a few times and stood around telling me nasty jokes while he stared at my butt. Altogether not my kind of person. I wasn't exactly thrilled when he was announced as a contestant for the race.

The two male voices in the trailer were still arguing. As crazy as it seemed, it sounded like Reggie and Alex Pardini. I knocked on the back door. "Everything okay in there?"

Reggie pushed open the door a crack, not enough for me to see inside. "What do *you* want?"

"I was just checking on you." I smiled. "Anything wrong?"

"Mind your own business, Zoe Chase. I'm getting ready for the race." Reggie slammed the door closed again.

I didn't see Alex, but it had certainly sounded like him.

"Well, at least he's okay," I said to Crème Brûlée as we walked away. "I wonder what he and Alex were arguing about."

I walked back to the Biscuit Bowl and put Crème Brûlée in the passenger seat of the truck again. "Try to be good," I coaxed. "This is only the beginning of the race."

"How's he doing?" Miguel asked, startling me.

"He's fine." I smiled back. "Just a little homesick, I think."

He shrugged. "Me, too. I haven't left Mobile in a long time."

"Me, either." I stroked Crème Brûlée's head. "I know how he feels. I'm always more comfortable at home."

"Me, too." Miguel smiled. "I'm sure you're going to do well during this race."

I *really* loved his smile.

"Thanks. I'm happy you could be here to help. I really appreciate you taking the time to come with us—to come with *me*."

"No problem. It sounded like fun."

I turned away with a sigh. We never seemed to get any further than polite Q & A like this. It seemed as though one of us should've been willing to step up and kiss the other person senseless.

Just not *me*.

There was a loud shout from inside the Biscuit Bowl.

Now what?

THREE

I joined my team in the cooking area. They were still making biscuits. The pile was steadily growing. *What a team!*

Miguel had to stand outside since the kitchen was so small. I wished it could be different, but the area wasn't meant to hold so many people and cooking supplies.

"I'll just wait out here until we're ready to get started," he said.

I hoped he didn't feel like I was pushing him out of the way. I silently cursed my ex-boyfriend for making me doubt myself like this and took a deep breath to calm my frazzled nerves.

Maybe being part of a food truck race wasn't the best time to explore my relationship with Miguel. It had seemed like a good idea when I'd asked him to come. We'd be in different places with different ideas. Different things, like romance, would just happen naturally.

It's going to be all right. Miguel likes you.

We just had a few details to work out. And trying to win this race was as good a time as any to figure it all out.

Ollie was nursing his hand like a hurt bear. "I burned myself taking the biscuits out of the oven."

"He's making such a fuss." Delia brought out the tube of aloe I always kept in the kitchen. "It's hardly anything."

"To *you*!" He wouldn't let her see his hand.

"Big baby!" She pulled his hand toward her and slathered on the aloe. "There. Doesn't that feel better?"

"Thanks." He sniffed—with a wink at me over her head. He was *enjoying* it!

"What's happening out there?" Uncle Saul asked. "Was that Crème Brûlée?"

"Yes, but something else, too." I told him about Reggie and Alex. "Reggie's always in a bad mood. I wonder who he got to sponsor him anyway. I'm surprised at him arguing with Alex, though. We're a long way from Mobile to lose so soon and have to go home."

"It would probably take more than that to send him home," Ollie said. "I watch programs like this on TV all the time. People like Reggie always make it through. It's the nice ones who have to worry. Like *you*, Zoe."

"What were they arguing about?" Uncle Saul mixed a new batch of biscuit batter with mashed sweet potato.

"I'm not sure. I couldn't tell what they were saying." I tasted some of the apple raisin filling. "This is good. Let's spice it up some."

Uncle Saul glanced into the bowl. "Sounds good. Between us, Zoe, we have a good sense of these things."

"Seems odd for the host of the food truck race to be arguing with *anyone* behind closed doors. If he's doing it for ratings, he'd want everyone to see it, right?" Delia was still holding Ollie's hand. She suddenly realized and put it down.

Ollie grinned.

I ignored them so I could concentrate on the forms we

were going to have people fill out after they ate our food. "I think one of us will have to approach people about their opinions. We'll have two selling the biscuits. That leaves two in the kitchen."

"That might be a good job for Miguel," Ollie said. "He's awesome at talking people into things. If he wasn't, I might be in jail right now."

"Ollie might be right." Uncle Saul ignored Ollie's assessment of his life. "Would that fit his definition in the rules as an outrider?"

I scanned the rule book. "It looks like he can do anything I need him to do except cook. He's kind of like a joker in a deck of cards."

"Good comparison." Uncle Saul smiled. "Why don't you go out there and ask him what he thinks about getting opinions?"

Uncle Saul knew my devious plan to go back home with a different kind of relationship between me and Miguel.

"I'll do that." I glanced around the kitchen. "It looks like we're ready to go at six. Thanks for all the hard work. Everybody take a break."

I went back outside into the cool morning air. I knew it wouldn't last for long. It was summer in the South, which meant hot weather. I was grateful that my food truck had air-conditioning as long as the portable generator was working. Not all food trucks were so lucky.

I found Miguel sitting on a bench near the Biscuit Bowl and sat beside him. There was a small magnolia tree hanging over us. I thought it was a very romantic place to talk. I wished I had something to say to him that didn't involve what I wanted him to do for the food truck race.

"Everything ready?" he asked.

"I think so. The oven worked better than I thought it would."

"Good." He smiled and nodded.

Seriously? I was thirty years old and this was the best I

could do? It was like I couldn't get my tongue to say what I was thinking.

"I—uh—need you to get people to fill out these little forms on whether or not they like the food." I showed him, deliberately leaning closer to him.

"I can do that." He took the forms and scanned them. "I do this after you sell the food?"

"Yes."

"No problem."

"Thanks." I sighed. *Now what?*

"Zoe?" He looked down into my face.

"Yes?" My heart was beating fast.

There was another loud noise from the Dog House. It wasn't arguing this time—more like a dull thud followed by a loud groan.

"That didn't sound good." Miguel got to his feet. "I'll check it out."

"I'll come with you."

Whatever he'd been about to say was lost as we walked to the back door of the Dog House. Leave it to Reggie to ruin my perfect moment with Miguel.

Miguel knocked on the back door. There was no response. He pounded, and I called Reggie's name. Still no response.

"Is there a problem, sir?" a burly Charlotte police officer asked. "Ma'am?"

"We're from the other food truck." I pointed behind us. "We heard a strange noise up here and were worried about our friend, Reggie. This is his trailer. We're both from Mobile."

I wasn't really worried about Reggie. I was talking nervously because I was wondering what Miguel was thinking and feeling. Had he planned to kiss me before this happened?

The faster we got through this, the sooner Miguel and I could sit on the bench and talk again. Or kiss.

The officer frowned at my words, but he took our concerns seriously. "Step aside, please. Let me handle this."

Reggie had a pickup truck hauling the Dog House behind it. There was no access between the two vehicles. The side window on the trailer, where Reggie sold hot dogs and sausages, was closed and locked. It would probably break if the officer forced it open.

Miguel and I followed him as he circled the truck and around the other side of the trailer. The only logical way into the cooking area was to open the back door as Reggie had done earlier to yell at me.

By this time, another officer had joined us. The two officers discussed the situation for a moment as they tried to decide what to do. There was no way to be sure it was an emergency. We didn't even know for sure that Reggie was *inside* the trailer. One of the officers called in the problem while the other decided to use a crowbar to open the back door.

Alex Pardini had seen the commotion and had brought his cameraman with him to investigate. "What's going on, officers?"

"We're not sure, sir. Step back, please."

"We heard a bad sound inside." I filled Alex in on why Miguel and I were there.

"What kind of sound, Zoe?" Alex wondered.

"I'm not sure."

He conversed with the officers as they worked. "What are you hoping to uncover here? What do you think happened? Should our other drivers be worried?"

The officers stared at him like he was crazy.

The camera was taping everything when the officers finally managed to pry open the door to the Dog House. It splintered away from the side wall. Reggie wasn't going to be able to use it again.

But it didn't matter.

Reggie was on the floor with a refrigerator on his chest. It looked as though he might not need a door, or a food truck, ever again.

FOUR

"Is he dead?" Alex asked with a look of revulsion on his handsome face that wouldn't have been good for his ratings. "I mean, seriously, someone should call an ambulance in case he's still alive."

The two officers assured him that they had already called for medics and an ambulance. They asked us to move away from the trailer again.

Everyone affiliated with the race was suddenly there with us, pressing closer to find out what had happened. There were murmurs of disbelief and horror that one of the food truck drivers had been seriously injured or killed—and a few unsportsmanlike comments about there being one less competitor for the fifty thousand dollars.

Miguel stayed there to hear what he could about Reggie's condition. I went to the back of the Biscuit Bowl to tell everyone inside what had happened. My team had remained hard at work despite what was happening outside. I could hear the sound of sirens as other police cars and the ambulance arrived.

"That poor man," Delia said after I'd told her. "Is he going to be okay?"

"I don't know. I couldn't tell." I shivered, thinking about the look on Reggie's face. "I hope so. I think the strap broke that was holding his refrigerator in place." I felt guilty after I'd thought such terrible things about him. I was going to feel *really* bad if he was seriously hurt—or the other.

"Accidents happen in the food industry just like any other," Uncle Saul added.

"It seems strange that I was just over there talking to him. Well, he was *yelling* at me, like always, but still."

"You mean when you heard him arguing with Alex." Ollie shook his head. "Too bad you couldn't hear what they were saying."

"I don't think Alex had anything to do with it. Miguel and I were sitting outside, talking about filling out the tasting forms, and I think we heard the refrigerator fall. Alex wasn't anywhere around then."

"I thought the big fridge was a good idea," Ollie remarked. "I guess I was wrong. But I'm not shedding any tears for that jerk anyway. There were a few times I wanted to *kill* him back in Mobile!"

"You shouldn't say that now," Delia cautioned.

"Just 'cause he's hurt doesn't mean he's suddenly a good guy," Ollie argued.

"I'm sure it was only an accident," Uncle Saul said. "I saw Reggie putting in the refrigerator when we were getting ready to leave Mobile. I was wondering how he was gonna manage to keep it in place."

I shrugged. "It was terrible anyway. I hope he's okay." It didn't really look like it, but I knew looks could be deceiving. It wasn't a great way to start the race.

"He's probably fine," Uncle Saul said as he drank a soda. "One time I dropped a truck on myself as I was changing a tire. I pushed myself out from under it. I was banged up and had a few broken ribs—well, all of them were broken—along with my collarbone, both shoulders, and one hand. But I'm alive, and I drove that old truck until I had to send it to the scrap heap."

"I had something similar happen to me." Ollie began telling another amazing, and improbable, tale of survival after something had fallen on him.

Miguel burst in after their colorful tales. "He's dead. Reggie is dead."

"How do they know so soon?" Uncle Saul asked. "Didn't they have to take him to the hospital?"

"They did," Miguel agreed. "But they had already called it before they transported him."

I glanced at Miguel. "How did he die?"

"The police said he didn't tie down his refrigerator well enough and it fell on him."

Uncle Saul removed his hat for a moment and stood with his head bowed, eyes closed.

"That isn't a fit way for a man to die." Ollie shook his head.

"I wonder what we'll do now," Uncle Saul said. "Will the race go on or will we all go home?"

There was a loud meow from the front of the Airstream. I knew what Crème Brûlée's vote was on the matter.

"I heard the producers are deciding what they should do," Miguel said.

There was heavy pounding at the back door. Alex's assistant peeked inside. "Everyone stay put for now. We'll let you know what's going on when they make a decision about the race."

"So all this was for nothing?" Delia grabbed a biscuit and started eating.

"Good idea." Ollie grabbed one, too. "We might as well eat them. They won't be any good after a while."

"Maybe we could give the biscuits away." I considered the possibilities. "It would be better than all the food going to waste."

"Couldn't we sell them?" Ollie wondered.

"No. We don't have a sales license for Charlotte. The show's producers handled all of that for the race," I explained. "But there's nothing saying we can't give them away."

Chef Art knocked at the door to tell us what Alex's assistant had already said. When I told him I was going to give away the biscuits, he was thrilled. "What an opportunity! You have a great mind for business, Zoe. Let me round up a few local reporters."

At seven A.M. we were out on Trade and Tryon streets in the heart of downtown Charlotte. Chef Art had found a few interested reporters. We gave them biscuits, and they did some live feed to go with the story about what had happened to Reggie.

It wasn't long until all the food truck drivers were taking the food they couldn't use out on the streets, too. It was much better to be out on a sunny morning giving people food than to sit inside and worry about what would happen next with the food truck race.

If we went home, we went home. I wasn't sure that wouldn't be for the best anyway after what had happened to Reggie. Maybe I hadn't liked him, but his death had put a pall on the whole idea of the race.

We got the trip to Charlotte and a night out at a hotel. The show would probably pay for our trip home, as they had for our trip here. Chef Art and the other sponsors got their names out there for their time and money. The rest of us had a chance to have our names on all the advertising.

I wouldn't lose any sleep over it.

It was a little sad to have to tell enthusiastic Charlotte customers that they could only get my biscuit bowls in Mobile, but that went with the territory. When I could get my products online, they could buy them frozen there. The biscuit bowls wouldn't be as good but at least they could experience them without a trip to Mobile.

Delia had stayed with the Biscuit Bowl and Crème Brûlée while we'd given out all the biscuit bowls. We got back two hours later, and she told us the producers were ready to make a statement about the show.

"You go on, Zoe," Uncle Saul said to me, sweating from the hot, humid air on the street. "It's your food truck. The rest of us don't need to be there."

"We don't *need* to be," Ollie said, "but we *want* to be. I want to know what happened with Reggie."

"Me, too," Delia added.

"That's fine," Uncle Saul said. "You all go. You can tell me what happens next when you get back."

"We're supposed to meet at the cool-down tent," Delia said.

- - - - - - -

The cool-down tent was set up to help alleviate the summer heat that everyone would be working in with a fine, cool mist. We were supposed to be in some of the hottest weather of the year from Charlotte to Mobile in the next five days. The large tent was also set up to be a meeting place, centrally located in the group of food trucks.

Miguel, Ollie, Delia, and I went back out on the street. Food truck teams were making their way toward the cool-down tent.

Alex Pardini was on a stage with a microphone beside the tent. Cameras were up there with him and panning on us out in the crowd.

"Don't get your hopes up, Zoe," Miguel cautioned as we waited for everyone to arrive at the stage. "I don't think they'll go on with this after Reggie's death."

"I'm prepared for that," I told him. "It was a fun trip, if nothing else. I haven't been to Charlotte in years."

When it looked like everyone from the nine remaining food trucks (including ours) was there, Alex greeted us and gave us the news.

"A terrible thing happened here this morning," he said. "Food truck driver Reggie Johnson, the owner of the Dog House from Mobile, Alabama, was found dead in his trailer.

He was accidentally crushed by his refrigerator. We will never forget him as a daring and valiant competitor."

Everyone applauded. The cameramen moved from place to place in the street to best get images of our reactions to the news. Police officers held back reporters and the crowd that had come to watch the race.

"We had a big decision to make, folks." Alex bowed his head for a moment as though it was a difficult, *personal* decision for him. "Should we continue with the Sweet Magnolia Food Truck Race? Or should we end it right here? The producers made their decision. Now they want to hear from you."

There was only a moment before food truck drivers began yelling out their answers.

Alex acknowledged a few of them after admitting that he couldn't hear everyone at the same time. "Daryl Barbee from Grinch's Ganache; what do you think we should do?"

Daryl stood beside his wife, Sarah. He was a very short man with a large cowboy hat that seemed to swallow his head. "I think we should honor Reggie by continuing the race."

There was a loud round of applause following his words.

Maybe I was uncharitable, but I was thinking—*He's got cupcakes ready to go.*

Alex held up his hand, and everyone got quiet again. He called on Bobbie Shields from Shut Up and Eat, a food truck that served loose meat sandwiches and the biggest pickles I'd ever seen.

Bobbie was a large woman who liked wearing colorful Hawaiian dresses and dozens of bracelets. She shouted out her answer. "We should go on! Reggie wouldn't want us to stop."

The applause was deafening on the street around me.

I felt like I knew Reggie well enough to guess that he wouldn't really care if the race went on or not. I'd pegged him as more the *if I'm not in it, it doesn't matter* category. But I was probably being negative again.

"All right." Alex smiled fabulously at all of us. "It's time for the vote. Everyone who wants to continue, raise your hands."

It wasn't even close. The only two food trucks that *didn't* want to continue were Chooey's Sooey, an Asian food vendor, and Stick It Here, the pot sticker and kebab food truck.

Everyone else cheered when they saw their victory.

I admit that I voted to continue. Maybe if Reggie and I had actually been friends, it would've been different. Fifty thousand dollars is a lot of money. If that made me a bad person, so be it.

I was curious, too, as I looked at Alex's dazzling smile. What was going on in *his* head? Did he feel like a bad person for arguing with Reggie before he'd died? And what had they been arguing about?

Maybe Reggie didn't like the interview Alex had done with him.

The producers had moved the challenge to noon. That gave everyone time to prepare—even teams like ours who'd given away all their food. Miguel raced for his car. He'd already located a supermarket where he'd shopped last night. I was sending a list of what we needed to the email on his phone.

Ollie, Delia, and I ran back to the food truck. Everyone around us was moving fast. Most had given away their food, as we had. That probably meant shopping and cooking for all of them. Anyone not out of their food truck at noon, and selling their primary food with sweet potatoes in it, would be disqualified.

"I guess I was right staying behind." Uncle Saul laughed and enjoyed his moment of foresight. He'd peeled and cut the rest of the sweet potatoes we hadn't used. "Let's get going."

I had never planned to have more than two or three people working inside the Biscuit Bowl at one time. It wasn't really big enough for more than *one* person. Four people trying to bake, deep-fry, fill, and finish one hundred biscuits was almost too much.

We managed somehow.

Miguel got back with the supplies. We'd had enough
sweet potatoes to get some cooked and mashed to add to the
biscuits while he was gone. If I'd been at the diner, it would
have been too early to get started. Because the camping oven
was slower and smaller, it took right up until noon to get
everything ready again.

We'd decided to send Delia out to sell the biscuit bowls
on the street. Lunch traffic had begun, with plenty of people
on foot making their way to benches and restaurants where
they would eat and spend time away from their offices.

Ollie wanted to go with Delia to sell biscuit bowls. I
wasn't sure. But I decided he could take food to her so she
wouldn't have to come back each time she ran out. He was
happy with that.

It would be up to me and Uncle Saul to keep food ready
for Ollie to take to Delia.

That was my strategy. Smart, right?

It was a relief when we began at last. Ollie was already
taking a second, finished group of biscuit bowls to Delia.
The bacon and cheese biscuit bowls smelled *deelish* (made
with sweet potatoes instead of shortening). The spicy apple
raisin filling had a dusting of powdered sugar and a swirl of
white icing.

"It was getting a mite crowded in here." Uncle Saul heaved
a sigh of relief when it was only the two of us. "What is wrong
with that boy, anyway? Has he never had a girl before?"

I knew he was talking about Ollie and his disastrous
efforts to court Delia.

"Miguel told me that Ollie was actually married before,
when he was still in the Marines. His wife was a marine,
too. She had PTSD and opened fire on him one morning at
breakfast. She shot him twice before he had to kill her. He
almost died, too."

Uncle Saul put a hand to his forehead. "Holy smoke! That
boy has been through the wringer! No wonder he's making

such a mess of things. It would only be Christian for me to take him under my wing. I used to be pretty hot with the ladies of Mobile, you know? During carnival, I was the king of hearts."

He chuckled to himself as he filled five more apple biscuit bowls.

"Maybe you should show Bonnie that side of you." I grinned. "I'm sure she'd be interested."

"Are you trying to be a matchmaker or what?"

Everything was going well until we reached the ninety-five biscuit mark. We were *so* close.

Then one of the cameramen barged into the Biscuit Bowl and knocked over what remained of my apple raisin filling.

I turned to him, angry. "What are you trying to do?"

"Uh—sorry, ma'am. I was—uh—trying to get a close-up of your *apples*." He stammered and pulled at his network ball cap.

Uncle Saul slapped his hand on his leg. "Never heard *that* term for it before!"

We looked at where the cameraman had stopped record-ing on the screen. It was an in-depth view of my cleavage above the red tank top.

I was flattered—in a lame kind of way. But now we had only the bacon cheese filling. "It's all we have. It will have to do. We only have five more biscuits to sell. Let's make this work."

Ollie was back for more biscuit bowls. "Delia's kicking butt on sales. You should see her sell!"

"Take these." I gave him the last bacon cheese biscuit bowls. "How are the customers holding out?"

"The crowds are getting smaller as everyone goes back to work. Good news is that a lot of people are hanging around to see what's going on." Ollie grabbed the biscuit bowls and was gone.

The cameraman was done with us—our crisis was past. Had he done it on purpose to create drama?

Miguel popped his head into the food truck. "How's it going? I've got twenty statements from people saying they loved your biscuit bowls. But Pizza Papa just sold their hundredth slice. I guess they win this challenge."

"Sweet potato pizza—and they sold out?" I turned off the deep fryer. We were done.

"They were selling them really cheap."

"Don't they have to sell at their normal price? Isn't that covered in the rules?"

"Not sure." He shook his head. "One interesting thing I heard while I was out there—the police are wondering if Reggie Johnson's death was really an accident."

FIVE

"What do you mean by that?" Uncle Saul asked him. "The police think someone pushed a refrigerator on top of the man? In that small area?"

"It's something about a strap that had been holding the refrigerator in place," Miguel said. "It looks as though it's been cut."

I listened as I started cleaning and putting things away. We'd have to move the truck today, and everything had to be strapped down.

How could the police even tell the difference between a strap breaking and a strap being cut?

"I hope that's not true," I finally remarked. "Why would anyone want to kill Reggie?"

Uncle Saul laughed. "Maybe it was someone who ate his food."

"Now that's mean." I stored away the remaining flour, baking powder, and shortening. I hoped never to work with sweet potatoes in biscuits again. It was possible to do, but the biscuits weren't the best I'd ever made.

Ollie and Delia weren't back yet, which meant they hadn't sold the last five biscuits. Oh well. I hadn't expected to win all the challenges. I hoped we wouldn't be sent home yet, but it was a possibility. Each day, team members who didn't win the challenge could be sent home.

I took off my hat and let Uncle Saul do the rest of the cleanup. I had a small bottle of cool water that I shared with Crème Brûlée in the front of the truck.

Crème Brûlée rolled on his back, showing me his soft, fuzzy tummy. I tickled it gently while he pretended to swat at me as though he didn't like it. Everything was a game with him—except looking for his food.

The police were still swarming all over the Dog House right in front of me. I thought about poor Reggie making it all the way here, only to end up under his refrigerator before he had a chance to take the first challenge of the race.

I always checked all of the appliances, shelves, and supplies in the back of the Biscuit Bowl before I moved it from place to place. I made a mental note to double-check from now on. It was always better to be safe.

Courtesy of the Sweet Magnolia Food Truck Race, all the teams would be put up at hotels for the night. The idea was to finish in one location and announce the winners— and losers. Everyone who wasn't kicked out would go on to Columbia, South Carolina. We'd spend the night there and then face our challenges in the morning on Tuesday.

Mobile felt a long way off. I wasn't joking about being homesick for my normal, appreciative customers and my friends. I missed my old diner. Being part of the race was exciting, but strange.

Sweet potatoes in biscuits? I was amazed anyone would eat them.

The loud buzzer that sounded could be heard up and

down the main street. That meant the challenge was over.
Everyone would gather at the cool-down tent again.

"I guess that's me." I stroked Crème Brûlée and we
rubbed noses. "I'll be back soon. Don't worry. I'll leave the
air on for you. No scratching or potty on the seats!"

He meowed and snuffled my hand a little, flipped over,
and went back to sleep.

I hoped we'd at least managed to stay in the race. I
glanced in the back. Ollie and Delia were there.

"We sold the last biscuit bowl a minute before the buzzer
went off!" Ollie was excited, even though it wasn't neces-
sarily something that would help us stay in the race. He
almost lifted me up off the floor when he hugged me.

"I knew I sent out the right girl," Uncle Saul said to Delia,
hugging her.

Ollie frowned. "It was a *team* effort. One person couldn't
have done it alone."

Miguel came to join us. "You were great! It looked like
Pizza Papa won the challenge. We'll see what happens now.
Let's get over to the cool-down tent." I led the way and
everyone else followed.

Alex was back on the stage again. The food truck drivers
were slowly making their way toward him. Some were covered in food stains. Others already looked defeated.

"Most of you met your first challenge," Alex said. "Give
yourselves a big hand."

Of course everyone applauded.

"But we can't all be winners. It was decided that, despite
the sad death of Reggie Johnson, and the subsequent loss of
his food truck, the Dog House, that one other food truck
will still be taken out of the running after this challenge."

Everyone groaned. Really, I guess we'd all hoped the
producers might let Reggie's truck be the one that didn't go
on. He obviously couldn't participate. Wasn't that enough?

I could see from the faces of the other food truck owners

standing close by that they had felt the same way. A certain amount of grumbling was to be expected with that disappointment.

"Okay. I know a lot of you figured it would only be the Dog House eliminated from the race." Alex smiled at everyone. "How fair would that be since Reggie didn't participate?"

His attempt to placate the crowd wasn't very popular. He conferred with a group of people on the sidelines that I'd decided were "the producers." He was back a minute later with his arms stretched out like Moses parting the Red Sea.

"I'm sorry, but that decision is final," Alex said. "I have the names of the contestants who will be going on to Columbia with us. I also have the name of the winner of the challenge. Does anyone want to hear it?"

The crowd yelled in a halfhearted fashion.

"I can't hear you." Alex cupped his ear with one hand. "Does anyone want the *good* news?"

The group managed a louder response, with Ollie leading the way as he screamed his answer. I wasn't sure I'd ever be able to hear out of my left ear again.

"That's better." Alex opened a large envelope. "The winner of the sweet potato challenge is Our Daily Bread, according to all challenges."

Everyone applauded as Reverend Jay Jablonski ran to the stage. Our Daily Bread was manned by a group of ministers from Jacksonville, Florida. They'd started the truck selling breads, rolls, and coffee cakes as an outreach project for their church.

Alex congratulated Reverend Jablonski. The stocky, balding minister took the microphone to thank his team and race officials.

"We owe it all to God," he said with a big smile on his face.

There were also prizes awarded daily to challenge winners. Reverend Jablonski won a new air conditioner for his food truck.

"Of course he won." Bobbie Shields from Shut Up and Eat complained loudly as she stood next to me. "Sweet potatoes aren't all that noticeable in bread."

Reverend Jablonski left the stage after another round of applause. Alex took over the microphone again.

"And now for the contestants who will continue on to Columbia." He took out another sealed envelope.

I wondered when someone had time to make up those envelopes. The challenge had only been over for such a short time.

"Are you ready?" Alex tried to rev up the group again. His excitement was falling on disappointed ears. "Traveling on to Columbia and the second leg of the race will be: Our Daily Bread. Shut Up and Eat. Fred's Fish Tacos. Chooey's Sooey. Stick It Here. Grinch's Ganache. Pizza Papa. And the Biscuit Bowl."

"That means the mushroom woman didn't make it," Uncle Saul said loudly over the cheers and moans from the winners and losers. "Darn! I was looking forward to trying her mushroom soup."

"At least we made the cut," I said. "I wonder how they came to that decision."

Alex tapped on his microphone to get everyone's attention again. "And of course, our friend and fellow food truck owner Reggie Johnson travels with us to Columbia in spirit. That's it, people. See you tomorrow."

Everyone filed into the cool-down tent for a briefing on what we could expect tomorrow. The challenge would be selling our normal menu but on roller skates. It also included singing and a taste challenge.

"I'm not doing that." Delia made her feelings plain. "I don't dance and I don't sing."

We were each given vouchers for meals and hotel rooms for our teams. I reserved judgment on the singing and roller skating until tomorrow.

I'd been a roller-skating carhop when I was in college. That had been so many years ago that I could hardly remember. I wasn't even sure I knew *how* to skate anymore. And singing was really not my forte.

At least we were able to serve our normal menus! I wasn't worried about a taste challenge. I felt sure we could beat anyone at that.

Everyone left the area after that. Police were waiting to reopen the downtown streets we were taking up. When we got back to the Biscuit Bowl, I saw a tow truck hooking up to the Dog House.

I wondered if there would be an investigation of what had happened to Reggie. Had he been murdered or was it an accident?

Despite my feelings about him, it was hard to imagine someone had followed him up here from Mobile to kill him. What were the chances he knew someone here who hated him that much?

I felt the police would figure out it was a simple accident once they'd had a chance to look into it.

Packing up so many food trucks was noisy and messy. There was a lot of shouting as things went wrong—Fred's Fish Tacos had a flat tire, and Stick It Here lost their outside menu board.

Everyone was free to do what they wanted for the rest of the day. We could hang around in Charlotte and take in the sights or go on to Columbia. The only thing that mattered was stocking up and being ready for tomorrow when the next challenge began.

"Do you want to give me the list of supplies that you'll need?" Miguel asked as I was checking the Biscuit Bowl one last time before we left.

"Let me talk to Ollie and Uncle Saul later in Columbia before we plan what we're going to make tomorrow, now that we know we can serve our normal menu." I shifted Crème Brûlée's bed to the back of the food truck. There had to be room up front for Ollie to sit. Delia and Uncle Saul were riding with Miguel.

Ollie nudged me in the side before we left the kitchen. "I want to ride in the car with Delia and Miguel."

"Okay. That's fine."

"I'm not letting your uncle take up all of Delia's time. This was supposed to be an opportunity for Delia and me to get to know each other."

"Okay. I'm good with that. But maybe you should have told Delia that's what this was supposed to be."

He frowned. "Why?"

"Have you even told her that you *like* her?" I looked into his big face and had to smile. He was totally clueless.

"No. It's not necessary. When someone likes you, you can tell."

"Maybe *you* can. Most people need a hint. If you don't give Delia a hint about the way you feel, she'll never know."

He made a sound somewhere between a *humph* and a snort. "Like I should take advice from *you*. You haven't told Miguel the way you feel about him. I'll do things my way—in the car with Miguel."

"Okay. I'll see you in Columbia."

"That's right." He started to walk out of the kitchen and suddenly turned back. "And I'm not roller skating or singing in Columbia."

I laughed at that. "You got it."

After Ollie was gone, I got Crème Brûlée set up in his bed and gave him a little kiss for the road. Luckily the kitchen area was air-conditioned. It was only going to get hotter the farther south we went.

I made sure everything was secure, no falling refrigerators or microwave ovens. I closed the back of the Airstream and turned around to find myself face-to-face with a stranger.

He flashed his police badge at me and nodded. "Zoe Chase? I'm Detective John McSwain of the Charlotte-Mecklenburg Police Department. Could I have a few moments of your time?"

SIX

"Sure. I guess." I shrugged nonchalantly, but my heart was pounding. "What's this about?"

"I looked at the list of food truck owners involved in the race and noticed that you and Reggie Johnson were the only two from Mobile. Were you acquainted with him?"

"Only in the way that we're both food truck vendors. I didn't know him personally."

"What can you tell me about him?" He wrote down everything I said.

What could I say? He smelled like old grease and looked like he'd been in too many fights? That hc played dirty tricks on me to get better vendor spaces?

None of those things seemed right to say considering that Reggie was dead.

"I didn't know him well. When I was researching food trucks to start my own, I had one of his hot dogs. It was okay."

The detective finished writing and glanced up at me.

"Anything about his finances? Was he a gambling man? Did he have a family?"

"I think you should use your resources to find out if Reggie Johnson had a family." Miguel came around the corner of the food truck where he'd obviously been listening.

"Who are you?" Detective McSwain asked him.

"Miguel Alexander. I'm Miss Chase's attorney. I'm also from Mobile, if you'd like to question me about Mr. Johnson."

"Miss Chase doesn't need an attorney." The detective gave me a dirty look, like I had called Miguel for help. "I was only asking a few *friendly* questions about the deceased."

"If you have enough *friendly* answers, Miss Chase needs to drive to Columbia for the next part of the race." Miguel's tone was polite but firm.

"That's fine. I guess neither of you knew Mr. Johnson very well. I won't take up any more of your time." He nodded to me. "Miss Chase."

We watched him walk away.

"Did I miss anything important?" he asked.

"No. At least I don't think so. I couldn't tell him anything about Reggie—at least anything he'd want to hear about him. Reggie wasn't a very nice man, but his hot dogs were pretty good."

He smiled. "I don't think he wanted to hear that."

"That's what I mean. You must be right about the police suspecting Reggie's death wasn't an accident. I was thinking before about who might want to kill him. If it was another vendor, maybe they knew him in Mobile."

"Unless it was another vendor in the race and they wanted to eliminate some of the competition."

"I guess that's true." I bit my lip. "I felt a little bad not telling him about hearing Reggie argue with Alex in his truck. Do you think I should tell him?"

"I don't think we should even consider that idea, or any other idea that pertains to Reggie's death. We're here to win the race, right? Let's concentrate on that."

He was right. I let go of the questions that had wandered into my mind.

"Are you driving to Columbia now?" I asked him.

"I am. I'd like to get the supply part out of the way in Charlotte in case you have something difficult to find."

"There shouldn't be any problem. I don't make complicated food for the Biscuit Bowl."

"I guess I'll see you down there then."

I smiled at him, wishing I didn't feel so sweaty and full of grease. I smelled like biscuit bowls and bacon. Not a bad combination, usually. "Thanks again for being here, Miguel."

"I'm having a good time, Zoe. That's what vacations are all about, right?"

"You used your vacation time to be here?" I felt bad about that.

"Actually, I haven't had a vacation in so long that I'm not sure what I'm supposed to do with one. Besides, I'm the boss—like you. I get to take off when I want to." He smiled back at me. "I just haven't had a good reason to until now."

Our gazes locked and we moved a little closer to each other. I closed my eyes, excited that this would be our first kiss. My heart was pounding and my stomach was in knots.

Ollie came running around the side of the Airstream. "Forget Miguel's car. Delia has decided to stay in Charlotte and hop a ride with a friend of hers who lives here. She'll be down in Columbia later."

"What does that have to do with my car?" Miguel took a step back.

The golden moment was gone.

"Nothing." Ollie shrugged his broad shoulders. "I want to ride down in the Biscuit Bowl."

A *brilliant* idea sprang to mind. I flipped him the keys to the Airstream. "You and Uncle Saul can ride down in the truck. I'll ride down with Miguel. We can talk about tomorrow's menu on the phone."

I was so proud of myself. My stomach was doing flip-flops.

It was about an hour to the next stop. Miguel and I would have time to talk by ourselves with nothing getting in the way. If I managed to get the shopping list done in time, I could go shopping with him, too. Then maybe we could eat dinner together.

It would *almost* be a date.

"Anything you think we need on the supply list?" I asked Ollie before he left.

"I guess the usual—flour, water, shortening, fruit, and meat. Have you thought about doing drinks for the crowd in Columbia? We had a lot of people ask about that today. If so, we need sodas. You ditched what we usually carry to make room for other things."

"You're right about the drinks. I'll check on that before we go. Thanks, Ollie."

"I'm ready when you are," Miguel told me. "No hurry."

"I'll be back as soon as I ask someone about the drinks and find Uncle Saul."

Uncle Saul was easy to find. He was wandering around through the other food trucks that hadn't left the area yet. His hands were full of pork pot stickers, a few fish tacos, and a chocolate cake pop.

"Are you worried about going hungry between here and Columbia?" I asked him with a laugh.

"They made too much. There was good food about to be thrown away. I took what I could."

I knew he was right. That was one of the problems with finding the right balance between how much food you made each day and how much you could sell. Some basic staples could be used over again. When I had deep-fried biscuit bowls left over, I either had to find someone who wanted them or I had to throw them away. It looked like every other food truck vendor had the same problem.

It was different with the race, but with the excitement and having made food twice, it was easy to see how some vendors made too much.

I told him about the travel arrangements.

"This is good." He rubbed his hands together. "I want to give Ollie some pointers about how to attract a woman. He sure needs some help. We can discuss it on the way."

I wasn't sure if Ollie was going to want to take romantic advice from a man who lived in the swamp with an alligator and probably couldn't remember when he'd had his last date. But I didn't say anything. Whatever they talked about was up to them.

I needed to plan *my* strategy for talking to Miguel.

"I'll see you down there." I hugged him. "Thanks for all your help."

He winked at me. "Are you gonna do the roller skating and singing tomorrow?"

"Probably. So we better come up with some great biscuit bowl ideas to compensate. I might still be able to roller-skate, but I've never been able to sing. And let's not forget the taste challenge."

We talked for another few moments, laying out some ideas on fillings for the biscuit bowls. I left him getting into the food truck with Ollie.

I needed to find one of the people in charge who could tell me about selling drinks tomorrow. The cool-down tent was already gone. Most of the stage and equipment was packed up, too. I couldn't find Alex or any of the producers in the area. I had some phone numbers but wasn't sure who to call. Making up the rules as they went along made it tough on the contestants.

I finally spotted the big RV that I knew Alex was traveling in. There was a line of expensive trailers, most elegantly appointed, as Chef Art's was. They were completely out of the food truck league and weren't intended to be part of that scene.

I knocked on Alex's RV door. There was no answer. I didn't know who the other RVs belonged to. I decided I would go and knock on each door until I found someone

who could either answer my question about drinks or point
me to someone who could.

I was walking along the side of Alex's RV, almost reaching the back of the vehicle, when I heard someone talking.
Thinking it was someone on a cell phone having a private
conversation, I paused to let them finish.

"I don't *want* to know the whole plan." Alex's voice
sounded angry. "I paid *you* to take care of the problem. It
was stupid to kill that food truck vendor."

So Alex *was* involved with Reggie's death? What plan
was he talking about?

"It's gonna be harder to make anything look like an accident now," Alex continued. "The cops are all over. What
were you *thinking*?"

There was a moment of silence as Alex was probably
listening to the person speaking to him. I could hear him
nervously pacing the street.

"Yeah, well, it better look right. If it looks suspicious in
Columbia, the sponsors could stop the race. This is my best
chance to make it happen."

Time to panic!

Alex was talking about what had happened to Reggie in
a way that sounded as though he was responsible. Even worse,
it sounded like there could be more "accidents" to come.

I thought about Detective McSwain. I could tell him what
I'd heard. He might not have jurisdiction in Columbia, but
if he hurried, he could stop the problem in Charlotte.

Forgetting my need to know about soft drinks, I ran like
a crazy person through the hot afternoon. The Biscuit Bowl
was already gone from its location. The tow truck had taken
the Dog House. There were only a few food trucks left on
the street.

I spotted a group of uniformed police officers who were
starting to direct traffic around the food trucks and the other
RVs. Detective McSwain stood out among them in his dark
blue sports coat and jeans.

"Detective." I glanced uneasily across my shoulder when I finally reached him. "Could I have a word with you?"

"You're free to go, Miss Chase." He barely noticed me as he spoke to an officer.

"You don't understand. I have something important to tell you about Reggie's death. It can't wait. You need to know before everyone leaves Charlotte."

The detective shrugged and excused himself. "What is it, Miss Chase? Where's your lawyer?"

"Look, I'm sorry. Miguel was only looking out for me."

"Okay. What do you want to tell me?"

I explained the argument I'd overheard between Reggie and Alex. Then I carefully pointed out Alex Pardini's RV where I'd heard him on the phone. "I think Reggie was murdered, and there may be more to come."

He nodded, taking me seriously. "Did you actually *see* Mr. Pardini in the trailer with Johnson?"

"No," I admitted. "But I recognized his voice. That was about an hour or so before we heard the refrigerator fall."

He shook his head. "There may not be much I can do with this unless I get more evidence. You're sure about what you heard Mr. Pardini say on the phone—and that it *was* him? Would you be willing to swear to that in court?"

I thought about what that could mean. Charlotte was a long ride from Mobile. I didn't like Reggie, but he didn't deserve to die in whatever game Alex was playing. "Yes."

"Thanks for telling me. I'll look into it."

"Will you please keep my name out of it for now? I don't want to be booted out of the race if Alex isn't really involved."

"Sure. I'll ask a few questions, okay? Let me have your cell number so I can get in touch with you later."

I gave him my business card. "I hope I'm wrong."

He smiled. "You know, I get a lot of tips from people who overhear things or see things they aren't supposed to. A lot of times that's where convictions come from."

I thanked him and went to find Miguel. I didn't want to

be standing there with the police when Detective McSwain went to talk to Alex.

I glanced around for Miguel. He was leaning against his older black Mercedes, talking to a very beautiful woman who looked elegant and cool in a green crepe dress, despite the heat.

She probably didn't smell like biscuit bowls, either.

She laid her hand on his arm and lifted her chin as she smiled up into his handsome face. He smiled back as he looked deeply into her eyes.

I didn't like the way this was going at all. Maybe I'd waited too long to make my move.

I stood off to the side until *she* left. I didn't want to make it any worse by barging in like a total idiot. I didn't want Miguel to think I was desperate or something. I was still going to have to drive to Columbia with him since the Biscuit Bowl was gone. There was nothing I could do but wait.

"Where have you been?" Miguel asked when the other woman was finally gone. "Were the police bothering you again?"

"No. It was just the opposite." I explained what had happened as Miguel drove his car toward the interstate highway and Columbia.

I didn't ask about *her*.

- - - - - - -

"Why would someone involved with the race want to kill off the contestants?"

We were gridlocked in heavy traffic leaving the city.

"I was wondering the same thing." I longed to ask about his beautiful companion but couldn't make the words come out of my mouth. We weren't a couple *yet*. I had no claim on him. Besides, they were just talking.

And asking now would mean admitting that I'd seen them together and hadn't casually walked over and spoken to them. I felt stupid either way. I wondered what Delia would have done in these circumstances.

"It doesn't make any sense," Miguel continued about Reggie's death. "The sponsors would lose their money and the charities wouldn't get anything. The whole thing would be ruined."

"Sometimes it's hard to figure why people do the things they do."

"I know." He glanced at me as traffic began to pick up. "So, are you going to sell the food while you roller-skate and sing tomorrow?"

"Probably skate, if I can find a cheap pair of skates." I felt so awkward even talking to him. "I don't know about the singing."

"Not a problem about the skates." He inclined his head toward the backseat. "Compliments of the race. They gave out a pair of skates to each team. I went ahead and grabbed a pair in your size."

"How did you know what size to get?"

He glanced at my feet. "I noticed when you kicked your shoes off in the car the other day. Six and a half, right?"

I arched my brows and smiled in what I hoped was a provocative manner. "It's nice to be noticed."

Ugh! That was awful.

I'd never been good at one-liners. I should have known better. Maybe he wouldn't notice.

Oh, right. He smiled and didn't seem to take it the wrong way.

I really liked his smile. His eyes were such a perfect shade of brown—sort of like chocolate, but sexier. *Very nice.*

"I notice you *all* the time, Zoe. I can't imagine a man who wouldn't."

My heart beat fast. *Is that good? It sounds good.*

Or was he saying I flirted a lot? I did flirt a *little*, but not so much.

After that, I tried to keep the mood going. I brought up all kinds of subjects—except the one I *really* wanted to ask about.

He responded and admitted all kinds of crazy stuff about himself—really opening up for once. We laughed about the floats at carnival last year. It was great. It felt natural to be there with him. I hoped he felt the same.

There were several accidents on the road and police everywhere as we were leaving North Carolina. I decided it would be a good time to get out my cell phone and start making my shopping list since Miguel was going to have to concentrate more on the road.

Uncle Saul had already left me a few voice mails about food ideas.

Even though we weren't talking, I was thinking about Miguel and the death of his wife and child ten years ago. It had happened around the same time that he was framed for falsifying evidence when he'd run for district attorney in Mobile.

It was as though his life had stopped then. He'd quit the DA's office and opened up his own legal practice. Everyone in the city now knew him as a street lawyer who would help anyone in a jam. That's how I'd met him. He'd been Ollie's lawyer.

I knew Miguel was still getting over that tragedy—if anyone could ever really get over something like that. From what I could find out—and I had investigated *extensively*— he'd never even dated during the last ten years.

It didn't matter to me. I was willing to wait for the butterfly to emerge from the cocoon. I wanted to be the one he thought about when it was the right time for him.

I just hoped the mystery woman in Charlotte wasn't in line before me.

My cell phone rang as I was making my list. It startled me, and I dropped it on the floor. It was the Charlotte-Mecklenburg Police Department.

"Miss Zoe Chase?" the unfamiliar voice asked. "We're gonna need to talk to you again."

SEVEN

Miguel and I were less than thirty minutes outside of Charlotte. We turned around and drove back to police headquarters.

The man on the phone had been vague. It wasn't Detective McSwain, and yet the caller had said it was *about* him.

"I gave Detective McSwain my business card after I talked to him about Alex Pardini and Reggie," I explained to Miguel. "He said he might need me to testify about hearing the argument and the phone conversation. This seems too soon for that."

Miguel didn't like it. "They need to work on the investigation. They shouldn't call you for more information every few minutes."

I knew he was trying to protect me, and I felt good about that.

I couldn't afford to pay him. I could hardly ask him to act as my legal counsel if I needed one.

My father had paid my legal fees with him last year when

I'd been investigated for murder. I wasn't involved in the same way this time—although Reggie had been part of what had happened last year, too.

I didn't have much money of my own—everything I had was sunk into the business. I could offer him food. That was about it.

We parked the car and went inside the police station. I asked for Detective McSwain. The officer at the desk looked at me a little strangely and then asked us to wait. He said someone would come and talk to us right away.

A few minutes later, Detective Macey Helms came out and shook our hands. She was an attractive, heavyset black woman with braided hair. Her deep purple suit was very nice. I complimented her on it.

"Thanks." Her voice said she wasn't impressed. "If you two will come this way."

We went with her to a small conference room. The metal bar on the table reminded me that criminals were interrogated here. It made me uncomfortable, which was probably a good thing. I have a way of running off at the mouth sometimes. I was sure this wasn't an appropriate moment for that. I clamped my lips closed as I sat down.

Just let Miguel do the talking. Don't say anything you'll regret.

Another detective, who introduced himself as Stanley Marsh, stood at the side of the room while Detective Helms sat down with us. He looked like he was in his thirties, maybe, with dirty blond hair and blue eyes. His clothes were worn and dirty. Maybe he was an undercover cop.

I could tell Miguel was a little agitated. His face was alert as he spoke to the two detectives. "What's going on? Miss Chase understood that she was here to speak to Detective McSwain."

Detective Helms put a card on the table. "Recognize that, Miss Chase?"

That was easy enough. "Yes. It's my business card. Was there something wrong with giving it to Detective McSwain?"

The two detectives glanced at each other.

"We found your card on Detective McSwain's *body* a short while ago," Detective Helms said in an accusatory tone.

I sat forward in my chair. "Body? He was perfectly alive and well when I saw him last. You can ask all the police officers who were out there with the food truck race. I barely even talked with him alone."

"A short while ago, Detective McSwain was found dead. He appears to have been the victim of a hit-and-run."

"That happened very quickly," Miguel added. "We were only thirty minutes out of Charlotte."

"So the two of you were together?" Detective Marsh asked.

"Yes. We've been together since I left Detective McSwain." I peeked at Miguel. He didn't seem to have a problem with me saying that.

"What did you and Detective McSwain talk about?" Marsh was standing against the wall with his arms folded across his chest.

"He asked me a few questions about Reggie Johnson the first time. Later, I told him that I'd heard Alex Pardini from the race talking about killing Reggie."

Helms nodded to Marsh. "The dead man from the food truck."

Marsh moved toward the table. "And what did you tell him?"

"I told him that I barely knew Reggie. We were both from Mobile and had food trucks. That was about all we had in common. I was walking past an RV when I heard Alex talking to someone about Reggie's death like it wasn't an accident and there could be more to come. Alex was talking about covering it up."

"And you and Mr. Johnson were both competitors in the food truck race, no?" Helms suggested.

"Not really." I smiled at both of them, not wanting to sound superior, but let's face it—the Dog House wasn't a real competitor with the Biscuit Bowl. "I make most of my food from scratch. Reggie put hot dogs on buns and dressed them up."

Marsh slammed his hand on the table. "Did you kill Reggie Johnson, or were you in *any* way responsible for his death?"

Miguel sat forward. "What's this about? I was with Miss Chase when she was speaking to Detective McSwain. He never said anything about her being responsible for Mr. Johnson's death. In point of fact, Miss Chase was constantly with others, who will be glad to vouch for her entire morning."

Detective Helms made a dismissive motion at Detective Marsh. The man immediately backed off to stand against the wall again.

"Here's what we've got," Helms said. "We have a food truck driver who was found dead after a strap was cut that held his refrigerator in place. That happened *before* the race. We had reason to think it might be suspicious even without what Miss Chase just told us. We have a fine detective who was found dead as he was investigating that death. We know Detective McSwain wasn't *accidentally* struck by a vehicle. And we have your business card in his coat pocket, Miss Chase. How do you think all those things go together?"

I started to speak. Miguel put his hand on mine.

"Miss Chase isn't a police officer. She doesn't have any idea how those things go together."

"Okay." Detective Marsh tried a new approach. "Why was your business card the *only* one Detective McSwain took from all the food truck drivers that were here in Charlotte?"

I started to speak again. Again Miguel said I shouldn't answer.

"You did your part," he argued. "Let them do their jobs."

- - - - - - -

An hour later, Miguel and I were walking out of the police station. The police had asked a lot of the same questions over and over. I only had the same answers. Eventually I guess they got tired of my answers, but there was nothing they could charge me with so they let me go.

"So you think it's okay to go to Columbia now?" I asked him.

"Yes. I think you were very clear on what you had to say." He squeezed my hand. "Good job, Zoe."

"Thanks. I hope they didn't think I had anything to do with it. Reggie was obnoxious, but I wouldn't have killed him—although Ollie said he would have."

"I'm glad you *didn't* say that." Miguel smiled as he opened the car door for me. "The police didn't suspect you of anything. They were just trying to get an idea on what occurred here. You happened to be part of that."

I had ten calls from Uncle Saul on my phone. He kept asking where we were and how close we were to Columbia. I suppose we would've already been there without the police detour.

After I talked to him, I turned to Miguel. He was intently staring at the interstate highway again.

"Do you think Detective McSwain was killed because he was investigating what I told him?"

"I think we should leave it alone, Zoe. We don't want to be involved in this any further."

"I kind of feel responsible, if that's what happened."

"The police will take care of it. It might not be safe for you to walk around asking questions, in case Alex is involved with what happened. You don't want to end up like Reggie."

I looked out of the side window, watching the landscape change from big city to rolling hills and small communities. Charlotte was a nice place, although my memory of it might be colored by the two deaths that had just occurred there.

I had a lot of questions that Miguel didn't want me to ask. I was a little afraid to ask them, too.

Not only because someone might kill me, but with Alex involved, I could be kicked out of the race.

I was happy to see the signs for Columbia. I hadn't exactly been up for initiating another conversation like the one we'd had before as we were leaving Charlotte. I was worried about Reggie and Alex, and Detective McSwain. The food truck race had suddenly become even more stressful.

Columbia was a clean city, smaller than Charlotte. It was also warmer and more humid. I had the GPS coordinates in my phone for the hotel we were staying at. Miguel's Mercedes was a little too old to have GPS built in, even though it was in immaculate condition.

"Pull off on this exit," I told him. "It looks like the hotel is close to downtown this time." In Charlotte, the hotel had been outside the city.

"What are you doing about Crème Brûlée tonight?" he asked.

He was asking because I'd had to sneak my cat into the hotel last night. The hotel wasn't pet friendly. I'd already looked up the hotel in Columbia. It wasn't pet friendly, either.

I had to leave the air-conditioning on in the food truck all night anyway, but I didn't want Crème Brûlée to get scared and start howling.

"I'm sneaking him in with me again, I guess," I said.

He shrugged. "Where's the next turn?"

I glanced at my phone. "One mile on the right. We should see the signs for the hotel from the road."

Maybe he was making conversation by asking about Crème Brûlée. Maybe he was looking for a way to break the silence between us without bringing up the police problem in Charlotte. Either way, I was happy to oblige.

I told him about the biscuit bowl fillings we were working on for tomorrow, and the plans I had to remodel my restaurant at home, if I won the prize money.

"You really love making food, don't you?" A smile tugged at his lips.

"I do. Food makes people happy. They go out and have a good meal and leave their problems behind them for a while. There's nothing wrong with that."

"No." He reached over and squeezed my hand. "There isn't."

We found the multistory hotel easily. Uncle Saul and Ollie were waiting in the bar on the ground floor. Miguel and I checked in at the front desk and then joined them.

I was reluctant to bring up what had kept me in Charlotte, but I knew they were going to find out anyway. I explained the whole thing when we sat down.

Miguel sipped his Corona and didn't say a word.

Ollie was full of questions. "So they think Reggie was murdered and this cop was killed because you asked him to look into the conversation you heard between Alex and some mystery guy who might have killed him?"

"When are you gonna learn to keep your pretty mouth *shut*, Zoe?" Uncle Saul shook his head. "You didn't get that from your daddy's side of the family, I can tell you that. The Chases know how to keep secrets."

Miguel saluted him with his bottle.

I was conscious of the fact that there were dozens of people from the food truck race in the bar and felt exposed by the conversation. "I don't want to be the next victim, do you?"

"What about Alex?" Ollie said loud enough to turn heads.

"*Shh!*" I reminded him. "We don't know what's going on with that yet. Let's not rock the boat until we're ready to swim."

"Right." Ollie scrutinized the other patrons of the bar. "The killer could be right in here with us."

"Maybe." I glanced around. "But why would anyone want to kill Reggie? He wasn't a great threat as a competitor. He was by himself, unlikely to win the race. It doesn't make sense. Why not kill someone from Grinch's Ganache or Our Daily Bread?"

Uncle Saul made a disbelieving face. "You think those two are the front-runners, Zoe?"

"I think so. What can't you do with bread? Who doesn't love cupcakes? It won't matter what the challenge is; bread or cupcakes will win every time. Besides, the bread truck people are *ministers*. Everyone loves ministers."

"What about Stick It Here?" Ollie said. "Everyone loves pot stickers."

"Not so much, maybe," Uncle Saul observed. "And they weren't very creative with the last challenge."

Miguel called for another Corona. Ollie and Uncle Saul both had their drinks refreshed.

I decided I only needed one margarita. I got the keys from my uncle to go out and check on Crème Brûlée. I'd have to decide if it was late enough to try and sneak him inside.

There was an underground lot where all the food trucks were parked. It was easy to tell that the hotel had been chosen because there was plenty of room in the parking area. The trucks had to be plugged in and air-conditioned to keep the food fresh.

The Biscuit Bowl's twirling ceramic biscuit wouldn't have fit inside anything less than twenty feet high. There were colorful additions on some of the other food trucks, too, like the giant loaf of bread on Our Daily Bread and the sticks coming out of Stick It Here. Grinch's Ganache had a big cowboy hat on top.

My twirling biscuit was the tallest, and that made it easy to find in the pack. I was very proud of the design. Uncle Saul and Ollie had come up with the idea when the truck was being renovated. I added on to it later.

It struck me as soon as I opened the door that the inside of my food truck was too hot and completely dark. There were usually little colored lights on the appliances and a clock on the microwave. Nothing was on.

I found Crème Brûlée. He was a little warm with his heavy coat, but he seemed fine. I checked the circuit breakers in the truck. Everything seemed okay, but the power wasn't working.

Holding my cat because I was afraid he might make a slow jog for the door, I checked the outside plug. That was the problem.

Someone had deliberately not only cut my power cord but chopped it into pieces.

EIGHT

I got on the phone right away with Uncle Saul. He, Ollie, and Miguel ran down to the garage after snagging the hotel security man.

I kept Crème Brûlée hidden while the security man looked at everything. If the hotel found out I was sneaking my cat inside, they might kick us all out.

"Yep." Sid, the security man and part-time parking attendant, verified the results. "Somebody cut up your cord all right."

By this time, other food truck vendors were parking their trucks. Other vendors who were already checked in heard what was going on. They raced down to make sure their trucks weren't damaged. The space was suddenly filled with food truck teams.

Everyone checked their trucks. The new arrivals were safe. The damage had been done before they'd arrived. Someone called the police, and the entire garage erupted in chaos.

I took advantage of what was going on and sneaked Crème Brûlée up to the hotel room in a large tote bag. I wasn't able to bring his food and litter box. That worried me some. I decided to put him in the glass shower stall with some water.

"You're going to be fine," I told him as he meowed at me. "At least you'll be cool. Don't make too much noise or we'll both be sleeping in Miguel's car tonight. And you know how he'll feel about *that*."

Actually, Miguel had never really had a problem with my cat riding in his car. But Crème Brûlée didn't know that. Maybe it would encourage him not to start howling.

I went back to the garage. It was really a mess by then. There were a dozen police officers walking around, searching everything, and taking pictures. The garage was cordoned off with crime scene tape.

The food truck vendors were upset. Alex was there with the sponsors and producers. The garage wasn't meant to hold that much angst.

"What am I supposed to do about my fish?" Fred Bunn asked whoever would listen. He was the owner of Fred's Fish Tacos. He was a short man, barely five feet, with crazy, curly red hair and millions of freckles.

I liked him just for his curly hair. It made me go to him and sympathize. Curly hair attracts curly hair.

"I know. I've lost a few things, too. Will we be compensated for our loss?" There wasn't enough milk, butter, or eggs left over in the mini fridge for the next challenge, and what had been left from Charlotte was spoiled.

We were lucky we hadn't shopped yet as Miguel had wanted to. I'd preferred to head straight to Columbia and shop there after being detained so long in Charlotte.

Fred looked at me like I was crazy and turned away to complain to someone else. It seemed as though my sympathy wasn't what he was looking for.

I found Miguel, Ollie, and Uncle Saul at the Biscuit Bowl. "Have you heard anything yet?"

"They're saying it was vandalism because the hotel

announced that vendors from the race were staying here tonight to get publicity." Miguel shrugged. "I don't know what they were expecting."

"I'm not buying that explanation," Ollie said. "Maybe if Reggie weren't dead, I might see it their way. Now I'm thinking someone is trying to sabotage the race."

"For what purpose?" Uncle Saul asked him. "They don't like food trucks? You're being paranoid, Ollie."

"It seems more likely that one of the vendors did this to cut out the competition," Miguel suggested. "Anyway, the police said to stay with our food trucks and they would take our statements."

"You don't have to stay," I told them. "You can go upstairs and get some rest for tomorrow."

"If there *is* a tomorrow," Ollie grumbled.

"I'm not leaving you alone down here," Uncle Saul said. "I don't like the looks of this, Zoe. Who knows what will happen next?"

Uncle Saul tended to be a little paranoid, too.

Alex came around to our side of the Biscuit Bowl with a big grin on his attractive face. "Don't you worry about a thing, Biscuit Bowl team. We'll pick up the tab for your damages and get these cords fixed before tomorrow."

"Thanks." I tried not to show my dubious feelings toward him. He might not be guilty of anything.

"There's only one thing," Alex finally said. "I can get these cords repaired *tonight*—won't cost you a cent. I can't do the same with reimbursing you for your loss on supplies. If you'll send me an itemized list of what you lost, and how much you paid for it, I can get a check cut for you by the end of the week. Best I can do."

Bobbie Shields, wearing another colorful Hawaiian dress, came around to complain to him. "You know, I looked at my losses. I already shopped. I can't replace what I need to start again tomorrow without a check from you *tonight*. I'm not made of money."

Alex looked uncomfortable. "I wish I could do something more, but this is it. You might be able to get a payday loan or some such in the city."

Dante Eldridge, the owner of Stick It Here, also joined us. He was a large black man who was covered in tattoos. He wore a red handkerchief around his closely cropped hair. His tight red tank top showed the power and size of his chest and arms.

"Don't give me that poor story, Pardini. Get some money from those rich sponsors over there. Give *them* a check at the end of the week. The rest of us can barely afford to be here. We can't afford to lose all our food."

Alex was definitely on the defensive. "Good idea! Why don't you ask each of your sponsors for money? They could get you a check. No problem."

Dante stepped closer to him, dwarfing Alex. "I *am* my sponsor, fool. Get me some money to replace what was lost, or your luxury ride might be too damaged to drive tomorrow."

Several other vendors had stepped closer to hear the conversation. They agreed loudly and adamantly with Dante and Bobbie.

It was almost amusing watching Alex gauge the mood and then do a quick cut and run to his RV. I could imagine that he locked himself in, too.

"Now what are we supposed to do?" Dante was furious. "There's not gonna be much of a race if there's no money."

Reverend Jablonski came toward the group with his arms outstretched. It seemed to be a popular pose.

"Ladies and gentlemen. I, and my fellow team members, would like to help you in your hour of need. We have sufficient funds to give each of you a stake, so to speak, to begin your sales tomorrow. We incurred no losses—flour and water don't go bad. We would enjoy helping you."

I was surprised and pleased by the offer from the members of Our Daily Bread food truck. It was truly inspiring.

I felt sure we'd be fine in the Biscuit Bowl. Our losses weren't that severe. Repairing the electric cord was good for us. We could settle up with Alex later.

Bobbie, Fred, and Dante all took loans from Reverend Jablonski. It made the vandalism a lot easier to bear. Maybe Alex would even be able to come out of his RV.

"I'm going back upstairs for another drink while we're waiting for the miracle-working electrician who's going to get all these rigs repaired tonight." Uncle Saul slapped Ollie on the back. "Are you coming?"

"Sure. Anybody hear from Delia yet?"

"We probably won't hear from her until she gets here," I said. "She's a big girl. She can find her way here."

I asked Miguel if I could get the roller skates from his Mercedes. "I might as well see if I can still do this. I'd like to know tonight if I have to withdraw from the challenge."

"Are you going to practice down here?" He glanced around at the crowded garage.

"No. I think I'll hit the pavement upstairs once I've given my statement."

Miguel got the skates and waited around with me for one of the police officers.

We talked about all kinds of things—I stayed away from any discussion about Reggie's death or what had happened to Detective McSwain.

Instead we talked about carnival and taking boats out on Mobile Bay. We both enjoyed eating French pastry and good coffee. He even told me a few things about his legal practice, which was set up in one of the worst parts of town.

"I guess you have to go where the customers are, like I do." I said. "Ollie told me the two of you met when you got him out of jail. I know I'll never forget how kind you were when the police thought I'd murdered the taco truck driver."

"You're a different case. For one thing, you *paid* for services. I have a problem collecting from a lot of my clients.

I'm thinking about living in my office the way you live in your diner."

I smiled but pointed out the major difference between us. "You could go back into practice where people pay you. You don't have to build up a reputation for what you do. Everyone knows you."

"That may be true." He watched some of the vendors pulling spoiled meat from their freezers. "But most of my reputation isn't very good. I don't know if I could ever do legitimate legal work again after the fiasco of the election. I don't know if anyone would trust me. And there are so many people who can't afford legal advice. I think I'm where I need to be—as long as my expenses stay low and I don't have a life."

"Well you can always come and eat at my place for free. Consider it a night out."

"And I can give you free legal advice." He smiled at me.

I hadn't asked, and I was dying to know. Now was as good a time as any. "Why did you agree to come with me on the race? I know you have better things to do. Not that I'm complaining. I'm just curious."

"I thought we could spend some time together away from our normal routines. I didn't know it would be so crazy, but it's good to talk, right?"

"It's *very* good to talk," I agreed.

Whee!

One of the many police officers in the garage finally came to take my statement. Under Miguel's watchful eye, I left out the part about what had happened in Charlotte. I probably would've added it on otherwise. I like to tell the whole story.

After the officer had nodded and given me his card, Miguel helped me hide Crème Brûlée's collapsible litter box and his food. We sneaked those things up to my room, along with the skates. My cat was genuinely glad to see these little pieces of home when I'd set them up.

"Have you sent me the supply list yet?" Miguel asked

when I'd closed the bathroom door to give Crème Brûlée some privacy.

I took out my phone and pushed send. "That should be it. Thank you again for doing this. And for waiting with me downstairs. *And* for helping me with the police."

"You're very welcome."

We stood there awkwardly. My cell phone rang and so did his. We exchanged quick good-byes and he was gone.

I sighed and answered my phone. It was my mother in Mobile. She'd heard about the problems we were having with the race and wanted to check on me.

Wanting to check on me was the story of our relationship. My mother was a high-powered corporate attorney who was running for a judgeship even as we spoke. Her goals in life included driving me crazy and pushing me to be more like her.

Instead, I was more like my dad who wasn't a slacker but had never had the urgent need for greatness that my mother enjoyed. I looked like him, too—like Uncle Saul. The three of us shared black curly hair, even though my dad cropped his down to nothing so it wouldn't curl. I guessed it was his way of controlling what he could of his life, especially while he'd been married to my mother.

"So what's going on? The food truck murder is all over the news. Maybe you should come home before it gets any worse," my mother suggested.

I could imagine her sitting in her perfectly organized office with her well-toned body and sculpted blond hair. We shared blue eyes, and that was about it. I loved my mother, Anabelle Chase. I just wasn't like her.

"It's okay, Mom. It didn't happen anywhere near me. I'm pretty sure the police were wrong about it, too. I think it was just an accident. They're making a big deal out of it to get more publicity. You don't have to worry."

"Too late. I'm worried. I should send someone down there to take care of you."

"Uncle Saul is here."

"Exactly. That's why you should come home *now*. Don't make me come up there and get you."

My mother had never appreciated Uncle Saul's free spirit lifestyle. I was sure that was why their relationship was quickly over when they were very young, and she'd made her play for the other Chase brother.

Uncle Saul could've run the Bank of Mobile with my father. It had been in their family for more than a century. It was his birthright. Instead, he'd opened a successful restaurant and then left to live in the swamp.

She didn't understand that he needed to be different. It had only gotten worse when she'd divorced my dad.

"I'll be home in a few days. Everything will be fine."

"Zoe, I get your strange need to express yourself with food. But I don't want you to die doing it."

"Mom—"

"I'll send you a plane ticket in your email. Talk to you later. Love you."

I looked at the phone. My mother's pretty face still lingered there, even though she'd hung up on me. Crème Brûlée was scratching at the bathroom door for me to let him out.

I took a deep breath and went to grab my bag. I'd brought duct tape to protect the corners of the room, even though his claws were cut short. I didn't want to take any chances that I would have to pay for damages.

I certainly wasn't going home until I got kicked out or the race was over. My mother claimed to understand, but I knew she didn't. Winning this race meant a lot to me—more than a few cut cords or even Reggie's death.

I was there to win!

NINE

Despite Alex's promises that we'd be reimbursed for the losses on our food trucks, I went ahead and called my insurance agent. I figured that was why I paid those high premiums every month.

I thought Alex sounded a little sketchy about the whole thing. I didn't need the money back right away, but I wanted my losses covered at some point. I wasn't made out of money, even if I won the race.

I was headed down to try out my skates, and when I opened the hotel room door, Delia was reaching for it. We both laughed. We were sharing a room for the night.

"You *really* did some shopping," I remarked as she passed me. A young hotel worker brought in several bags and boxes, which he put on the bed.

Delia tipped him well and thanked him for his help.

"I don't shop all the time. A girl has to have something to wear, especially if she's going to be on TV." She sat down on the bed and stretched her long, slender body. "How are things going here?"

I told her about the food truck vandalism. "The Biscuit Bowl is supposed to be repaired by tomorrow. I hope so. I sent Miguel out to buy a couple hundred dollars' worth of food."

Delia smiled at me. "How are things going with you and Miguel?"

"We talked. He waited for me at the food truck until the police came for my statement." I included a big grin with this information. "Good, huh?"

She yawned. "Good—if he's your *brother*. Not so good if you want him to be your *lover*."

"I wasn't thinking so much about being his lover as going out on a real date." Maybe I was wrong about getting tips from Delia.

"Same thing. You need Miguel to look at you as more than somebody he picked up in his business portfolio. You have to step up your game, Zoe. Make him see you as a beautiful, desirable woman."

I sat down on the bed beside her. "That would be nice. I think he still considers me a client that he helps out. I've tried to change his attitude. I'm not sure what else to do."

Delia got up and grabbed one of the dress bags. "I have just the thing. Once he sees you in this during dinner tonight, he won't be able to think of you as *anything* but the woman he wants in his bed."

I swallowed hard. *Big step!* "Okay. But could we start by dating first? You know, dinner, dancing, that kind of thing."

She laughed. "Oh, Zoe, you're such an amateur. Just put yourself in my hands. Miguel won't know what hit him."

I hoped I'd know what to do with that kind of reaction, but I agreed. *What did I have to lose?*

"By the way," she said softly with that strange smile again. "Is Ollie involved with anyone?"

I cheerfully told her that he wasn't. He'd be thrilled when he found out she liked him back.

We talked for a while about Ollie and what I knew about him, which wasn't much.

"Ollie's *sexy*, don't you think?"

Sexy? Ollie?

"Maybe, but it's hard for me to see him like that. I've never seen him with a woman."

"I can see it in him." Her tone was fairly purring. "You probably just don't notice, Zoe. He's more like your brother."

"I think Ollie is handsome, in a rugged kind of way. He's much younger than he looks, I think. It may have been a while since he had a relationship."

Should I tell her what I knew about Ollie's past? I only had it secondhand from Miguel. I decided it wasn't my story to tell. When he was ready, he'd say something to her.

"Ollie's a real man." Delia brushed her long brown hair, looking at herself in the mirror. "He's exactly my type."

She was about to show me the dress that would be perfect for me when my cell phone rang. It was a call from the front desk. Someone was there to see me.

"Hold that thought," I said to Delia. "I'll be back in a few minutes."

"I'm meeting someone. It's a while until dinner at eight. Let's meet back here at seven, shall we? We'll have you looking fabulous in no time. Miguel won't be able to keep his hands off you!"

I wasn't at all sure that Delia understood the concept of dating.

But it *was* a plan, and I didn't have any other bright ideas on how to make Miguel notice me. I decided I could deal with the consequences *after* the plan had worked.

I was definitely going to need a shower, and my hair needed some extra conditioning after being under Chef Art's hat all day. I'd have plenty of time to get to that. I took my room key and went down to the front desk.

I thought it could be Alex or Chef Art waiting for me downstairs. Instead, it was Detectives Helms and Marsh. I was surprised to see them since I was in another city and state.

"Let's sit down over here for a moment," Detective Helms said after our initial wary greetings.

At least the greetings were wary on *my* part. What were they doing here?

We sat down in a few chairs near a window and a pretty fountain with some plants growing around it. I was glad Miguel wasn't there, on one hand, and sorry that he wasn't on the other. I'd have to mind my own tongue.

"Miss Chase." Detective Helms smiled in a much friendlier manner than she had that morning. "May I call you Zoe?"

"Sure. What's up?"

"We have special permission to be here with the race after what happened in Charlotte to Mr. Johnson and Detective McSwain. Our chief believes we've found evidence that proves the hit-and-run was intentional."

"What kind of evidence?" I wondered how they could tell the difference between a hit-and-run being intentional or not.

"That's on a need-to-know basis." Detective Marsh still had his hostile attitude toward me.

"I guess that means I don't need to know." I smiled as I got to my feet. "I don't know why you're here, but I'm stressed enough with the food truck race—not to mention everything else that's happening. I don't need your stress, too."

Helms nudged Marsh with her elbow and nodded at me.

"Oh, all right. We need your help, Miss Chase. Our lab techs found video footage of what happened to McSwain. The car didn't even try and stop for him. In fact, it went faster and swerved *toward* him. It was murder."

"We believe it's all wrapped up with the information you gave him and the food truck race." Helms smiled at me again, trying to look pleasant. She wasn't very good at it, even though she looked fabulous in her black suit.

"I don't know what I can do to help." I sat back down in one of the comfy chairs. "I told you what I knew earlier. Believe me, I didn't hold anything back. You can ask Miguel, my lawyer."

"We understand that there were more problems involving the race when you got here today," Helms said. "Piecing these murders together might be a lot easier for us with someone on the *inside*."

I understood. "I'll be glad to tell you what I know when I know something else."

"That would be a good start," Marsh said.

"It was vandalism here. No one was hurt or killed. You can probably find out more from the Columbia police. I gave them my statement."

"You didn't see anyone hanging around the food trucks before it happened, did you?" Helms wanted to know.

"I went down there to check on things. The food trucks are in the underground parking area. The damage was already done. I didn't see anyone down there."

"Were *all* the food trucks damaged?" Marsh had a bored expression on his face.

"Only the ones that got here early. There were a few that were just arriving. Someone got in and out before that."

"I'd like to give you my personal cell phone number." Helms handed me a business card. "You can call me here anytime, day or night. If you see or hear *anything* suspicious, let me know. I promise we won't follow you around. Just keep us informed."

I put the paper in my pocket. "Okay. I hope there isn't anything else. Tempers are short already."

Detective Marsh thanked me. "We appreciate your help."

I went back upstairs to think about everything. I took a nice hot shower, put on a cucumber facial mask, and let my hair conditioner sink in for a while. Delia was gone. It was still a long time until dinner.

I looked at the roller skates on the floor near the bed. I

thought I might as well give them a try. I could still opt out of tomorrow's challenge. Maybe better that than to look like an idiot.

Not knowing if I might fall a few times, I put on a new pair of jeans and a Biscuit Bowl tank top. I'd noticed a back area in the parking lot outside that might be a good place to practice without an audience.

My hair was still damp but was already perking up after a day of abuse. It was good to get the deep fryer smell and feel off me. I realized I was lucky that Miguel hadn't tried to kiss me while we were waiting downstairs for the police. That might've been disgusting, and a little sweet potato flavored.

Outside, it was warm, but the sun was lower and a cool breeze was skittering around between the buildings. I sat on the curb and put on the skates. I hadn't worn skates since college and my job as a carhop. It had been fun at the time, but it didn't sound like much fun now.

Fifty thousand dollars was a powerful motivator. I could skate and sing. The worst that could happen might be that someone would ask me to shut up. I'd sing *quietly*.

There were large trash bins in the area where I'd chosen to practice. I held on to one as I got up from the curb. My legs felt like spaghetti. I would have fallen if it wasn't for the trash bin.

Maybe I was wrong about the whole thing. Maybe this would be a good challenge for me to sit out.

"Having any luck?"

Miguel's voice startled me. I felt the skates slip out from under me and panicked, flailing around like an octopus. I would've fallen on my rear end, but Miguel caught me before I hit the ground.

"Thanks." I was a little breathless. Our faces were very close together, and his arms were around me. "You always seem to show up at the right time."

"Just another part of my service, ma'am."

"I don't know how I can ever repay you, sir."

"We'll think of some way, Zoe." He slowly bent his head and kissed me.

I couldn't believe it. No fancy dress. No brilliant conversation. Just him and me, the skates and the smelly trash bin. I was glad he already had his arms around me or I would've been on the concrete for sure.

"Now what?" I was *so* glad that I'd taken a shower before I came down.

He helped me stand up. "Can you sing, skate, and pass out food at the same time?"

At that moment, I wasn't sure I could talk and walk at the same time. I felt like crying with relief. *Miguel more than likes me, too!*

"I'm not sure I can skate—*without* singing or carrying food."

"Just hold on to me and ease into it."

I held his hands as I moved my feet around on the concrete. I was hoping it would start feeling natural, the way it does when you get on a bicycle again or drive a stick.

"Can you do it on your own now?"

Not as well as I can when I'm holding your hands. "It's getting there."

He let go of me and the skates took off down a tiny hill, back to the trash bins. He put his hands on my waist. As I started to fall, he caught me again, my head on his shoulder, his arms around me. We were both laughing.

"Maybe we should forget the roller-skating challenge tomorrow," I whispered.

"It might be for the best."

He was about to kiss me again when a loud voice called out, "Zoe Chase! This is your backstage moment to let the world see the *real* you!"

TEN

I straightened up right away. Miguel was slow to release me, obviously not as distressed by the booming voice.

A camera was thrust in my face. Alex was there, and so were two interviewers I remembered seeing in Charlotte, wondering when it was going to be my turn. It was my turn *now*.

Miguel was pushed out of the spotlight.

Yes. This was my backstage moment—in roller skates—standing next to the trash bin I didn't dare let go of if I didn't want to fall. It was pathetic.

"Could we go inside?" I asked. "Wouldn't it look better if I were inside?"

"Not at all," Alex responded. "That's why we call this the *backstage moment*. So people following the race can get a feeling for the *real* you."

That's just great.

"Tell us about you, Zoe," one of the interviewers said. "The world is waiting to hear all about *you*!"

I started talking about myself hesitantly. I was so unprepared. I tried to keep it simple.

"We hear you have a boyfriend." The second interviewer cut me off and glanced at Miguel. "Is this him over here?"

Miguel frowned and waved his hand.

"Come on!" the interviewer encouraged him. "Help us make Zoe's backstage moment better!"

"No, thanks." Miguel smiled at me. "She's doing fine on her own."

"Obviously the shy type." Alex grinned. "But we have someone who isn't so shy. Someone we found at home in Mobile. Can you guess who that is, Zoe?"

"No." I bit my lip. "Not really."

"It's your ex. Tommy Elgin, a financial wizard from the Azalea City!"

Tommy Lee? Oh no!

Tommy Lee and I had gone out together for many years. He was pretty much the only man I'd dated since college. Our families had expected us to get married.

Our relationship was good—until I'd quit my job and started the food truck. He hated the idea of me being in the food service industry and had started seeing another woman. We parted on very bad terms.

And there was Tommy Lee on a video, talking about me and how obsessed I was with my business. He said it had ruined my life. *It was terrible.*

"Okay. Can we just cut that?" I asked. "I'm not with him anymore. He's not backstage with Zoe Chase."

"But this is the juicy part," the interviewer insisted with malicious glee.

He was enjoying himself *way* too much.

"If you want to talk to someone who *is* part of my backstage, you should talk to my team. They're the ones who really know me. We're in the Biscuit Bowl together all the time. No one knows me better."

Alex signaled the interviewer to turn off Tommy Lee's rant. "What have you got for me, Zoe?"

I thought quickly. "Uncle Saul is part of my team. He lives with an albino alligator in the swamp."

"Yeah?" He seemed interested.

"Yes. He used to have his own restaurant in Mobile, too. He'd be a good person to talk to about backstage Zoe Chase."

The three men mulled it over. *Please, please get away from Tommy Lee.*

"Okay," Alex decided. "He sounds interesting. And it would be better from here anyway. Where is he?"

"At the bar, probably. He'll be glad to talk to you. You can ask him anything you like about me."

"All right." Alex made his *let's end this* movement with his hand. "Let's find Uncle Saul. See you later, Zoe Chase!"

Miguel helped me up to the room I was sharing with Delia. I didn't wait to take off the skates because I wanted to get upstairs before something else embarrassing happened.

I took out my key and let myself into the hotel room. "I guess I didn't realize what we'd be in for during the race. I'm sorry."

"That's okay. I knew there'd be some odd things going on. I don't mind."

"Thanks. I hope you weren't *too* embarrassed. At least they didn't call you my boyfriend on TV."

"I've had people call me a lot worse."

We both laughed at that.

"Maybe we should get those skates off. I delivered your supplies to the Biscuit Bowl before I came to find you. The power is back on."

"That's great news. Thanks." I sat on the edge of the bed. Delia was still out.

Crème Brûlée walked over to me and meowed for me to pick him up. He'd never try something as big as jumping up on the bed next to me. I lifted him, and he cuddled next to me, purring.

"I guess you already know my history." He knelt in front of me and untied my skate laces. "I'm not a stranger to bad publicity."

"I know." Should I have admitted that I knew almost *everything* about him?

"Then you know about my wife—and the scandal, as my grandmother calls it."

"Yes. I know you ran for district attorney and you were accused of breaking the law."

Was this leading up to something?

He smiled up at me as he eased my right foot out of the skate. "Then you know why I'm a little camera shy. I hope I didn't hurt your feelings back there. I certainly wouldn't mind them calling me your boyfriend, except for that."

"Really?"

He took off my left skate and helped me to my feet. "Really."

He was going to kiss me again. We were so close, and then the hotel phone rang.

"Did you want to get that?" His lips were only a breath away from mine.

"No. Not really." I moved the short distance between us and closed the deal.

The phone continued to ring and we continued to ignore it. Then came the pounding on the door.

"Oh, for goodness' sake!" I moved away from him, reluctantly, and went to answer it.

"Excuse me, ma'am." A hotel employee interrupted with a red face. "I'm looking for Zoe Chase. There are two police detectives downstairs to see her."

He smiled and held out his hand. I certainly wasn't going to tip him after he'd interrupted something wonderful between me and Miguel to tell me about Helms and Marsh.

"Thanks!" Miguel put some money in his hand and then closed the door. "Zoe?"

I explained about meeting with the two detectives from Charlotte while he was gone to get supplies. "I didn't promise them *much*, really—just that I'd let them know if I heard or saw anything unusual."

"This potentially puts you in a very awkward place," he said. "If anyone finds out that you're working with them, it could be bad for you. If a killer *is* part of the race, your life could be in danger."

I kind of laughed it off. "It's not like I know anything, at least not anything that anyone else doesn't know. I thought it was better to humor them, you know? They promised to stay out of my way. What have I got to lose?"

Before Miguel could answer, there was another loud rap at the door.

"Zoe?" Alex's voice came through the door. "It's *me*. Could I have a word?"

Miguel opened the door. He and Alex exchanged a few inquisitive stares and shook hands while I put on my shoes. Miguel left the door open, standing right in the middle of the opening. The smile on his face was challenging.

I didn't like Alex, knowing what I knew, but it wouldn't do me any good to antagonize him. I looked up and smiled. "What can I do for you?"

Alex chuckled. "Working on tomorrow's challenge, I see. Good job! I'm sure you'll be fabulous."

"Thanks. Was there something in particular you wanted to talk about?"

"Zoe, I've heard an ugly rumor about someone in Charlotte saying that *I* had something to do with what happened to Reggie Johnson. You wouldn't know anything about that, would you?"

"No. I can't imagine who'd say such a thing." I couldn't resist adding, "You *didn't*, did you?"

"Absolutely not! I'm all about the food truck show. Reggie's death hurt us all. It's a black mark on this race that can never be removed. I want you to remember that."

If his words had been any more rehearsed, I would've been able to see him practicing in the mirror.

I thought about what he'd said—what *could* he have to gain by killing Reggie?

I could understand why Detective McSwain was killed. He was asking questions. At least that made sense. Poor Reggie didn't know much about anything.

"I understand, Alex. I don't want anything else bad to happen during the race, either. I came to win the money and show people my food. That's it."

He nodded. "That's what I thought. Let's keep the competition fair and friendly. I'll do my best. I know you'll do yours."

I closed the door behind Alex as he left. For a moment, Miguel and I didn't move or speak.

"I think he knows that I told the police about what I heard. Somehow he found out. I'm *doomed*."

- - - - - - -

There wasn't enough time for Miguel and me to continue where we left off before Delia returned.

"Oh!" She smirked when she saw the two of us together. "Shall I leave and come back later?"

Miguel cleared his throat. "No. I'm the one who should be going."

"Thanks for your help with the skates. Will I see you at dinner with everyone else?"

"I won't be at dinner tonight, Zoe. I have to meet someone. I'll see you in the morning at four. Bye, Delia."

I immediately thought of the beautiful mystery woman from Charlotte. Did she follow him here?

He left quickly, and Delia put her hands on her hips. "Well, that's a fine kettle of fish. What's so important that he couldn't be here for dinner?"

"I don't know."

"He'll be fine." She put down her bag. "Now, let's get you

all dressed up, just in case he puts in a surprise appearance!"

I didn't get dressed up, despite Delia's blandishments. What was the point? Miguel wasn't going to be there. I was exhausted and wouldn't have gone down at all if it wasn't a requirement of the race.

I had to keep reminding myself that just because Miguel kissed me didn't mean we were going to sit around holding hands and gazing at the stars together all the time. He had a life. I had a life. I wanted him to be part of my life. Hopefully he wanted me to be part of his.

All the talking to myself, and to Crème Brûlée, as Delia showered and changed clothes, didn't help at all. We headed downstairs for dinner with Ollie, Uncle Saul, and Chef Art.

Delia was beautiful in her slinky, sparkly gold dress with matching spike heels. I was just me in jeans and a Biscuit Bowl T-shirt. My black curly hair was looking good, though. I put on some eye makeup and lipstick since the dinner would be taped and shown on TV, too.

I told Delia about Miguel kissing me by the trash bin. She wasn't all that impressed. I wasn't sure what *she* was looking for, but *I* thought it was a good start.

We got out of the elevator on the ground floor, and I immediately saw Miguel near the front door of the hotel. He was wearing a nice suit and had his arms around the same woman I'd seen him with in Charlotte.

She was tall and beautiful, dark haired, and dressed in a fabulous red cocktail dress. They walked out of the hotel with her hanging on his arm. What an awesome couple they made.

Delia patted my arm. "Don't worry. It looks like he has something going on with her right now. You're bound to be next in line. He's just getting his feet wet with you right now. That's the way it is with men. He's probably getting ready to break up with her."

I didn't argue with her even though my careful research

into his life hadn't included a woman he was close to besides his sister and grandmother.

Race officials were springing for a big dinner each night where we would talk about what had happened that day and what we were doing the next day. They were using one of the hotel's private dining rooms.

We were supposed to wear the clothes we wore in our food trucks to identify ourselves to TV viewers. Most of the other teams and sponsors were there already. Hardly anyone was dressed like they had been in Charlotte earlier. I felt a little underdressed in my T-shirt and jeans, but at least my Biscuit Bowl T-shirt would be clear on TV.

I saw our table and waved to Uncle Saul.

I avoided the chair beside Ollie, figuring that he had probably left it open for Delia. He was already staring at her like a large puppy with a tattooed head. It was probably all he could do not to let his tongue loll out!

"Ladies!" Chef Art greeted us, pushing to his feet.

With Delia taking the chair beside Ollie, I took the open spot beside Chef Art. The single open chair taunted me. It was where Miguel would have sat if he wasn't out with that exceptionally beautiful woman.

"Have you talked to Alex yet?" Chef Art asked after I sat down.

"You mean has he accused me of trying to get him in trouble?" I ordered a margarita from the passing waiter. "Yes. I assume he talked to you, too."

His bright blue eyes were worried. I could tell because his left one was all twitchy. "There's a lot of money riding on this thing, Zoe. Don't screw it up. I like you. I really do. I like my money better. Leave Alex alone, and stay away from the police. Let this thing play out."

"I will." I thought about Helms and Marsh. They probably weren't too happy with me right now after I'd ignored their summons.

They were supposed to *wait* for my reports on the race,

I considered sulkily, not call me every few minutes. How was I supposed to keep our arrangement a secret if we met in the lobby all the time?

Everyone had ordered their drinks and dinner. I was working on my second margarita. It was almost nine when Alex addressed the crowd. I was beginning to think he was born with a microphone in his hand.

"It was a good challenge today, people. Tomorrow will be *even* better."

"What about the dead guy?" Daryl Barbee yelled out, still wearing his oversized cowboy hat.

"And our money that we lost in the vandalism," Roy Chow from Chooey's Sooey called out. "My power is still not on in my truck."

Roy was dressed conservatively in a suit and tie. When he was in his food truck, he and his three-man team wore matching New York Yankees baseball uniforms, down to the cleats on his shoes.

Not sure what that was supposed to mean to his customers, but he *was* from New York.

Alex grinned and took their questions. "We're working as closely as we can with police to find the answers to what happened with Mr. Johnson in Charlotte. You know, Charlotte has a high crime rate, right? I personally think someone tried to rob him. Anyway, we'll find out soon enough."

"And the power?" Dante, from Stick It Here, asked.

"Dante, your truck and Roy's are the last two still being worked on. I promise they'll be ready for tomorrow."

Alex made promises like he was running for elected office.

"That won't give us much time to get our supplies ready," Roy reminded him. "How about you give us a few minutes' head start?"

"Or extra points," Dante suggested.

"You two are a couple of jokesters, aren't you?" Alex laughed, but I could see him sweating in his nicely cut tuxedo.

Lucky for him, dinner was served before things got any

uglier. Not that I blamed Roy and Dante for being upset. A lot of work went into their food each day. The vandalism had caused them extra work with no guarantee that they'd be ready tomorrow when the rest of us were.

There was some good-natured joking between tables about people singing as they sold their food for the next challenge. Everyone was worried about the taste challenge. I thought that was the easy part.

To make the rest of us feel even more insecure about singing in public, Reverend Jablonski and his fellow ministers from the Our Daily Bread food truck got up and performed several hymns for us.

"They sound like the freaking Vienna Boys Choir," Ollie remarked. "How are we supposed to compete with *that*?"

Chef Art squirmed in his chair. His usual white linen suit seemed to fit a little tighter than normal. "I'd say the singing isn't going to sell biscuits. Zoe doesn't have to be a great singer tomorrow. She needs to show a little cleavage and a lot of leg. The biscuit bowls will do the rest."

Everyone turned to me. *No pressure*. I sighed and started eating.

I had to resign myself to doing whatever was necessary to win the money. It was *my* food truck, after all, and *my* idea to be here.

The sliced roast beef was dry and the gravy was lumpy. I longed for a good burrito but was too exhausted to go out and find one. It was unfortunate that there was no food truck in the challenge tomorrow with Mexican food.

Delia was working hard to impress Ollie. She was looking at him like he was a chocolate-covered donut.

Maybe that was the part I was missing with Miguel.

Chef Art looked unhappy and impatient. He left before dessert. I went with him. Four A.M. would come early, and I was ready for today to be over.

We talked about my menu plans for tomorrow, and he reminded me how important it was to keep the food ideas fresh.

"Everyone is trying to come up with great ideas, sensational eats," he warned. "I hope you are, too, Zoe. You know how essential that is to the food truck business. Don't pay any attention to Saul on this. He's got his food brain stuck in the 1980s."

I agreed with him before the elevator chimed as it reached my floor. "I'll see you in the morning, Chef Art." I borrowed a page from Alex. "You know I'm all about the food."

"I hope so. Good night, Zoe." I got out of the elevator. The doors had closed before I saw Helms and Marsh standing in front of my room.

"Zoe, it's important that we talk to you right away."

ELEVEN

I let the two detectives into my room. I should've known they wouldn't leave me alone just because I'd ignored them. I shouldn't have agreed to help them.

Miguel's threats of possible dire consequences for my actions were running around in the back of my mind.

I sat on the edge of the bed. Crème Brûlée hadn't moved from his perch on it since I'd left. Helms took the soft chair and Marsh took the chair by the desk.

"What's wrong?" I was hoping this would be over quickly and I could go to bed.

"We know you have to be up early—so do we, of course—to go out with the food trucks." Helms smiled at me. She was really a very attractive woman.

"Something has happened that you should be aware of." Marsh leaned forward with his elbows on his knees. "We have a possible suspect in the death of Reggie Johnson. Our person of interest may even be involved with Detective McSwain's death."

"Who is it?" I was ready for anything.

"We think Miguel Alexander is involved."

Okay. "What in the world makes you think that?"

"Mr. Alexander got a sizable deposit in his bank account the day he left Mobile." Helms stared at me as though I should immediately understand what that meant.

"Are you monitoring *all* our bank accounts?" That shocked me more than the stupid idea that Miguel had anything to do with the deaths in Charlotte.

They exchanged glances.

"We needed to keep track of a *few* accounts, yes," Helms agreed. "There were some standouts in the group. We aren't keeping track of *yours*, Zoe, if that's what you're worried about."

Actually, I was more worried about Uncle Saul's bank account, if he had one. My dad always said his brother was into a few shady dealings.

"I'm sure Miguel got paid for a job," I shot back. "He does a lot of work on credit. I think you should pick another suspect."

"Twenty-five thousand dollars is a lot of credit," Marsh said.

"Have you been to a lawyer lately? That's like two hours of work." I wished they'd go away. I didn't want to hear any more.

"The money was wired to him from an account in the Caymans," Helms continued. "That's what raised the red flag for us. We can't tell whose account that was. We'll have more information in the next twenty-four hours."

"I don't believe Miguel has any ties to the people putting on the food truck race." I yawned, hoping they'd take the hint. "Why would he kill Reggie?"

"He does have two ties," Marsh said. "You and Reggie Johnson. We think he may have exploited the tie with you to get involved with the race so he could kill Mr. Johnson."

"Why is he even *here*, Zoe?" Helms's face was earnest. "Have you asked yourself that question? He's not an official member of your team. He doesn't work for you."

"I asked him to come. He's an outrider. He gets supplies. Each team is allowed one person with a car for that job." I didn't want to go into why Miguel was *really* there. That was between him and me.

They both nodded as though that meant something sinister.

"What about Alex?" I demanded. "Have you found out anything about the phone call I overheard?"

"We got his phone records, but that was a dead end." Marsh shrugged. "There's nothing there we can use."

"Keep an eye on Miguel," Helms said. "That's all we're asking."

"It's for your own good," Marsh added. "If we're right, and Alexander was paid by someone to disrupt the race, he'll keep trying. He may have killed at least once. If so, he won't hesitate to kill again."

"And he may have someone working with him, so stay sharp," Helms said. "We think someone else killed McSwain, but it was definitely part of this whole scheme."

"That doesn't sound like Miguel," I insisted. "I think you should find another suspect. I won't spy on him for you. You'll have to find someone else. Now, if you don't mind, I'm going to bed."

Helms was apologetic. Marsh had more to say on the subject, but I insisted on escorting them both to the door.

When they were gone and the door was locked behind them, I took off my jeans and lay down beside Crème Brûlée in my T-shirt and underwear.

"Can you believe that? They think Miguel killed Reggie and had someone kill Detective McSwain. I suppose he cut the power cords to the food trucks, too. How stupid is that?"

Crème Brûlée rolled on his back and meowed for me to pet his tummy. He slapped at me with his paws.

"Yeah. There *is* the mystery woman. They'd have to be pretty brazen to meet right here at the hotel if they'd killed people, though, right?"

He hissed and rolled over.

"I know. Miguel *is* probably seeing that woman. She was really gorgeous, and she's not his sister. But that doesn't make him a killer." I sighed. "I'm going to sleep now. Let's handle all this in the morning."

— — — — — — —

I had terrible dreams about singing and roller skating all night. I was glad when the alarm clock finally rang and it was time to get up.

I tied my skates to each other like I used to when I was a kid. I showered and dressed in jeans and a tank top after tying a scarf over my hair. I put the skates across my shoulder and got everything—except my cat—down to the food truck in one trip.

It made me feel better to see all the other food truck owners in the parking deck getting ready for the day. I'd been a little nervous going down there after being the first one to find the vandalism last night.

I'd thought later that it was lucky for me that whoever was responsible for what was going on had only wanted to cut a few power cords instead of killing someone else. Otherwise, I would've been a likely candidate.

A likely candidate for Miguel to kill?

Stupid thought. Where did that come from?

I shrugged it off as I stowed away my stuff and went back up to get Crème Brûlée. Delia was getting her things together. She hadn't slept in her bed at all last night.

Was she with Ollie all night?

Eww.

My mind needed a cleansing cup of coffee after *that* thought. It was almost as bad as thinking about my parents doing it.

"I'm glad to see you're back," I burst out to keep from thinking.

She smiled, her eyes dreamy. "Ollie is *quite* a man."

Double eww.

I grabbed my cat. "I have to get back down to the food truck. I'll see you in a little while."

So they were together. I was glad for Ollie. I hoped it wouldn't complicate the rest of the race. Not everyone could couple-up and work together.

Crème Brûlée was already snuggling into the truck seat when I left him. A few of the other food truck drivers called out a greeting to me as I opened the back door to the Biscuit Bowl. I was completely thinking about the day ahead—not so much the roller skating or the singing as the food and how everything would go together. It was a normal thought for me each morning as I set out.

"Zoe?"

I jumped and stifled a small scream. It wasn't because Miguel had crept up on me, I told myself. It was because I was tense.

"Sorry." He smiled. "I didn't mean to startle you."

"That's okay. I'm getting ready to go."

"Did you get your cat out here already?"

"Yeah. Sure. No problem."

"Look, about dinner last night—"

I didn't really want to hear it. I hailed Ollie and Uncle Saul when I saw them. I don't know what Miguel thought of that, but I was a little irritated with him. I didn't think he'd killed anyone, but he'd ditched me to go out with the mystery woman.

Was it my imagination or was Ollie a little more *peppy* than usual?

"Let's go sell some biscuit bowls," he said loudly and then eyed me critically. "Is that your idea of sexing up to sell biscuit bowls while you're singing and skating?"

Of course *everyone* had to turn and examine what I was wearing.

"This is my idea of what I'm going to wear today," I retorted. "I'm sure we'll do fine."

Delia joined us. She and Miguel stowed the rest of everyone's gear in the trunk of his car. Nothing else was said about my taste in clothes. I was ready to go out and win the challenge.

I noticed that several of the other teams were smacking hands and doing joint cheers to get themselves going. Maybe we needed to do something like that, too. I thought we'd wait and see how we did that day. Tomorrow we'd be in Atlanta, if we made the cut. If not, there wouldn't be much to cheer about.

Uncle Saul moved Crème Brûlée into the middle of the seat between us. He rode with me in the Biscuit Bowl. Delia and Ollie rode with Miguel.

It was almost like carnival back home, watching all the big, colorful trucks roll out of the underground parking lot. I turned on the spinning biscuit on top of my truck. I might as well give everyone in Columbia a peek at what they were missing because they didn't live in Mobile.

There was very little traffic headed to the downtown area at that time of the morning. It was an eerie feeling. I suspected this was why we were setting up so early. The streets were empty where we were directed to park. It was just like the day before in Charlotte. As soon as the food trucks were in place, everyone began jumping out. The race directors got the cool-down tent in place, next to the stage again. As we were getting everything ready for the challenge, we could hear Alex trying out the microphone.

Chef Art poked his head in the kitchen for a moment. "Don't forget your hats. I don't want you to win the challenge and not have everyone see my hats on TV."

"We'll do it," I told him.

"Zoe, why aren't you wearing tight, short shorts? People want to see some skin out there. The tank top is good. Can you pull it down some—show a little cleavage? What are you thinking? Can you change into something a little more *indecent* before the challenge?"

"I could, but I'm not going to. I own the Biscuit Bowl. I can't sing, but I can skate. If I fall, I don't want it to be on bare knees. This is what I'm wearing."

He shrugged. "Just say you don't want to win. I'll understand."

I looked back to tell him that the kitchen was crowded enough with four of us back there, but he was already gone.

The biscuit dough was ready. I'd already mixed it up, rolled it out, and cut some biscuits. It had to be baked in muffin trays to make the indentation for the filling. Ollie was putting the first tray into the little oven.

"Alex wants everyone down at the stage in five," one of his assistants told us.

"You don't need me," Ollie said. "Go find out what's happening. I'll keep the biscuits baking."

"I'll stay here, too," Uncle Saul said. "I'm working on our savory filling—spicy chicken and eggs. I think I'll do better with more space."

I knew our sweet filling was going to be peaches. I could work on that when I got back. I'd been saving a recipe for spicy peaches that I'd found in January for this moment.

"I guess it's you and me," I said to Delia. "Let's see what Alex has to say."

Miguel joined us outside and walked across the street with us. The tall buildings of downtown Columbia were lit up against the dark sky. There was a hint of rain in the air that I hoped would pass. I could probably make it roller-skating down the city sidewalks if they were dry. If they were wet, I wasn't sure.

"Good morning, everyone," Alex called out. It may have been dark all around us, but the stage where he stood was bright as day. "How are you all this morning?"

He went on to acknowledge the sponsors again. He explained the rules and concept of the food truck race. Everyone was waiting for the reason we were all called together. We stood impatiently, hoping he'd come to the point so we could get back to work.

"I know you're all anxious to hear everything about today's challenge. You all have your packets with the basics. You already know that you'll need one of your team to skate and sing as they try to sell their food to people who are on their way into work this morning."

We nodded.

Antonio Stephanopoulos from Athens, Georgia, the owner of the Pizza Papa food truck, made a rolling motion with his hands. His thin gray whiskers shook. "Let's get going, eh?"

"I *love* your enthusiasm," Alex yelled after he asked for applause. "What you don't know about today's challenge is that one of the people you'll be trying to sell your food to this morning has twenty-five hundred dollars in cash for the first person to find him."

That brought some enthusiasm and a few whistles.

Delia and I looked at each other and grinned, too.

"Besides singing and skating, part of the challenge is to be the first team to sell a hundred and fifty dollars' worth of product on the street today. The taste challenge will be met by us interviewing people on the street after they've had your food. We'll look at those tapes after the challenge to determine the winner. Now go out and make your sponsors proud!"

"That's a lot of extra money," Delia said. "You could really use that, Zoe."

"If I win it, we'll split it."

"Don't be silly. You're already helping me and Ollie. Maybe you could take us out for a night on the town when we get home." She hugged me and ran back to the food truck.

"I hope you win," Miguel said. "Don't worry about the skimpy shorts and top. If you fall, you'll be glad you're wearing jeans. Besides, you're already the best-looking food truck owner here."

I laughed. "Is that comparing me to Antonio Stephanopoulos or Roy Chow?"

"Good luck out there."

I stepped inside the Biscuit Bowl kitchen. Delia had already shared the news with Ollie and Uncle Saul.

"Stay focused. Look for someone who doesn't *appear* to have any money," my uncle suggested. "Maybe a street person or another vendor."

"No," Ollie argued. "This is gonna be on TV. Whoever has the cash is gonna look *good*. Maybe not dressed in a suit, but *good*."

I took their advice, such as it was. Delia looked me over and tied my T-shirt in the back so it was tight on my chest. She also rolled the legs on my jeans so they were up to my knees, but still covering them.

I didn't have the heart to tell her that most of that bare skin she'd exposed below the knee would be taken up with my skates.

I thanked them for their help and got the peach filling ready. Uncle Saul's spicy chicken and egg filling smelled wonderful. Biscuits were baking up light and fluffy. Ollie turned on the deep fryer.

I looked at my team. They made me want to cry. They were all such great people.

"Thanks again for all your help. I wouldn't be here without you."

Delia winked. "Don't forget to thank Miguel, too."

"I won't. I'm going to put on my skates and get ready. We can be on the street at five thirty. I don't know how many people will be out there looking for breakfast, but the early biscuit maker hopefully sells her quota early, too."

I tried not to worry about the biscuit making. It was easy to start thinking you were the only one who could make your headliner food. The biscuit bowl was my creation, but I knew I could trust my team to do a good job.

I put on my skates and cleared my throat. I was more

worried about being able to stand up and move around than whether or not I could sing.

I looked around for Miguel. I couldn't find him, or the Mercedes, anywhere on the street. I started to call him, but I didn't want to be a nag or someone who's always trying to keep tabs on him. I didn't really need his help.

Ollie brought out the first tray of biscuit bowls, savory. I took it from him, got ready to sing, and fell down hard on the sidewalk.

TWELVE

There were only three spicy chicken biscuit bowls that could be saved. The other five had to be thrown away.

What made it even worse was that we were the first team up and running so we were getting extra coverage from the cameramen. They didn't stop taping when I fell, either. The whole mess—including the ripped, bloody part of my jeans where I'd hit my knee on the concrete—would be preserved for the TV audience.

Ollie helped me up and yelled for Delia. "We have to get that knee cleaned up."

Delia ran outside with Uncle Saul. They both groaned and said how sorry they were, asking if I was okay.

In the meantime, one of the ministers from Our Daily Bread (not Jay Jablonski) was already on his skates, singing loudly in his professional choir voice and heading into the waiting crowd of spectators with a trayful of cinnamon rolls.

"Never mind that," I told my team. "We need another

tray of biscuit bowls. Delia, could you get me a wet paper towel? Let's get over this and move on."

The cameraman had his lens right in my face as I was talking. I wished I could yell at him to move away. I'd agreed when I registered to allow the cameras complete access. What good was a food truck race if they couldn't capture every single detail?

Delia, Ollie, and Uncle Saul moved quickly. I was on my feet—wobbly but standing. A wet paper towel got most of the blood off my knee. My jeans were only going to be good for making shorts later.

Ollie and Uncle Saul got another tray of eight biscuit bowls ready.

By that time, Fred was skating away from his fish taco truck. Believe me, the cinnamon rolls smelled a lot better than fish tacos at that time of the morning.

Another minister was taking more cinnamon rolls to the first one, who was now lost in the crowd, probably selling his hundred and fifty dollars' worth of product before I could even get on my feet.

"Come and find me when you have another tray ready." I started slowly skating down the sidewalk again.

"Be careful," Ollie said. "And sing. Don't forget to sing!"

It looked as though Bobbie Shields's daughter, Allison, who was part of the Shut Up and Eat team, was a worse skater than even me. She was a pretty young girl with waist-length blond hair that gently floated in the breeze as she fell, over and over again.

Finally, her loose meat sandwiches and giant pickles spread out around her, she gave up. I passed her on the sidewalk as she sat there crying.

I felt terrible not offering her my help. It wasn't just that I'd lose the challenge. I didn't think I could stop without falling over, too. I couldn't remember how to use the brakes on the skates.

Lucky for me, I skated right into a man on the edge of the crowd that stopped me. He smiled and steadied me before buying one of my biscuit bowls.

"This looks really good." He took a big bite. "*Mmm.* Tastes good, too. Let me have another one."

I stuffed the money into my pocket, glad I didn't have to make change at the same time. I pushed my feet a little and glided forward again. A woman stopped me and bought another biscuit bowl.

I should've been better prepared. My pockets weren't going to be adequate for the money I was going to have to put into them. I wasn't used to street selling. I had my cash box at the food truck. It usually wasn't a big deal.

I noticed that a member of Chooey's Sooey was skating around like a pro with dim sum on a tray. He was also wearing a money pouch around his waist. *Great idea.*

When Ollie came to find me, I only had one biscuit bowl left. I was singing my heart out, any song that came to mind.

"I need one of those." I pointed to the money pouch.

"You mean a fanny pack?" He shook his head. "Nobody wears those anymore."

"I don't care." I dug in my pockets until I found all the money I'd made and stuffed it into his hands. I still had the money for change that I'd put in there. So far everyone had given me exact change, and a tip.

"Okay. Let me call Miguel." He massaged my shoulders quickly and then took the empty tray and the money before he left.

What I really needed was some pain-relieving antibiotic spray for my knee. It had been a long time since I'd had a scrape there. I'd forgotten how much it hurt. I couldn't get to my phone to call Miguel and see if he could find some in the cool-down tent where they kept the first-aid supplies. I was going to have to live with it.

The crowd was much bigger today than it had been in Charlotte. They were all there to watch what was going on and wave to the camera. It seemed like I'd skated through a sea of them before I reached the other side.

Ollie brought more biscuit bowls after I'd emerged from the crowd. He took the money again. "I can't get in touch with Miguel. I don't know where he is. I sent Delia to the cool-down tent for some salve for your knee. I'm gonna kick Miguel's scrawny butt when I see him."

"Thanks." I continued skating. "How are we doing on the money?"

"We've got a ways to go." He held up a cup with a straw in it. "Uncle Saul says hot water with lemon is good for your throat. I'd like to kick his scrawny butt, too, but we have to get through this challenge first. Are you okay?"

"Great."

On the other side of the crowd were the real people heading in for jobs at the downtown businesses. Some were white-collar workers in their suits and ties. Others were retail shop people in various other outfits—more colorful than the suit people. None of them looked very happy.

I heard them grumbling about the delays in traffic because of the food truck race. They were in a hurry to get to their jobs and didn't have time to stop for a before-work snack. They didn't mind telling me about it, either.

I saw the minister from Our Daily Bread praying by the crowded sidewalk. A few people stopped, prayed, and bought cinnamon rolls from him. Maybe they felt sorry for him.

I tried my best to think of something I could do to draw positive attention to my biscuit bowls, which were getting cold waiting for me to sell them. Cold biscuit bowls were bad biscuit bowls. I had to come up with something. I realized this was why everyone had expected me to wear tight shorts and a low-cut top.

But I didn't want that kind of attention. I saw Dante from Stick It Here in his red scarf, talking to a crowd of women who were buying pot stickers and kebabs from him. He was letting them taste first before buying.

I knew what I had to do.

When Ollie came back with the next tray of biscuit bowls, I had him break two of them into smaller pieces.

"We're going to need a few extra biscuit bowls to give away," I told him. "Maybe you should bring some napkins back with you, too."

"Okay. You sound a little hoarse. Drink some more water." He held the cup again. "I hate to tell you this, but somebody said that Grinch's Ganache has already sold enough cupcakes to win the challenge."

"We should keep going anyway. Who knows if that's true or what else is involved or how they're going to decide who gets kicked out? Has anyone found the man with the money yet?"

"Not as far as I know." He squatted in front of me and carefully sprayed antibiotic pain relief on my knee. "Is that okay? I can pull up your pants leg if you need me to."

I breathed a sigh of relief right away. "No. That feels better already. Thanks, Ollie. Any word from Miguel?"

He snorted. "Nothing, otherwise he'd be running this stuff out here. Is something wrong with him?"

"Not as far as I know." I pushed what Helms and Marsh had told me out of my thoughts. No way Miguel had anything to do with the cords being cut in the parking garage or Reggie's death. I didn't believe that for a second.

I had to focus on finishing the challenge.

The camera crews had switched from following the food truck team members to interviewing the people on their way to work—probably for the taste challenge. I heard a few workers curse at them. One man loudly told a cameraman to get out of his face.

What happened to the South being so friendly?

My voice sounded a little stronger after the lemon water. I switched to all the patriotic songs I could think of—"The Star-Spangled Banner," four verses; anything I had ever heard that sounded like "God Bless America."

I engaged the slightly hostile crowd and offered them free samples as I skated by the steps of another large building. People were really starting to pack into the city. I glanced at my watch; it was seven thirty.

A few more people bought biscuit bowls from me. One man bought a peach biscuit bowl for breakfast and a spicy chicken biscuit bowl for lunch. I sold two peach biscuit bowls to a woman in a dashing red suit with a matching hat. Loved her look!

I had to tell her how gorgeous she was. That was when I was struggling to make change for her twenty-dollar bill. I didn't say it just to sell her a biscuit bowl.

One of the members of Pizza Papa's team had dropped his tray of mini pizzas on the sidewalk. I'd thought when I saw him skating with a tray in each hand that he was doomed. He was shaky on his skates and had forgotten all about singing. Antonio pushed through the crowd to help him. The closest cameraman took pictures of the whole thing.

I was down to one peach biscuit bowl when Ollie finally came back.

"We're having a few issues with the deep fryer." He replaced my empty tray with a full one. "That's the bad news."

I groaned. "How bad is it?"

"Like it-will-never-deep-fry-another-biscuit bad."

Oh no. At home, I'd know where to get that fixed, or replaced, on credit. *What are we going to do out here?*

"Don't give up yet. Saul is looking at it. He thinks he might be able to do something with it."

My legs and feet hurt, especially my knee. My lips were chapped and my throat was sore. I was ready to sit down with a cup of coffee and take a break.

"The good news is—this is it! Sell this tray, and you're done with the challenge." He held up the lemon water again.

I waved it away. "I can't drink any more of that stuff."

"You have to. You have to stay hydrated. The fish taco

truck was out in front until his assistant passed out from dehydration. They had to take him to the hospital. They dropped out of the challenge because they only had one skater. Drink the water. Sell the biscuit bowls. Keep singing."

I did as he said because I knew he was right, but I was almost too tired to care.

When Ollie was gone, I pushed myself to sell the last eight biscuit bowls. I wished I'd thought to ask if anyone had won the money yet. I knew it didn't really matter. I had to concentrate on getting rid of the biscuit bowls.

I thought for a few seconds about buying them myself and eating them, but I knew that would be the moment all the cameras would focus on me.

I saw a group of businessmen in nice suits walking toward a building with a double green door on the front at street level. I skated toward them, and into them, when I couldn't stop.

Miraculously, I didn't drop anything.

"Sorry." I smiled as they helped me settle my tray and held me upright for a moment.

"What's a pretty girl like you doing out here selling food on the street?" One of them was a handsome man who had a sweet, smoky drawl that even managed to tingle my weary senses.

"It's that food truck thing," one of the other men told him—not so handsome and a little nasal.

"These look very good," smoky, sweet said, not *only* looking at my biscuits, either. "I think we could use five of them for our morning meeting, don't you, Roger? Pay the woman."

Roger (nasal) quickly took out his wallet and gave me forty dollars for the five biscuit bowls. "Keep the change, and look for a new job."

Forty dollars! That was well over my hundred-and-fifty-dollar goal. I almost started crying, I was so grateful to be done with it. I still had three biscuit bowls left, but that didn't matter since the challenge was for the money and not how much product we could sell.

"Thank you so much. I really appreciate it."

"You're welcome." Sweet and smoky smiled and went inside the green door.

I was ready to skate back to the biscuit bowl before my legs gave out on me. I saw a man putting newspapers into one of the dozens of newspaper boxes. His big delivery truck was parked at the curb.

I knew the remaining biscuit bowls wouldn't be any good. We'd have to throw them away when I got back. I thought I might as well give them to this man to enjoy. I could also give him a business card.

Who knew when he might be in Mobile?

"Excuse me. I have these yummy peach biscuit bowls that I can't use. I was wondering if you'd like to have them."

He squinted at me, his baseball cap pulled down low on his face. "They look delicious. Are you sure you don't want me to buy them?"

I explained about the food truck race and the daily challenge. "So I'm good for the day. Usually my customers have hot, fresh biscuit bowls, made to order. I don't want to sell them to you cold and a little stale."

He nodded and took the whole tray in one hand before he threw his ball cap up in the air and congratulated me. "You've just won the twenty-five-hundred-dollar cash prize!"

THIRTEEN

I was stunned. I was sure I looked like it, too, as the cameras all zoomed in on me. I was such a mess, it made me cringe to think that everyone would see me like this on TV. I hoped my mother wasn't watching. She'd really think I'd lost it.

The man explained that he was part of the food truck race as he counted out the twenty-five hundred-dollar bills into my hand.

I was fortunate that someone had thought to tell Ollie, Delia, and Uncle Saul what was happening. They got there before I could drop all the money. There was no room in my pockets for any more cash.

"We won!" Delia danced around.

Uncle Saul hugged me, and Ollie took the initiative and pulled Delia into his big, strong arms.

She stopped dancing and kissed him hard for a minute.

Ollie left her and hugged me. "Was that too weird?"

I laughed. "Not at all. I'm happy for you."

"That's the way I like to leave 'em." His crazy eyebrows went up and down. "Pining for more."

It didn't take long before Alex had joined us with more cameras and his usual microphone. Local media types also took part, snapping hundreds of pictures. People asked me questions. All I could think about was getting the stupid skates off my feet. I never wanted to wear a pair of skates again.

While everyone was focused on Ollie, Delia, and Uncle Saul, I slipped off to a bus bench to take off the skates and socks. I had blisters all over my feet. No one ever said being in business was going to be easy.

I glanced up at the concrete stairs leading to one of the tall buildings and saw Miguel. He was talking to the same woman from the hotel the night before—the same woman who'd been in Charlotte.

So that's where you've been.

I watched him for a few minutes with her. He'd changed into a nice brown suit and a tie. A white shirt played up his dark hair and eyes. She was wearing a strawberry-colored dress with a little matching crocheted jacket that complemented it beautifully.

They were speaking intently to each other. Neither one of them seemed to notice anything else going on around them.

Who is she? Are they romantically involved?

Maybe they were talking about business. I massaged my tired ankles.

If it was business, it was something serious. Miguel had his serious face on, like when he told me I shouldn't get involved in what happened to Reggie.

I only had a second to wonder if his odd behavior was related to that.

Then I was swamped by the race proceedings again. Most of the teams had left their food trucks and wandered over to where we were. Everyone was shouting, happy, and enjoying the end of the Columbia challenge.

"All right, food truckers," Alex called out on his microphone. "Time to go over to the cool-down tent and look at our taste-test videos before we announce today's winners— and *losers*."

His voice was like squeaky thunder, even with the noise of the city around us. I glanced up at the stairs again. Miguel was looking down at me. I grabbed my skates and walked barefoot between Ollie and Uncle Saul back to the food truck. Delia ran ahead. She was afraid she was going to miss the announcements.

The way my feet and legs felt, I didn't care.

Chef Art was in the cool-down tent when we got there. That meant another round of photos with him. "You did good, Zoe. They're putting up a board outside to chart the standings of the teams. I have a feeling the Biscuit Bowl is gonna be at the top."

All the teams crammed into the tent to see what people thought of their food. I kind of cringed after a few videos had people saying bad things about other vendors' food. Most of the comments were positive.

When they finally got to mine, three people who had biscuit bowls in their hands said they were delicious. One man said my biscuits were dry. Another man said he didn't like the filling. That was three out of five—not too bad. Some teams only had one good response.

Alex announced that Our Daily Bread was the winner of the taste challenge with five positive responses. The team of ministers received a bunch of freebies from Disney World, airplane tickets to exotic locations, and dinner at several nice restaurants.

Oh well.

We moved back outside. Ollie hugged me and said not to worry. Chef Art frowned but didn't say anything.

Alex unveiled the big electronic board once there was a

crowd on the street. It lit up with all the teams listed, even though the names were scrambled and jumping around. They called for someone to take care of the problem while we waited.

Finally, a tech fixed it. The Biscuit Bowl wasn't number one—but it was number two— right after Our Daily Bread.

"Those ministers are gonna kill us," Ollie growled. "The only thing I dislike more than a pious person is a pious person who outsells us."

"Okay. These are the standings," Alex announced. "As you can see, there are eight of you still alive. These standings are based on how well each of you did in the challenges. It reflects your continued effort as well as meeting the individual challenges. Your score will be higher if you finish the challenge, and if you win the side challenges, like Our Daily Bread with the taste challenge, or winning the cash, like the Biscuit Bowl."

A producer whispered in his ear.

"That is to say there are still eight of you *in the race* at this moment. Excuse me."

"Cut the PC stuff and get on with it," Bobbie Shields yelled. "We all know Reggie is dead."

He ignored her. "Grinch's Ganache is the winner of today's challenge!"

Daryl and Sarah Barbee took a bow. They were the only ones on their team. I didn't envy them.

"The prize for the winner today—specially chosen by the food truck race committee—is a *free* paint job for the outside of their truck at any of more than one thousand locations of Ray's Airbrush Central nationwide. Congratulations, Grinch's!"

Everyone applauded, but we were all still tense, waiting to see which of the food trucks were going on to Atlanta, and who was being left behind.

Alex dragged it out. I was sure that was his job. He announced the Biscuit Bowl again as the winner of the cash prize. He commended everyone's efforts at the singing and skating challenge. Not all eight food trucks had met the challenge. Shut Up and Eat and Fred's Fish Tacos had both been sidelined.

"I know all of you are anxious to hear the new list of trucks going forward to Atlanta," Alex said. "But instead of me telling you, why don't I *show* you instead?"

The electronic board went blank again. The tired vendors groaned.

The tech walked up and hit it a few times on the side. The lights came on, and the remaining teams showed up in the seven slots still left.

"I knew it!" Fred Bunn threw his fish-shaped hat on the street and stepped on it. "They didn't get rid of Stick It Here when they didn't make the challenge yesterday. I'm getting a lawyer."

Uncle Saul and Ollie were jumping up and down. Delia was applauding. The Biscuit Bowl was going to Atlanta!

- - - - - - -

We were packing up the food truck when Miguel returned. Uncle Saul had worked on the deep fryer as much as he could. He couldn't repair it. We were going to have to head to Atlanta knowing we had no way to make biscuit bowls the next morning.

Chef Art arranged a press conference for the two of us to talk about me facing certain failure the next day since I had no deep fryer. He coached me to not sound cheerful about it and wear his hat.

I managed to look really depressed and even squeezed out a few tears for him, bless his heart. The camera took a close-up of my scraped knee. If I hadn't been so tired, I would've laughed at all of it. After all, I was here. People were eating my biscuit bowls. The rest was all drama and didn't matter.

"That was good, Zoe." He slapped my back when it was over. "This is gonna be a difficult, emotional moment for the team. Even though the Biscuit Bowl has made the cut, *will they live to fight another day?*"

Chef Art laughed and congratulated himself before he was picked up in his big RV—his face and name painted on the sides.

Delia, Ollie, and Uncle Saul were cleaning and working on a list of supplies needed for the next day.

Miguel walked over to me with his hands in the pockets of his brown suit pants. He'd removed his jacket and tie. "Sorry I was out of commission for a while."

"We got by."

Okay, I was a little angry. I was also *burning* with curiosity about the woman he was with. I wanted to tell him about Helms's and Marsh's accusations against him. I couldn't do it then.

"I know. I wouldn't have done it, except that it was really important."

"I understand. It's only a food truck race." I smiled at him. "Who is she?"

He looked a little surprised that I'd even noticed he was with her. Not a man who knew much about women, obviously.

"She's an old friend. We went to law school together. Her husband is divorcing her. He wants everything, including their young daughter. She asked me to help her."

Hmm. Did that mean she was an old flame kind of friend? It sounded like it to me.

"So you're leaving the race?" I took off my stupid hat. "It's okay. It must be important."

"I'm not leaving the race. The trial isn't for a few weeks. I didn't want this responsibility. I haven't done this kind of law in a long time. Not since Caroline died."

Caroline. That was his dead wife's name. It was the first time he'd mentioned her name to me.

I'd had to find out her name the hard way, by asking around at the courthouse where I frequently parked my food truck. A few free biscuit bowls went a long way.

"I'm glad you're not leaving." I searched for the right words that would help me find out if he was romantically involved with his "friend."

I couldn't think of anything clever. I blurted instead, "Are you romantically involved with your old friend?"

Well, there it was. Not too clever, but I hoped it would get the job done. He'd kissed me and acted like I could expect more. I figured I had the right to know.

He smiled and kissed me again. "No. She really *is* just an old friend. You're the only woman I'm interested in being romantically involved with."

Wow! Just what I wanted to hear.

I threw my arms around his neck. There were a thousand other questions I wanted to ask, but I was willing to be content with that one for now.

"There's something I have to tell you." I explained what Helms and Marsh had told me about the large amount of cash deposited into his account.

"They better have good justification for going into my bank account. You said they're here, right? I think I'll contact the Charlotte police for some answers. Why would I even be on their person of interest list?"

I shrugged. "I think it was the money. They said it was a red flag. And they feel like you stand out like a sore thumb at the race. I'm sorry. I didn't tell them you were here because I invited you. I felt like it was none of their business."

"I'll take care of it. I guess it was good, after all, that you were involved with them. Let's hope it stays good in the future."

We were ready to roll. Uncle Saul rode with me in the food truck. He'd called an old friend of his from his days in the restaurant business who'd agreed to meet us in Atlanta with a used deep fryer to replace mine. It was lucky that I won the money. It would help a lot getting us a replacement.

I thought I understood why Miguel's old friend asking him to help her could be very important to him. Ten years ago, his life had been very different. He had a great career, a family. He'd probably thought everything was going his way. He'd lost everything.

I knew a little bit about his childhood. I knew he came from a large family that had very little money. He'd had to work hard to go to college and law school—too hard to stay down forever after what had happened to him.

His old friend asking him to defend her might be the place where his life would change again. He might find out that he had the confidence to move forward.

Would he be interested in a girl with a food truck and a run-down diner if his life was different?

I hoped so.

"We did okay back there." Uncle Saul got my head back in the business at hand. "We worked really well as a team. There's only one little problem—Ollie and Delia. I don't know how much of the kissy-kissy stuff I can stand in a confined space."

I laughed. "I'm sure it will get better."

"I don't think the race will last that long."

"We'll have to be patient and understanding. Ollie has been alone for a long time."

"That's just it, Zoe. I think he's going at it too hard. I'm afraid, despite my coaching, that he's gonna crash and burn."

"Let's hope not. At least not during the rest of the race."

"It's made me think a lot about my own life," he said quietly. "You may not have noticed when you were out there last, but Bonnie has a thing for me."

"Which one is Bonnie?" I joked.

"Go on." He laughed. "I know you noticed. It's been that way since we met. I haven't wanted to encourage her. I'm not much of a catch."

"She seems to think otherwise. She's known you awhile now. She must think you're worth waiting for."

"You think?" He gazed out the side window. "It's been a long time for me, too, Zoe girl. I'm not sure I'm ready for it."

I kept my hands firmly on my cell phone and my eyes on

the traffic going out of Columbia. "I think you're probably thinking about it because you *are* ready, Uncle Saul."

"Maybe you're right. I don't know."

Atlanta was about four hours away, and it was supposed to be the turning point for the race. It would also be the toughest venue with more challenges, more prizes—and more than one food truck getting kicked out of the competition.

I hoped my team could keep it together. Once we got past Atlanta, it would be downhill. We'd go on to Birmingham, and end up in Mobile on Friday for the grand finale.

I really wanted the fifty thousand dollars. I could upgrade my diner with that money and only use the food truck for special occasions. It would be *awesome*.

"I'm willing to do my part," Uncle Saul conceded. "I can always hit Ollie with a biscuit if he and Delia get too annoying. We'll be okay for a few days."

"Let's focus on that. We need different sweet and savory fillings for the biscuit bowls in Atlanta. Stews and the usual hot foods aren't going to work in this weather. I'm thinking about chicken salad. You know, you used to make that chicken salad with the pistachios in it? Maybe we could do that."

He laughed and slapped his knee. "That was forever ago. But I remember. I made that special honey balsamic dressing for it."

"That's right. You tell me what you need, and I'll start working on a list for Miguel as we're driving. I want to be on top of this."

He laughed. "I'll work on the list. You're driving." He took out my cell phone. "How do I get this thing to make a list?"

"You might do better with a pen and paper! There should be some in the glove box."

He took out a pen and found some paper. "You know, I saw you and Miguel outside this morning. Looks like the two of you are having a few problems."

I dictated the supply list while Uncle Saul wrote what I said and added his own supplies.

It was a long trip to Atlanta. We stopped for lunch right off the highway. The restaurant was busy, but it was clean and the food was decent.

Delia flirted with Ollie while we ate. The two of them were acting like lovebirds, just as Uncle Saul had dreaded. It didn't surprise me, and it didn't bother me. I hoped he'd be okay with it, too. I thought he might be a tiny bit jealous since the object of his affections was back home.

I was worried about the honey balsamic dressing for the chicken salad. The ingredients that Uncle Saul had given Miguel didn't seem right. I was afraid he wasn't thinking about chicken salad when he wrote the list. It would be hard to get supplies at four A.M. the next morning if Miguel didn't get everything today.

"Are you sure this is right?" I asked him again.

We were at the restaurant, getting ready to go.

He glared at Ollie and Delia who were laughing at something, their heads together. "It's right, Zoe. Don't worry about it."

I checked the list again before I gave it to Miguel. I wanted to take a look at everything for the next day. Uncle Saul and I left Miguel, Delia, and Ollie as they were getting into the Mercedes. We weren't back on the highway for more than a few minutes, with Uncle Saul at the wheel, when he began slowing down.

"What's wrong?" *Please don't let something be wrong with the engine.*

"I think that's Dante Eldridge out there on the road. Where's his food truck?"

FOURTEEN

"I was hijacked," Dante said when we had pulled to the side of the road. "I stopped for gas, and someone hit me in the head and took my truck. I got a knot the size of a golf ball and a headache bigger than my truck. I'm gonna kill whoever did this."

In the meantime, he needed a ride. His cell phone was in Stick It Here, too. I let him borrow mine to call the police. He got in the car with Miguel, Delia, and Ollie. The plan was to get him to the next exit where he could wait for the police. It wouldn't do him any good to go on to Atlanta without his truck.

We were already in Georgia, with another hour or so to go until we reached the city. Uncle Saul and I got back in the Biscuit Bowl.

But Crème Brûlée was crying and unhappy. Before we could leave, I had to put on his harness and let him out in the grass on the side of the road.

"You should've left that cat at home, Zoe," my uncle commented as trucks and cars streamed by us.

"I couldn't. I took him to Mom's house and he didn't want to stay. You know Dad won't keep him."

"Probably just as well, unless you want the poor creature to starve to death." Uncle Saul watched Crème Brûlée, who was closely studying a dead moth in the grass. "On second thought, you'd have to skip feeding him for more than a week for that to happen. How'd that cat get so big?"

"He's got very large bones. And his breed can be quite large." I held up one of Crème Brûlée's paws. "See the size of that?"

He laughed. "Yeah. Like a lion."

He was making fun of my cat! I scooped Crème Brûlée up after he'd finished his business and carried him back to the food truck. He didn't like being lifted. He kept slapping at me and howling until he was back in his bed again.

"He's got a real attitude problem, too."

"Don't talk about him. He's right here between us. It hurts his feelings."

"You are too soft, Zoe girl. Your heart must be made out of marshmallow. I hope it doesn't get burned one day."

I didn't comment on that. Ollie called to make sure nothing was wrong. They were already at the next exit waiting for us. I explained that my cat had needed a pit stop. Uncle Saul started the Biscuit Bowl, and we headed toward the exit.

"This race is getting risky," Uncle Saul said. "Vandalism. Hijacking. Murder. I've never seen the like. What are people thinking? Fifty thousand dollars isn't gonna make that big a difference in anyone's life. Well, it's really more like twenty-five thousand after taxes."

"It's a lot of money, however you look at it," I replied. "And there's the prestige. This is going to be broadcast all over the country. People are going to see the Biscuit Bowl in California and New York. All of us will be famous—but not as famous as whoever wins the race."

He patted my hand, reaching over Crème Brûlée between us. Of course my cat had to swat at him a few times.

"Hey!" Uncle Saul yelled at him. "Don't worry, Zoe. I'll do what I can to help you win."

"Thanks."

I thought about Dante. He'd been alone in his food truck, like Reggie. I hoped there were enough of us to keep our truck from being hijacked.

"What would someone want with Stick It Here anyway?" I asked.

"I don't know. The whole thing is crazy."

We went off at the exit and found the others at a more heavily traveled gas station close to the road. It was a surprise to see the highway patrol already there and talking to Dante. I decided we should wait until they were finished. The chances were the police wouldn't find the food truck right away. Dante was going to need a ride to Atlanta.

"It's easy to spot," Dante explained to the officers. "There are sticks coming up out of the top with big, fake pieces of meat on them. The truck is white and has a lot of writing on it. You can't miss it."

One of the officers glanced at the biscuit on top of my food truck and nodded. "I get it. One of those food truck people. They told us you'd be coming from Columbia this way."

"That's right," Dante agreed. "Can someone call me if you find it out here?"

The officer handed him a business card. "We'll do our best, sir."

There was nothing else to do but head for Atlanta. I felt so sorry for Dante even though we were competitors. He was doing so well in the race. It had to be hard to want it so badly only to have someone snatch the victory away.

Not to mention that Dante made his living with his food truck in his hometown, Jackson, Mississippi. Even if he had insurance, which many vendors didn't, it might be months before he could work again.

Putting that behind us, Uncle Saul and I talked about

sweet fillings for tomorrow's biscuit bowls all the way to the hotel in Atlanta. We decided to make strawberry filling, if we could find some fresh strawberries. We could drizzle white icing over the top of each one. *Yum!*

Atlanta was so much bigger than Charlotte and Columbia— bigger than Mobile, too. It was like the tall buildings were mountains surrounding us. I wished I had time to wander around the shops and look at kitchen gadgets, but I knew that wouldn't happen during this trip. Maybe next time.

Traffic was terrible. We were stuck trying to get into the city for an hour. When we finally arrived at the hotel, the sponsors of the race had sent security people to watch the food trucks. No one wanted a repeat of what had happened in Columbia. It was bad press for all of us.

The hotel was nice, and right in the heart of the city. After checking in, Delia and I found out we were sharing a room again. Neither one of us cared.

"I'm going up to take a shower, Zoe," she said with a yawn and a stretch of her lithe body. "I'll see you later."

Dante went to find someone from the race to report what had happened. He was very generous with his thanks for picking him up. He offered us free kebabs when they finally found his food truck.

Miguel took the supply list from me and went to see if he could find everything on it. "What if I can't find fresh strawberries?"

"Blueberries would do in a pinch," I told him. "Thanks for doing this."

He smiled. "You're welcome."

I really wanted him to kiss me good-bye, but Ollie and Uncle Saul were leering at us. He walked away with the list. I knew there was going to be a lot of ribbing about our budding romance. I could take it. I hoped Miguel could, too.

Ollie, Uncle Saul, and I went to find one of the security guards for the race after that. We talked to him about the extra security they were supposed to give us. The head of the security group was a little vague. He acted as if he couldn't believe we were questioning him.

"We've already been apprised of what happened in Columbia, Miss Chase. We won't let anything like that happen here."

We left him setting up his workers around the parking lot. Most of them were yawning and inattentive.

"Anyone have the feeling they aren't that interested?" Uncle Saul asked.

"I'll camp out in the Biscuit Bowl," Ollie volunteered. "No one is gonna cut anything while I'm there."

"Thanks for offering, but I don't want you to sleep down here." I glanced around. The food trucks were all in an underground parking deck again. "The fumes from the cars and trucks could kill you."

"I've been in tougher situations, Zoe. I can handle it."

"No. That's why they have security. It will be okay. I'd rather have them steal the Biscuit Bowl than have you hurt, Ollie."

"Really?" He stared at me as though he found that hard to believe.

"Really." I kissed his cheek. "Let's go upstairs."

He shrugged, and we went for the elevator.

Uncle Saul and Ollie went to locate the room they were sharing. I went to have a margarita in the bar by myself, hoping to have a few moments to organize my thoughts.

I wasn't on the stool five minutes before Detectives Helms and Marsh joined me. My margarita showed up a few minutes later.

"We heard about the hijacking." Helms ordered a club soda.

"Let's move this to a booth." Without warning, Marsh picked up my margarita and walked over to a secluded booth.

"Hey!" I followed as quickly as possible considering my legs still felt stiff from roller-skating that morning and my knee was beginning to throb again. "Are you two allowed to work in Atlanta, too? Don't you have to get some kind of special permission?"

We sat down together. Marsh ordered coffee.

"We have special permission, Zoe," Helms told me.

"What can you tell us about the hijacking?" Marsh quickly scanned the bar.

"Not much. Dante was attacked at a gas station. Someone took his food truck. We saw him on the side of the road and gave him a ride. He told the highway patrol, and we came here."

I sipped my margarita and wished I'd ordered it from room service.

"Something is going on here," Marsh said.

"I noticed." *Brilliant!* "Have you figured out what it is?"

"We still believe Miguel Alexander is involved in all this," Helms accused. "Someone is working with him."

I started to protest and tell them why Miguel had twenty-five thousand dollars in his bank account so they would stop being so suspicious of him. But realized that he hadn't told me, and I hadn't asked. He'd tell me if he wanted me to know. I could only guess in the meantime. And if they wanted to know, they should ask him.

"I think there's a lot of money at stake," Marsh said. "It's behind the scenes and not all what we're seeing up front. Have you got any ideas, Zoe?"

I took a big gulp of my drink to try and ease the pain. It was my own fault. I'd agreed to help them. "I'll tell you the truth. I've got two members of my team who are in love. I have a bad deep fryer that I'm hoping to have replaced by tomorrow morning. That's about all I can handle right now. If I actually hear or see something *important*, I'll let you know."

"It's vital that we stay in contact with each other," Helms said.

Another big gulp finished my delicious margarita. "I understand. But now I need a shower and a nap. You'll have to excuse me. If anything happens, I have your cell numbers."

The margarita really helped me get through that. I went back downstairs to get my clothes and Crème Brûlée. Everything seemed fine. There were some food truck vendors cleaning their trucks and a few pulling into the parking lot.

I grabbed my duffel bag and slung it over my shoulder, picked up Crème Brûlée, and pulled his blanket over him. I made sure all the doors to the Biscuit Bowl were locked.

I heard the elevator chime and started over to it, but before I could leave the passenger side of the truck, I heard an argument in the RV parked next to mine on the driver's side.

It was Alex's RV—again. I couldn't really understand what the two people were saying. It was something about money and a job someone hadn't done.

I recognized Alex's voice. The other voice was too low and raspy. It was probably the same person he'd been talking to on the phone after Reggie was killed.

This couldn't be good.

I inched around the front of my food truck to see if I could get a glimpse through one of the windows.

What am I doing?

Groaning, and not wanting to be involved, I started back the way I'd come. I stopped short as I heard a shot ring out in the parking deck.

FIFTEEN

I froze on the spot. Crème Brûlée started kicking at me with
his paws. I knew his next protest at being held was going to
be howling. I didn't want to be standing there when that
started.

*It could be nothing. Just a backfire from one of the trucks.
No one's running toward the RV. Where's everyone else?*

I was afraid to open the truck door and put my cat inside.
If someone *had* fired a shot, I didn't want him or her to know
I was there.

Instead, I opened my duffel bag and set him in there. I
laid it down carefully beside the tire. I covered him with his
blanket. He probably wouldn't move. He didn't like wandering around in strange places.

I crept around to the other side of the truck. There was
no visible movement. The door to the side was open. I waited
to see if anyone came running out. If someone had shot
someone else, I figured they wouldn't hang around long.

After a few minutes, I knew I couldn't wait any longer to see what had happened. If it was nothing, I needed to know so I could sneak Crème Brûlée up to the room. If something bad had just happened, I needed to know that, too, so I could call the police.

I looked around the parking area, but all the other food truck vendors were gone. I was alone out there—*again*. I had to stop hanging around in parking decks.

I kept my head low and cautiously crept to the door that was slightly open in the RV. I glanced inside without moving from the top step. "Alex? Are you in here?"

There was no response. I called again. Still nothing.

I went another few steps up the connecting stairs until I was standing in the threshold. "Alex? Are you okay? Do you need help?"

There was still no answer. I wasn't going inside any farther. It might be *nothing*, I thought, biting my lip. I didn't want to cause an uproar over *nothing*.

Still, there *was* the argument I'd heard.

I took out my cell phone and tried to dial 911. Of course there was no service. The closest open space that might have service was the big door going out of the parking area.

I turned around to go back down the RV stairs. Someone rushed by me from behind, pushing me out of the way. I dropped my cell phone and let out a small yelp of surprise.

As I tumbled down the remaining stairs to the concrete, I saw a pair of black boots and caught a glimpse of jeans. I wasn't sure if they belonged to a man or a woman. My head was spinning. I could taste blood in my mouth.

That was it.

I stayed on the concrete for a few minutes, afraid to move. I heard a car pull up and raised my head.

"Zoe?" Miguel was back with supplies. "What are you doing over there?"

- - - - - - -

"Where's security?" Miguel helped me up. "Are you okay?"

"I'm fine." I wiped away the trickle of blood from my cut lip. "Nothing serious."

He called the hotel and the police.

I told him what had happened and he went right inside Alex's RV.

I went to make sure Crème Brûlée was all right. I pulled back the blanket.

He was gone. Panic set in. My cat was alone in a parking garage. I wasn't sure what he'd do.

I started looking under the Biscuit Bowl. There was no sign of him—this from a cat that normally didn't even like to walk into the next room to eat.

Miguel came to tell me that Alex Pardini was dead. "He was shot in the chest at close range."

"That's *terrible.*"

"Are you sure you're all right? What are you doing, Zoe?"

"I set Crème Brûlée down. He's gone. He must've been terrified by everything going on out here. I have to find him."

We looked everywhere for him. We were still looking when the police arrived. They asked what we were doing, and I told them. They weren't much help, but then they had a murder to deal with.

An hour later, I was close to tears. What if I never found Crème Brûlée? What if he'd been hurt and *couldn't* come when I called him? He could've been hit by a car or someone could have picked him up and I'd never see him again.

Bobbie Shields came over to see what was going on. She offered to help look for my cat, too. "I have a sweet little Manx at home. I would hate to lose him."

No sooner had she joined us than Uncle Saul and Ollie came downstairs—they'd heard about the shooting.

"Was anyone hurt?" Ollie asked.

I told him about Alex.

He frowned. "I suppose it would be wrong to ask if any-one *human* was hurt?"

"Shame on you!" Bobbie said. "Alex was good at what he did! And they might call the race off for sure with him gone. Now help Zoe look for her cat."

A police detective in an expensive black suit finally arrived with the coroner.

"Hey! What are all you people doing out here? This is a crime scene. No one should be in this parking area except authorized personnel. Get out of here or I'll have to arrest you."

I wiped the tears from my eyes. I'm not a pretty crier. I knew my face was blotchy and unattractive. I didn't care.

"My cat is missing. He was out here with me right before the shooting. I'm not leaving until I find him."

"That makes you a witness. You can wait over here by my car. The rest of you have to go."

"I'm not going anywhere until we find Zoe's cat." Ollie towered over him.

"Me, either." Bobbie put her hands on her ample hips.

"We find the cat or we're all staying," Uncle Saul joined in.

"And I'm not a witness unless I find my cat," I added. "I didn't hear anything or see anyone leaving the RV."

The detective was obviously angry, but we were resolute. He threw himself into helping us find Crème Brûlée. He even assigned two of the police officers to help us.

I was close to the Pizza Papa truck when I heard a loud howl followed by cursing. The back of the pizza truck flew open and Crème Brûlée ran out. His little face was covered in pizza sauce.

"Stay out of here, you little devil!" Antonio Stephanopou-los shook his fist. "You spoiled a whole batch of pizza sauce with your paws."

I caught my cat and held him to me. Antonio was right. His paws and face—even his tail—were covered in pizza sauce. I looked at him in disbelief. "You came all the way over here and snuck into this truck to steal pizza? Bad, bad cat."

He meowed and looked at me so pitifully. It was past his usual time for dinner. He was probably starving. I hugged him, forgiving him, before I told everyone that he was okay.

"Is that blood all over him?" The police detective's eyes sharpened. "Where has he been?"

"No. It's pizza sauce. He was in the Pizza Papa truck. Crème Brûlée loves pizza. Well, pretty much anything Italian. I'm going to take him upstairs and give him a bath."

"You have to stay right here," the detective disagreed. "Let one of your friends take the cat."

Uncle Saul agreed to take Crème Brûlée to his room. "I'm not saying I'm going to give this monster a bath. I value my hands too much. But he'll be out of the heat anyway."

"Thanks." I wrapped my cat in his blanket. "I'll be up as soon as I can."

Ollie went up with Uncle Saul. The police were redirected to question everyone who had been in the parking deck. I told them what I knew, what I'd heard and seen. The detective asked me to wait until he was done looking at the crime scene.

"Here we are again." Miguel had finished putting away the supplies and was waiting with me. "We have to stop meeting like this."

I smiled, completely worn-out and soaked with sweat from looking for my cat. Not the most romantic way to feel. "This is how we met. Me, in trouble, waiting in the back of a police car. This might be how our relationship is going to go."

"I don't think so. This race has had a run of bad luck. That's all. Maybe the whole thing was about Alex and now that he's dead, everything will be fine."

"Or the whole race will be over since it's been cursed from the beginning. I don't know how many things can happen before they call it off."

"Was there anything else you heard or saw that you *didn't* tell the police?"

"No. It was over very quickly. I was scared. Maybe there was something else and I didn't notice it."

The detective came to find us and had me repeat what I'd already told him. He handed me his card. "Call me if you think of anything else. I know you're not going to be here past tomorrow. You can still let me know if you think of anything."

"I will." I pocketed his card.

Antonio Stephanopoulos was also talking to a police officer. From what I could tell, he'd been in his food truck the whole time. He'd been cooking, wearing his headphones, and hadn't heard a thing.

Helms and Marsh were by the elevators. They were talking to an Atlanta police officer. It looked like they were trying to explain who they were and why they were there.

Miguel and I left the parking area, along with about eight of the other food truck team members. I passed Helms and Marsh getting into the elevator. True to their word, they didn't acknowledge me at all.

"How much more can happen in this race?" Roy Chow asked as the elevator went up. "They wouldn't even let me make sure my truck was okay."

Daryl Barbee had tried to get into the garage, too. "You don't believe all this is real, do you? At the end of the race, Pardini and Johnson will pop out. The whole thing is a big stunt. They do these things to keep people interested. Really, don't take it so seriously."

"I didn't think of it that way," Miguel murmured as we got off on our floor. "Maybe he's right. It *is* part of a TV show."

"I don't know. I don't think they'd pretend to kill people. Maybe they'd take Dante's food truck and hack up our power cords. That's possible. They might have wanted to see how resourceful we are. I think pretending someone was murdered would be too far, even for reality TV."

I knocked on Uncle Saul's door. He opened it with a towel wrapped around his arm. "That beast is a menace, Zoe. I don't know why you keep him."

I noticed he was covered in soap and water and nursing two long scratches on his arm. "I thought you weren't going to try and wash him."

"I wasn't until I saw what a mess he was. I was afraid he'd get pizza sauce all over the furniture. Next time he can clean himself."

I apologized to my uncle and went downstairs to get bandages and antibiotic ointment for his scratches. I was lucky that the desk clerk had a first-aid kit.

Miguel had headed on to his room while I was gone. He had to pay for a separate room—he didn't want to stay in the room with Ollie and Uncle Saul. No doubt he was in need of a shower and clean clothes as well.

"I'm so sorry this happened." I dressed Uncle Saul's arm. "He doesn't like baths. He knows better than to scratch me, but that's as far as it goes."

"Why don't you get a cute little puppy?" he suggested. "Even my alligator isn't as much trouble as that cat."

"He isn't all bad." I picked up Crème Brûlée. He rolled around in my arms and play-slapped at me with his paws. "Anyway, it's too late. I love him. I think he loves me. It's hard to tell. Get some rest. They'll probably make an announcement about the race at dinner, like they usually do."

"You think the race will go on?"

"I don't know. I guess we'll find out."

SIXTEEN

I managed to get Crème Brûlée cleaned up and fed in my hotel room and then took a shower and changed clothes before going down for the race dinner.

Dinner at the hotel was a somber affair. Most of the food truck drivers and their team members wore black—even if it was only black shorts and a black tank top.

Sponsors, and the food network show, had already chosen a replacement for Alex. His name was Patrick Ferris. I'd seen him before. He was Alex's second-in-command. He looked surprisingly like Alex, blond good looks and all. He sounded a lot like him, too.

"This has been a dark day for all of us involved in the Sweet Magnolia Food Truck Race." Patrick's eyes were glued on a teleprompter. "The loss of our comrade, Alex Pardini, is a terrible blow to all of us."

Bobbie Shields snorted loudly. Patrick glared at her, cleared his throat, and continued.

"As I was saying, it's terrible to even contemplate going

on with the race, but we all know that's what Alex would've wanted."

Patrick sounded all choked up and even wiped a tear from his eye. There were a few snickers from the audience but also a few sobs.

Dante Eldridge abruptly stood up. "What am I supposed to do without a food truck? I want to know what happened to my truck. If you all took it to make the show more popular, I want to know."

"That's right." Patrick acknowledged him. "Another of our companions has had his livelihood brutally ripped away from him. Unlike problems we faced in the past, there are no quick cures for Dante's truck being hijacked."

"My fist is gonna cure your face if I don't get my food truck back." Dante surged past the other tables to the front stage.

Two security men came out of nowhere to stop him. When he saw they each wore a gun, he went back to his table.

"This is getting really interesting now." Ollie was excited as he rubbed his large hands together.

"Seriously?" Delia said. "Guns and dead people make the race *interesting*?"

"Like cars crashing makes NASCAR interesting," he responded.

Delia frowned and shook her head.

"*Shh!*" Chef Art was eager to hear what was going to happen next.

"We *are* going to continue the race." Patrick picked up where he'd left off. "We'll be going forward with our double challenge tomorrow morning in downtown *Hotlanta!*"

Despite the loss of Dante's food truck, and Alex, everyone applauded. Patrick nodded and smiled as did the sponsors of the race who were onstage behind him.

"There we go!" Chef Art grinned. "That's what I wanted to hear. Too much money invested for everyone to go home without a winner. It would look bad, you know?"

"Was there some question of whether or not it would go on?" I asked him.

He shrugged. "There were one or two sponsors worried about Alex's death and what folks would think if we pushed on. Most weren't so wimpy. We started this. We have to finish it."

As soon as he'd uttered those fateful words, two pretty young women in pretty blue summer dresses brought out the electronic board they'd had in Columbia earlier that day.

"Let's look at the board as we go forward."

At Patrick's signal, the board flashed and lit up. "This morning there were seven food trucks remaining. Please stand up when I call your names. Our Daily Bread. Shut Up and Eat. Chooey's Sooey. Stick It Here. Grinch's Ganache. Pizza Papa. And the Biscuit Bowl."

The owners of those food trucks were standing at their tables. We all looked exhausted and worried.

"We lost one of our trucks to foul play—Dante, please sit down."

As Patrick said the words, Stick It Here went off the board.

Dante refused to sit down. "You all are *crazy*. I'm not hanging around waiting for you to make me feel any worse about this. I'm out of here."

We watched as Dante strode out of the room, and the doors to the big dining room shut behind him.

"*Oooh!*" Ollie whispered. "The drama."

"*Shh!*" I felt like losing Dante was worse than losing Alex. Not to be indelicate, but Dante was one of us. What happened to him could've happened to anyone.

The board flashed a few times, and the pretty girls smiled brilliantly.

"So here we are now," Patrick announced. "Six food trucks left in the race. Two seemingly impossible challenges for tomorrow. Are you ready for it?"

"I might be," Bobbie said. "If you go ahead and tell us what the challenges are."

Patrick dramatically ripped open a large envelope. "The first challenge for Atlanta is making, presenting, and selling your signature dishes *upside down*."

We all looked at one another.

Daryl Barbee was the first to speak. "Are you saying we have to make, present, and sell our food standing on our *heads*?"

Patrick laughed. "No! You misunderstood me."

"Then what are you saying, son?" Reverend Jay Jablonski asked from the front table.

"I'm saying the *food* has to be served upside down." Patrick glanced behind himself for support from the sponsors. All of them shrugged and looked away. "For instance, upside-down cupcakes, upside-down pizza, and upside-down biscuit bowls. See?"

Everyone nodded. After a few comments, Roy Chow asked about the second challenge.

"You're gonna love this one." Patrick smiled, showing his perfect white teeth against his perfectly tanned face. "You have to sell one hundred dollars of upside-down product, and *all* of the money you collect has to be in change."

"Change?" Antonio asked.

"That's right. Dimes, quarters, nickels, and pennies."

"What about those gold dollars and fifty-cent pieces?" Reverend Jablonski asked.

Patrick glanced back again. One of the producers nodded.

"Those work, too. No folding money, checks, or credit cards," Patrick confirmed.

"Most people don't even *carry* change anymore," Bobbie complained.

"That's why they call it a challenge, right?" Patrick smiled and applauded.

"Is that it?" Ollie asked.

"That's it," Patrick responded. "Enjoy your dinner. Get some sleep. We'll see you at four A.M. tomorrow."

I did as he suggested and enjoyed some delicious chicken with risotto and a nice glass of red wine. I know you're supposed to drink white with chicken, but I liked the red better.

Halfway through dinner, Uncle Saul's phone rang. It was his friend from Mobile with the deep fryer. I started to get up and go with him. He told me to sit down and finish my meal.

"This way, my buddy and I have some private time to talk. We'll get the fryer in. He's gonna want to get paid. Want me to take care of it?"

"No. Take the cash." I grabbed the envelope that held my winnings from Columbia and gave it to him. "Call me if you need my help."

"Doubtful, but I will if it comes up."

There was a lot of grumbling and outright complaining as the food truck teams finished dinner and left the large room. Patrick and the producers were long gone. The electronic board and the pretty girls had gone with them.

Chef Art finished his dinner. "I'm going to meet with the other sponsors of the race and see where we stand in all of this. I don't know if anything has to be changed yet. I'll let you know. See you all in the morning. Get some sleep, Zoe. You're looking a mite peaked."

"Thanks."

Ollie went off with Delia to get drinks. Uncle Saul went to bed.

"I guess it's me and you." Miguel smiled and took my hand. "We could go out and take in some of the local night life if you want."

"I'm really tired. Maybe a drink and then I'm ready for bed. I know that's not very exciting. But you already know I'm not a very exciting person."

"I think you're pretty exciting. Almost too exciting for me. I lead a boring life in comparison."

I laughed as we wandered down the long hall with the

ugly, brown-flowered carpeting underfoot. We were walking in the general direction of the hotel bar.

I glanced up to reply and saw Miguel's beautiful female *friend* in a crowd of people filling the hotel lobby. The sponsors and producers of the race were answering questions from a large media group about Alex's death. *She* was right in the middle of it.

It was one thing to have seen this woman in Charlotte the first morning. A little odd to see her in Columbia the next day. Why was she here in Atlanta, too?

Lots of questions occurred to me.

We sat down in the crowded bar. We were lucky to get a secluded booth from a couple that was leaving. Miguel ordered a whiskey sour and I got my usual margarita.

"I know this isn't any of my business, but did you agree to come with me for the race so you could meet your friend here and in Charlotte and Columbia?" I smiled to take the edge off the question.

"I had already agreed to come with you when Tina called about meeting her somewhere to talk. She said she was going to be in Columbia, and that worked for me."

Our drinks arrived, and I pushed the subject a step further. "Does Tina know about the race?"

He shrugged. "Yes. Alex Pardini was her husband."

"What?"

After dropping that bombshell, Miguel leaned closer to me. "I told you about her husband trying to take everything away from her."

"I guess she doesn't have that problem now." I thought about those black boots and jeans that I'd seen before I fell down the RV stairs. "That's a very good motive to kill someone."

"What I didn't tell you, Zoe, was that there have been two recent attempts on Tina's life. Alex may have been killed because of those attempts."

I had to admit that the phone call I'd overheard in

Charlotte *could* have been about Alex killing his wife or hiring someone to kill her. I was still only guessing from the stilted words I'd heard. "But why have her killed during the race? Wouldn't someplace private had been better? And why is he dead instead of her?"

"Maybe to provide an alibi for himself. I don't know. I'm trying to understand it myself."

"Maybe that's the part I heard about payment right before Alex was killed. Maybe the killer wanted more money. But why would Alex kill Reggie?"

He shrugged. "To throw everyone off when he killed Tina?"

"I guess that's possible."

His phone rang and he stood up. "Excuse me, Zoe."

It only took a minute for Detectives Helms and Marsh to spot me alone at the booth and move in. They weren't exactly the faces I wanted to see across from me.

"How was the dinner?" Helms asked.

"It was pretty good for catered food. I enjoyed it. How was your dinner?"

"We haven't had dinner yet." Marsh sounded as though he wasn't too happy about it, either. "We've been in the parking garage with the Atlanta police investigating *another* murder involved with this race."

"Are they shutting the race down now?" Helms asked.

"No. Not at all." I sighed. "There were a lot of good words about Alex Pardini and that he'd want the race to continue. We'll be up and running again tomorrow at four A.M."

"What about the sponsors?" Marsh wondered. "Aren't they worried about bad publicity from being involved with the race?"

"I don't think most of them are all that worried. I know Chef Art wasn't."

"What about Pardini's death?" Marsh leaned forward after pushing Miguel's drink out of the way. "Have you remembered anything else that happened before he was killed?"

"No. I told the police what I heard and saw. It wasn't much."

"Zoe, were the boots you saw men's or women's?" Helms questioned.

"I'm not sure. I only caught a glimpse of them."

"If you think of anything else—" Marsh began.

"I have your cell phone numbers. I'll call." I wanted information from them, too. "Do you still think Miguel is involved with this?"

"We have some information about a woman he was seen with in Columbia." Helms looked at her notebook. "Tina Gerard. Ever hear of her?"

I was going to pass on that. I wanted their information, not the other way around.

"No. Who is she?"

"She's Alex Pardini's wife. We know she called Miguel in Mobile *before* the race started. She and Pardini have been going through a really nasty divorce. The way it looked, she wasn't going to get anything. Then she hired Miguel."

Marsh's gaze was intense. "Now, with Pardini dead, that changes *everything*."

SEVENTEEN

I understood what they meant. They knew about the twenty-five thousand dollars that had been wired to Miguel's account. It looked like Tina *could* have paid Miguel to kill her husband.

"We're building a case against your friend, Zoe," Helms added. "I hope you aren't involved in all this."

"Where does Reggie's death fit into it?" I asked.

"We're not sure yet," Marsh admitted. "Maybe he was the *first* hit man Tina Gerard paid to kill her husband."

"Meaning Miguel was the next?"

"Well, well." Miguel finally made it back. "A man can't leave his date anymore without someone else stepping in. Do you *mind*?"

The two detectives pushed out of the booth. Miguel sat down and took a sip of his drink.

"We'll be talking to you, Zoe," Helms said. "Good night. Be careful."

When they were gone, Miguel asked, "What did they want this time?"

"The usual." I studied his face. "They know it was Tina who sent you that money from the Caymans. They think you killed Reggie, too."

"Why would I kill Reggie?"

"Because he wasn't doing his job as the first hit man Tina hired to kill Alex. So she hired you."

"Nice to know where I stand. No wonder my ears were burning."

"The police have been keeping an eye on you and Tina. They think you're working together."

"That's okay. I have nothing to hide. I didn't kill Alex, Detective McSwain, or Reggie Johnson. I'll be glad to share my alibi with them if they'd like to question me. Instead they keep skulking around talking to *you*!"

"I'm sure they're waiting for enough information to arrest you. Are you sure your friend Tina has your back? If the police are talking to her next, that could be what they need."

"I don't know." His eyes narrowed. "This is a new one for me. I've never been under suspicion of murder for hire. Looking at it logically, I suppose I can see how they're putting it together."

I covered his hand with mine on the table. "Let's not look at it logically anymore. Let's pretend Tina is setting you up to take the fall for Alex's murder."

"Sorry. Absolutely not. Why would she do that?"

"Because she was going to lose everything. Now she'll get everything, whatever that is. Maybe she didn't need you as a lawyer but as a fall guy."

"I think Alex was wealthy," he admitted. "Tina told me she'd given up her legal practice years ago to raise their daughter."

"That makes it even worse." I yawned. "People will do even more for their kids than they will for money."

"That doesn't mean Tina killed him."

"No. It doesn't. But I'm more worried about you taking the fall for Alex's death than I am Tina. She sent you that money before the race and then *conveniently* met you along the race route. That sounds kind of suspicious to me."

"I hope *neither* one of us is guilty of killing anyone." He squeezed my hand. "You need to go to bed. You've been up for a long time, besides the skating and singing. Don't worry about the police. They think they have something, but it's all smoke and mirrors. We'll work this out."

He walked me to my room. We saw Delia laughing and going into the bar with Ollie.

"Poor Ollie," Miguel said. "I think he's in for a wild ride with Delia."

I slipped my key card into the room lock and the light turned green. "Maybe it will be just what he needs to get him out of his rut. But they may have to dial it down a bit until we get through the race. We have enough problems without the two of them going at it in the back of the Biscuit Bowl."

Miguel lightly kissed me. "Good night, Zoe. I'll see you at four."

I threw my arms around his neck and gave him a more satisfying kiss. "Don't worry. I won't let the police have you."

He laughed. "Better put on your Superwoman cape if you're going to keep me out of trouble."

"I can do that." I smiled and wished him a good night.

I locked the door behind me and didn't bother switching on the light. With the curtains open, the lights from around the hotel were enough to cast a dim glow through the room.

I looked out at the city of Atlanta spread around us. Tomorrow was sure to be a daunting day even without the police harassing me about Miguel. I hoped there were lots of people out there who got up early—with change in their pockets. I hoped they enjoyed eating upside-down biscuits.

And I hope Tina isn't leading Miguel into more than he, or Superwoman, can handle.

I shed my T-shirt and jeans and set the alarm clock. After getting into bed, I cuddled with Crème Brûlée, who was beginning to need a mani/pedi. My last thought, before sleep overcame me, was that I'd forgotten my cat's brush at home.

- - - - - - -

The alarm caught me in the middle of a particularly good dream. Miguel and I were at carnival and glitter was falling from the sky. We were the king and queen of Mardi Gras, riding through the streets of Mobile on a beautiful float.

That was over.

This was reality. I was in Atlanta. It was four A.M., and I was going to have to sell upside-down biscuit bowls.

I stumbled in to take a quick shower and wash my hair. There wasn't time to do anything elaborate with my curls. I scrunched a lot of conditioner through them and put on the scarf to hold them down until I wore Chef Art's hat.

In the light, I could see that Crème Brûlée was starting to look like a giant fuzz ball. I stroked his tummy as he rolled around on the bed and pretended to want to slap my hand.

"I'm gonna have to ask Miguel to get a brush for you when he gets supplies today. By tomorrow, I won't even be able to find your face if I don't. You don't want to be one of those cats that someone posts on Facebook, do you?"

He didn't really seem to care. I put him down on the floor in the bathroom and fed him as I got ready to go.

I noticed Uncle Saul had left a text on my phone around midnight. The fryer was in the truck and working. That was good news. I expected him to be out of the race today after such a late night. We'd have to work around his absence.

By the time I got all of my things together, Crème Brûlée had finished his morning rituals. I cleaned and folded his traveling litter box and then put that and his food into my large bag.

"I think we can walk out of here with you out in the open since I could hardly leave you downstairs after a murder."

I put my bags over my shoulder and hefted him in my arms. "Let's go."

Delia was just getting up. "What time is it?"

"Time to go," I whispered. "I'll see you downstairs."

"Okay."

I met Miguel and Ollie in the elevator going to the parking garage. I told them about Uncle Saul. Miguel volunteered to wait for him at the hotel and join us when he could.

"Don't worry, Zoe," Ollie said with a big grin on his face. "We can handle it—me, you, and Delia."

"You're in a good mood," I remarked with a yawn.

"I had a few drinks with Delia last night. It was good." He smiled and raised his eyebrows at Miguel. "You know. I think it was *very* good."

The elevator reached the underground parking lot. We were stopped by two police officers. "We'll have to escort you to your food truck. Our investigation is still ongoing. The captain doesn't want you foodies messing things up."

As long as they weren't keeping us from reaching the Biscuit Bowl, that was fine with me. An officer escorted us, and even looked around the outside of the food truck to make sure everything was as it should be.

I got a big surprise when I opened the passenger side door. Uncle Saul was asleep in the truck. Crème Brûlée meowed at him as I shook his shoulder.

"Zoe?" He yawned and stared at me through half-closed eyes. "Is it morning already? It looks so dark."

"It *is* so dark. We're in the basement, and it's not light outside yet." I smiled at him. "If you'd like to take a shower and change clothes, Miguel will wait for you. I have to get going."

"No. That's why I stayed down here. It didn't make any sense to go up to the room for a few hours. I'm ready when you are. I can shower and change later. You got a minute to look at the new deep fryer?"

"I've got about that." The other food truck drivers were

already leaving. I could hear them yelling at one another excitedly as they got started for the day.

We looked in the back. The new fryer was shiny and clean. It wouldn't stay that way for long.

"I went ahead and added the new oil last night so I could try it out. It seems good. He only charged me half price on it, too. It's a little different from what you're used to, but I think it will do the job."

I crouched down beside the fryer. The oil was so clean and clear. With it being new, it looked like it went on forever.

"Thanks for doing this." I hugged him. "You could skip working today, you know. Ollie and I can take care of it."

He looked up and around the small interior. "Where's Delia?"

"She's getting herself together. She might be down already."

We were getting in the Biscuit Bowl and Miguel's car when Delia came running from the elevator with a police officer by her side.

"Were you all about to leave me?" she asked breathlessly.

"Of course not! Get in. Let's go!"

"Okay! See you there."

I started the food truck. The engine kind of clunked. It was running. That was all that mattered. Ollie had made sure everything was tied down in back before he'd left with Delia and Miguel. We were off!

We drove through the not-so-quiet streets of Atlanta toward the heart of downtown. There was actually traffic out at that time of morning. The orange glow of streetlights directed us, and we followed the other food truck drivers.

"I hope our potential customers have a lot of change in their pockets," I muttered.

"As to that," Uncle Saul started with a chuckle, "I had an idea."

He went on to explain that his friend who'd brought the fryer from home was also a vending machine operator. "He had a bagful of change, Zoe. I bought it off him with the rest of the twenty-five hundred you gave me for the deep fryer. I was thinking that we could make change for people who don't have it."

I was amazed at the sneaky idea. "I wonder if that will be okay?"

"I already checked with Chef Art. He said there weren't any rules pertaining to it. I think we got his blessing."

"You have a devious mind."

"Thank you. I needed one growing up in the Chase family. All those rules and regulations weren't for me. Your father liked rules, I think. He still does."

I laughed at that. He was right. My mother was the same way. That's why Uncle Saul and I got along so well. That and the curly hair.

I saw the big white lights illuminating the area where the food truck event would take place. One of the assistants told us where to park and pointed out the cool-down tent and stage.

Miguel was right behind us as I pulled the Biscuit Bowl into the parking place designated for it. The space was a little tight, which made me a lot nervous, but I got it in.

We hopped out of the front of the food truck to begin setting up for the day. I waved to Miguel. Ollie, Delia, and I went around back to open the door.

I didn't see where they came from. It was like one minute, it was all food truck vendors, and the next, Detectives Helms and Marsh were there with what looked like an army of Atlanta's finest.

As Miguel reached us, the detectives stepped forward.

"Miguel Alexander, we need you to come with us."

EIGHTEEN

"What's this about?" Miguel asked.

"We'd like to have a talk with you," Helms said. "The Atlanta PD has been gracious enough to allow us to continue to pursue our suspects from Charlotte and Columbia. They're also letting us question *you*."

"What are you questioning me about?" He seemed completely at ease.

I wondered if he had a lawyer he called when *he* needed help.

"We want to discuss the deaths of Reggie Johnson, Detective McSwain, and Alex Pardini. Will you come with us, please?"

Helms's stern gaze said she was ready for a fight. She also looked like she hadn't slept. Had she managed to get information from Tina about Miguel?

"Am I under arrest?" Miguel asked.

"No. Not at this time. You're a person of interest in our investigation," Marsh snarled. "It would be to your advantage to come with us and answer our questions."

Miguel's gaze searched for mine. "I might be gone for a while, Zoe. You should have everything you need." He gave me his car keys. "If you need the car, take it. I'll see you later."

Marsh and Helms walked at the front of the pack. Two officers escorted Miguel until they reached the large group of police cars at the back of the food truck area. I couldn't see him after they'd reached all the flashing blue lights.

"What's up with that?" Ollie asked. "What do they want with Miguel?"

"They think he had something to do with what happened to those people." Uncle Saul shook his head. "Any ideas why, Zoe?"

I glanced at my watch. As much as I wanted to go with Miguel, I knew I wouldn't be able to help him—at least not then. I pocketed his keys and hoped for the best.

"We'll have to talk about it while we work if we want to stay in the race," I reminded them. "These upside-down biscuit bowls aren't going to make themselves."

- - - - - - -

I brought my team up to speed on what was happening with Miguel as we made biscuits, chicken salad with pistachios, and fresh strawberry filling.

Space was definitely at a premium in the kitchen area of the Biscuit Bowl. We had to make do with what we had, and walk all over one another's feet to do it.

Uncle Saul chopped up the ingredients for the chicken salad. It *was* his recipe. He had Delia helping him, making sure the chicken was cut up into tiny shreds. I made the biscuit dough, and Ollie baked tray after tray of biscuits in the tiny oven. I worked on the strawberry filling between trays of biscuits.

"This was bound to be about a woman," Ollie quoted with deep insight and a wicked grin at Delia.

"I don't think Miguel is involved with this woman other

than being friends." Delia smiled, reassuring me with her gaze as she said it.

"That doesn't mean she can't mess him up anyway," Uncle Saul said. "I don't like it. I can tell you that. Here we are, away from home. Who's gonna help him out of this scrape?"

There was a knock on the back door. It was one of the producer's assistants telling us that we needed to go to the stage.

Except for frying up the biscuit bowls, we were ready.

Chef Art joined us, taking my arm as we walked across the street to see what was going on. "What's this I hear about the police arresting Miguel?"

"Not arresting," I replied tersely. "They're only *questioning* him."

"Still," he mused, "it won't look good for something like this to get around."

"He's not guilty of doing anything wrong—except maybe trusting an old friend he shouldn't have trusted."

He patted my hand as he drew it through the crook of his arm. He smelled like lilac water and bacon. "All I'm saying is that appearances are everything. The media hasn't said anything about this yet. They're still too busy talking about the murders, and asking if there's a curse on the food truck race."

I laughed as we approached the stage, where Patrick Ferris was getting his hair and sound checked. "Well, there you go. I think our reputation is safe."

"Unless you *win* the race, Zoe. Then they'll come down on you like a ton of bricks for having a killer on your team."

I stepped away from him and stared hard at his friendly, famous face. "I'm not abandoning Miguel. I also have a homeless man, a waitress, and a man who lives with alligators in the swamp on my team. There will always be *something* if you want to find it."

He shrugged and peered up at the stage as he leaned on his cane.

"Do you want to withdraw your sponsorship?" I asked.

"No." He glanced back at me. "I still think you can win this. What happens to Miguel won't hurt me. It could make or break what happens for *you* from all of this. Will you be famous, or *infamous*?"

Our conversation was cut off by Patrick finally finishing his sound check. The cameras were on, and the producers' assistants urged all of us to applaud and cheer.

"Good morning, foodies!" Patrick's welcome was as bright and cheerful as if we weren't all standing in the middle of a dark street while most people were asleep. "Welcome to *Hotlanta*, and our third day of the Sweet Magnolia Food Truck Race. Just to remind everyone of our standings, can we have the big board out here?"

There was some problem finding the big board. Apparently no one had planned on using it first thing and it had been left in one of the production trucks. It took a few minutes to locate and set it up. The computer tech who'd programmed it was still asleep. He came running out of one of the RVs still in his pajamas.

The cameras stopped until the electronic board was set up. They started up again as the board flashed the names of the food trucks that were still left in the race.

Patrick had disappeared for the time that it took to locate the board and set it up. He bounded back on the stage a second before he needed to be on camera.

"So, we still have Our Daily Bread in the lead with points," he read from the board.

"Points?" Ollie whispered loudly. "Who said anything about *points*? I thought it was last food truck standing that won."

"Yeah," Bobbie Shields echoed him. "What do we get points for?"

The cameras stopped rolling again and the point system was explained again by the producers of the race.

"I don't like changing the rules halfway through the race," Antonio from Pizza Papa said.

"The rules are still the same as they were," I said. "They just didn't call it points last time. Nothing has really changed."

Bobbie muttered under her breath, but everyone else seemed to get it. The cameras came back on again, and Patrick took his spot.

"Okay. Our Daily Bread is on top. Biscuit Bowl is number two. Shut Up and Eat is number three. Chooey's Sooey is number four. Grinch's Ganache is number five. Pizza Papa is number six." He applauded and whooped for everyone.

The assistants on the sidelines did their best to try and get some love from the vendors. Everyone was tired, cranky, and on edge—it wasn't easy getting them to applaud.

Patrick laughed. "I know all of you have your challenges ready for today. Don't forget that your main menu item has to be served upside down. You have to simultaneously face the second challenge, too. You have to sell one hundred dollars in product, and your customers have to pay in *change*."

"We've got that," Daryl from Grinch's Ganache said. "Is that it?"

"I'm glad you asked. As a matter of fact, we've come up with a surprise challenge that will net the winner an additional one thousand dollars."

Everyone wanted to hear that.

"What do we have to do?" Antonio asked.

"I'm glad you asked!" Patrick pointed and winked. "It's another taste challenge! The first person to entice a customer to come here and be on camera with a short review of their food wins one thousand dollars. Simple, right? Sound good?"

Everyone in the group said it did. We were all ready to go back and get started.

The assistants started shouting and whooping, encouraging us to do the same. The crowd got louder, and Patrick began applauding. The whole thing looked good—for TV, anyway.

"All right, you crazy foodies! Go out and win those challenges!"

"Good luck, Zoe," Chef Art said as the morning ritual ended. "I hope you have a plan."

"I always have a plan. See you after."

- - - - - - -

We'd decided that Delia would go out and sell the biscuit bowls again this time around. She'd put on her tight white shorts and white stiletto heels with a bright red tank top that left very little to the imagination. She freed her hair from the ponytail and swung it around her shoulders.

"You look awesome," I whispered. "If you can't sell upside-down biscuit bowls, no one can."

She smiled at me. "You underrate yourself, Zoe. You're younger, prettier, and smarter. I'm sure you'd do as well out there on the street."

I impulsively hugged her. Her sweet perfume clung to me even after I'd let her go. "Thanks. But I'm better *in* the kitchen, and I don't mind a bit."

Uncle Saul was getting ready for the challenge inside the Biscuit Bowl. Ollie would be taking food to Delia again.

"Okay. I think we're ready," I called to Ollie who was also taking the change bag. "Let's go."

I stepped outside the Biscuit Bowl as they were leaving. It was still dark even though it was six A.M. There was a chill in the air. Fog swirled along the ground and in the taller building towers. I wished there were a cash prize for selling soggy biscuit bowls.

"Feels like rain." Uncle Saul sniffed the air as he came out of the kitchen. "I can feel it in my old bones."

"I wish you could feel what everyone else is doing to get

around this challenge." I watched Bobbie Shields walk by with her pretty daughter and wondered what they had in mind.

I didn't have to wonder what the other teams were going to do for long. There was a spotlight feature with Daryl and Sarah Barbee from Grinch's Ganache right outside our food truck. Daryl was clear on his plan.

"So what's your plan for making it through this challenge?" Patrick Ferris asked them.

"My plan is to sell all of our delicious red velvet cupcakes with real sour cream frosting for a quarter." Daryl smiled into the camera.

The big cowboy hat was off for once so I could see the rest of his face. He had a big nose and small eyes that looked like raisins in his leathery face.

Patrick laughed. "That's gonna take a lot of cupcake sales to make a hundred dollars, isn't it?"

Daryl's smile quickly turned to a frown. "I suppose so."

Sarah added, "But this way we don't have to worry about people having much change in their pockets. It was *my* idea."

It was one of the few times I'd heard her speak.

"Well, good luck to you. We'll see what happens when the challenge is over."

The lights went off, and the camera shut down. The assistants moved the table, umbrella, and chairs away.

Sarah and Daryl stared at each other as though they weren't sure about their plan anymore. Daryl grabbed Sarah's hand and squeezed it.

"That's what they need to get on camera," I whispered to Uncle Saul. "That's the kind of thing that keeps us all going."

He grinned and hugged me. "Like this?"

"Just like this."

He agreed. "We better get inside and fry up more of those upside-down biscuit bowls. That chicken salad is to die for. It was solid enough to hold on to the top of the biscuit. The strawberries are a little too juicy."

"Whatever." I laughed. "This wouldn't have anything to

do with you making the chicken salad and me making the strawberries, would it?"

At that moment, there was a loud roll of thunder. As the rain came pouring down, all the electricity in the Biscuit Bowl went out.

"That's just great," I muttered.

NINETEEN

We scrambled trying to get the generator up and running again. It seemed as though it had been affected by the storm, but Uncle Saul said it was just a power surge in the generator.

The thunderstorm raged around us, soaking us as we messed with the generator trying to get it started. When we finally had power again, Ollie and Delia came back, drenched, no sales, and all the biscuit bowls soggy with water.

"What now?" Ollie took off his T-shirt and wrung the water out of it.

"Wow." Delia admired Ollie's muscular physique when he'd taken off his shirt. "You work out?"

"Two hours most days." He preened a bit for her to admire his arms and back.

"You're in *great* shape." She touched his chest.

"Thanks." He examined her carefully from her feet to her hair. "You, too!"

"Thanks. I don't work out but I'm careful what I eat."

As she said that, I saw two members of the Chooey's Sooey food truck team passing by with umbrellas. Apparently they didn't believe the race organizers were going to shut down for the rain, either.

"I wish we had umbrellas." I shook my head for not thinking ahead that the weather could go bad.

"I could take Miguel's car and go get some," Delia volunteered.

"That's true. We could use GPS to find a store close by. It's too early for much to be open downtown."

"What about a drugstore?" Uncle Saul asked. "There's always one of those open twenty-four hours, and they probably have umbrellas."

"Good idea." I gave Delia my credit card. "Hurry! We don't have much time."

She took the keys to the Mercedes and my credit card and left.

"She's never gonna get back in time." Ollie looked out the customer window.

I kept making strawberry filling. "What else can we do?"

Uncle Saul retained his equanimity. "They're gonna have to give everyone an extra hour or something. You'll see. No need to fret over it in any case. You can only do what you can do."

Chef Art's assistant popped in from the back of the food truck. "He sent me with these umbrellas." She began speaking before she could catch her breath. In her hands were two large red and white umbrellas with Chef Art's face and logo on them. "He says to tell you the challenge isn't changing for the storm."

"Thanks, Lacie." I took off my apron. "We're going out, Uncle Saul. You've got the kitchen. I'll take Ollie and the change with me. Call Delia and have her come back. Good luck."

He laughed. "Good luck to you, too!"

The umbrellas were the huge beach-type ones. They weighed a ton but covered a large area. I couldn't balance one of them with the tray of biscuit bowls. It was a good thing Ollie was so much taller than me. He held the umbrella over both of us while I walked close to him.

"I was afraid of this." Ollie inclined his head toward the nearly empty, rain-soaked city street. "No one wants to hang around and buy food during a thunderstorm."

I knew he was right, especially when a lightning strike close by made me afraid we might become kebabs holding onto the metal umbrella.

As I was agreeing with him, I saw Patrick running up the sidewalk. His assistant was trying to hold an umbrella over his head. Lights came on, and the cameraman began taping another personal segment for the race.

"Zoe Chase, owner of the Biscuit Bowl from Mobile, Alabama, what is your next move during the thunderstorm? You only have"—he glanced at his watch—"ten minutes to meet the challenge of selling a hundred dollars in upside-down biscuit bowls for change."

"Actually, we assumed the challenge would be postponed until the storm was over," I said. "It makes more sense than all of us standing out here while the people we're trying to sell to are running into buildings to get away."

He laughed. "Then why are you out here?"

"Because I realized making sense wasn't what the race is about. I don't know if any of us are going to make the challenge, but we're out here, Patrick. I guess we'll see where it goes from there."

The camera followed my gesture toward the street where a few people were hurrying to get out of the storm.

"Thanks, Zoe." He put down the microphone and shivered as the lights and camera went off. "Let's get in the RV," he said to his cameraman. "It's nasty out here."

Patrick gave us a salute and ran off again.

"We might as well take off, too," Ollie said.

A city bus pulled up to the curb. It was packed with commuters.

I saw Sarah and Daryl run up to the door where people were making their way off. They immediately started selling their cupcakes for twenty-five cents each. A few hands reached out to exchange their quarters for cupcakes.

Brilliant!

"Let's do it," I said to Ollie.

"We can't sell enough biscuit bowls here to make the hundred-dollar challenge," he remarked.

"We can't, but we can stay good in the standings for trying. We'll take the back door."

I knew Ollie was right. I also knew we could sell more if the weather cleared, but why waste this opportunity in case it didn't?

A few of the disembarking passengers were grumpy at being detained while Ollie made change for the biscuit bowls so they could pay with quarters, dimes, and nickels. A few pushed around our customers who wanted what we were selling. I was surprised when the bus was empty to find that we had sold all but one biscuit bowl.

"What are we doing about getting more?" Ollie asked. "I can go back and get them, but if I leave the umbrella with you, they'll get soaked on the way. If I don't, you'll get soaked."

"There's no time left anyway." Sarah and Daryl ran by us on their way back to their food truck. "Let's go back together."

I saw other teams heading in with umbrellas. We'd made about twenty dollars. I knew Sarah and Daryl had probably done about the same. There might not be a winner for that one.

"We have to focus on getting the second challenge," I told my team when we reached the Biscuit Bowl. Delia was back, and in an apron, wearing Chef Art's hat. She was helping Uncle Saul make chicken salad.

"I've got another tray ready to go and biscuits in the oven," he said. "Are you going back out?"

"We have to try and find someone for the taste test if we

want to go on." I shook the water out of my shoes. "I don't want to go home from here."

Uncle Saul handed me the next tray of biscuit bowls, half of them chicken and half of them strawberry. "We'll get the next tray ready. You all be careful out there. You're walking around in a thunderstorm holding a lightning rod."

"Better than a trayful of soggy biscuit bowls," I told him with a smile.

Ollie and I went back out on the street. The rain had become lighter as the morning had moved on. The sky behind the big downtown buildings was a swirl of storm clouds that didn't look as though it was about to move off. All we could do was keep going and pray for a miracle.

Ollie had found a way to put the rest of the change into a money bag that he'd stuffed into the pocket of his water-proof jacket.

"What now?" He looked around.

The streets were as devoid of foot traffic as they were before. People from the food trucks stood around us trying to decide how to get a customer to come back with them. The cameras were rolling, even though Patrick wasn't out there. I thought we must all look a little pathetic standing around holding our food and not finding anyone to sell to.

The rain had lightened to a drizzle. There were plenty of cars in the street, filled with curious people staring at us. An Atlanta police officer was out there keeping an eye on things. There wasn't much to see, but for the life of me, I couldn't think what else we could do.

"Give me two biscuit bowls," Ollie said. "One strawberry. One chicken. Let's see if we can't drum up some business."

I watched as he ran out into the street at a crosswalk as the light changed to red. He went from car to car with his captive audience. I couldn't tell if he was selling or not until he waved to me.

I ran out into the street with him. The police officer

shouted, "That's what the crosswalk is for," but didn't try to stop me.

"Give me a strawberry biscuit bowl for this lovely lady in yellow." Ollie rolled his eyes at me, but he was smiling as he made change for the woman.

"Thank you. This is wonderful," she said. "Now I don't have to go out for lunch."

The light turned green. Ollie and I were stuck in the middle of the intersection with cars going by on both sides.

"This could work," I enthused. "You're the best for thinking of it."

"I'm not just good-looking, you know. I'm smart, too." He took two biscuit bowls from the tray.

By the time the light had turned red again, all of the food truck vendors were in the street. Ollie was working car to car. I followed him with the rapidly disappearing tray of biscuit bowls. When the light turned green again, we were out of product.

"I'll run back and get more." I was excited that we'd found a way around the problem.

"I don't think you need to." He pointed toward the sidewalk where a woman in a green Honda was parked. She waved to him. "I think we have our product review for the taste test! I told everyone who bought a biscuit what we needed. She agreed."

Ollie told the woman where to pull her car, and we walked her to the cool-down tent like she was precious cargo. I could see she was flustered and embarrassed, but she went through with it, giving us a glowing video review for our strawberry biscuit bowls.

"We met the extra challenge," he said after walking the woman back to her car and giving her a chicken salad biscuit bowl to say thanks. "That's pretty good, right?"

"I don't know. I guess we'll see. It shows initiative, right? I think a lot of teams are going to be washed out." I hoped so anyway.

We took our money to the cool-down tent as Roy Chow and Reverend Jablonski were taking theirs in, too. Some of the sponsors were there, along with the producers and Patrick Ferris.

I didn't know how this was going to come out, since we didn't make enough money but had completed the review.

After a few minutes of conferring and checking things out, Patrick announced what they'd decided. "Because of the bad weather, no team sold enough to meet the challenge. We had two teams who made the taste-test challenge, the Biscuit Bowl and Our Daily Bread."

There was appropriate applause, mostly from the producers' assistants.

"We have a question for the Biscuit Bowl team and the Our Daily Bread team," Patrick said. "You can take your thousand dollars now or use that win to improve your standing in the race. Your decision."

It was a no-brainer for me. "We'll use the money to improve our standing."

"So will we," Reverend Jablonski said.

"Then it looks like we have a tie for the winner of the second challenge," Patrick said. "No team will take home the thousand dollars for the taste-test challenge."

"So what do we do in case of a tie?" Jablonski asked.

The sponsors conferred with the producers. They gave their decision to one of their assistants, who delivered it to Patrick.

"Come on. Come on." Ollie urged them to move faster. "Who wins?"

"The decision has been made to break the tie using the taste-test videos from each of you. We're going to show the videos again, and whoever has the best compliments about their food wins."

"Like what?" Ollie asked.

"Words." Patrick fumbled trying to explain. "*Good. Excellent. Delicious.* That kind of thing."

We watched our video again and then Our Daily Bread's customer video. I couldn't tell much difference. But Our Daily Bread was declared the winner of the tie.

Ollie and Chef Art protested the decision. It still put us in the number two slot, so I was happy. All we had to do was hang in there until Reverend Jablonski messed up and the race was ours.

Chef Art, immaculate as always in his white linen suit, winked and nodded at me. I knew he was pleased despite his protests. It had been a difficult challenge in the bad weather. We were still doing better than the other teams, which meant someone else was going to be sent home.

There were high fives between the two ministers representing Our Daily Bread. Everyone was excited and congratulating one another.

Now that the challenge was over, I was starting to worry about Miguel. I thought we would have heard something from him by then. I had hoped he'd be back already.

It made me feel guilty. I'd been so worried about winning the race, I'd forgotten all about him until that minute. I wanted to help him, but I wasn't a lawyer. I hoped he'd called someone who knew what to do. All I could think to do was to go to the police station and demand his release.

Ollie growled as we left the tent. "We weren't prepared enough."

"I suppose not, but neither was anyone else. We did okay. Let's get cleaned up. I want to know what's happening with Miguel."

We walked back to the Biscuit Bowl and told Uncle Saul and Delia the news. We started packing up, even though we had to wait for the official word about who had won, and what they had won.

I went to the front of the truck and checked on Crème Brûlée. He didn't like storms. His howling during the bad weather was usually even worse than the thunder and lightning.

He seemed okay. Maybe I needed to run out to the food truck with him next time there was a storm at home. I stroked his soft white tummy, and he purred for me before he started slapping with his paws.

"You are so crazy." I kissed his little nose. "But I love you. I know I'm neglecting you a little, but I'll make it up to you later."

"Excuse me," a woman's voice said from behind.

I turned and faced Tina Gerard—for my money the one responsible for Miguel being questioned by the police. I would've blown her off. I felt like it was what she deserved.

Before I could, she said, "I know you're Zoe Chase. I'm worried about Miguel. Have you heard anything?"

TWENTY

There was a tense sadness about her that I hadn't noticed when I had seen her far away. She was beautiful and fragile, reminding me of a glass statue. Her clothes were expensive and well made. I felt sorry for her, too, knowing her husband had been trying to take everything away from her in their divorce settlement.

At least I *hoped* that's what had been going on. She may have been lying about the whole thing to implicate Miguel in Alex's death. I had to keep that in mind as I agreed to talk with her.

With everyone else packing up in back, and Crème Brûlée snoring in the front seat, I took a towel and dried off a pretty ornamental bench that was close to where the Biscuit Bowl was parked. We sat there as the heavy storm clouds moved slowly above us, promising more rain.

"I haven't heard anything from Miguel since he left with the police early this morning." I watched her face and eyes for any sign of what she was thinking.

She broke down sobbing. I went to the truck and got her a couple of napkins.

"I never meant for anything like this to happen when I asked him for help." She thanked me and wiped away her tears.

"What did you expect?"

"I thought he could help me keep my daughter. I didn't care anything about the money or the property. I haven't worked in years, but I'm a lawyer. I can make my own way. Alex was vindictive and wanted to destroy me. Miguel has always been a good friend. I realize now that everything I've done has made me look guilty of Alex's murder, and now Miguel is being blamed for it, too."

"So you didn't realize that putting twenty-five thousand dollars into Miguel's bank account could make him look guilty of killing your husband?"

"No, of course not. I never dreamed someone else hated Alex enough to kill him."

Someone else? I caught her meaning. *She* hated him enough to kill him.

"Did you kill him, or get someone else to do it, knowing Miguel would take the fall for it?"

Her face never changed. "I'd never do something like that to Miguel."

"Have you told that to the police?"

Her eyes shifted away from me. "I've talked to the police. They've asked me a ton of questions about Alex's death."

"But did you tell them that you put the money in Miguel's account for him to represent you?" I had to pin her down on this.

"They never asked me."

I stood up, anger propelling my legs like springs. "We have to go and tell them."

"All right. I can do that." She sniffled, getting slowly and gracefully to her feet.

The producers and sponsors of the race sounded the

buzzer. I knew I had to go to the stage for the last phase of the Atlanta challenge. That wouldn't take more than a few minutes.

"I have to take care of something, but I'll be right back. You can wait here or wait in the Biscuit Bowl. Then we can go to the police and get Miguel out of this mess."

"I'll wait. I don't want to hurt Miguel."

She looked sincere. She *sounded* sincere. All I could do was trust her.

Unless I found out better.

Ollie, Uncle Saul, Delia, and I walked over to the stage area. Chef Art met us there with a smug smile and a twinkle in his eyes.

"Are we going to Birmingham?" I asked.

"I think you'll be pleased with the outcome."

"Good morning, again, foodies!" Patrick yelled out.

There was a loud screech in his microphone. We winced and covered our ears.

He frowned at the technicians, who quickly made adjustments.

"Let's try this again. Good morning, foodies! The challenge is over, and we have a new board. Can we see that now?"

The same two women smiled and brought out the electronic board. After it was in place, it lit up briefly—then shut down again.

Knowing Tina was waiting, and that we could help Miguel, made me impatient. But I knew I had to be there to continue the race. *Two more minutes. Two more minutes.*

"Okay," Patrick said. "After these glitches, everything should be a snap."

They turned on the board again, and this time it stayed on.

"We have our winner—Our Daily Bread. Let's hear it for them." Patrick applauded, and everyone in the street in front of the stage applauded, too.

"No one won the first challenge because of the rain, but there were teams who worked hard despite the weather. A tie between our top two teams was settled, and we're ready to move on to the next stop in our race: Birmingham, Alabama."

Everyone applauded enthusiastically.

"Let's take a look at the new standings on the board, and who will be going on to the next leg of the race."

The numbers came up on the board. They were the same numbers as when we first got here. The group was silent as we waited for the decision of the producers as to who would go on.

The board went off again for a moment and then came up with the names.

Patrick read them off. "At the top is Our Daily Bread. Consistent high points. You guys rock."

"I wish he'd get on with it," Delia said.

"Me, too." I took a quick peek back at the Biscuit Bowl. The large biscuit on top was spinning, but I couldn't tell if Tina had waited for me or not.

"In second place, the Biscuit Bowl." Patrick located our little group with his gaze and pointed to us. "This team must try harder because they're *always* in second place."

Everyone applauded.

Ollie was offended by the statement. "What does *that* mean?"

"*Shh,*" Delia said.

"The third team moving forward is Shut Up and Eat. In this weather, their sandwiches have become looser than ever."

"Is he supposed to be a comedian, too?" Uncle Saul demanded.

"If he is, I don't think he's very funny," Bobbie Shields said.

"And in fourth place, we have Grinch's Ganache." Patrick finished out the lineup. "Pizza Papa and Chooey's Sooey will not be joining us for the next leg of the race."

The cameras panned on the two losing teams. They moved into the cool-down tent for their final interviews.

"You all made it!" Chef Art cheered. "You're going to Birmingham."

As soon as I got the word and the cameras were off the group in the street, I ran back toward the Biscuit Bowl.

"Where are you going?" Uncle Saul yelled.

"I'm going to help Miguel. Take the food truck to Birmingham."

"Zoe, there's not enough room in there for the three of us," Ollie reminded me.

"I'll go with her." Delia ran after me.

"What's going on?" Chef Art was losing his happy expression. "What are you doing, Zoe Chase?"

"I'll meet you in Birmingham," I promised. "There's something I have to do."

I looked at the bench. Tina wasn't there. She also hadn't waited in the food truck. She was gone, and her testimony about her relationship with Miguel was gone with her.

It didn't matter. I was going to talk to Helms and Marsh anyway. Maybe Tina was too scared to tell her side of the story. I wasn't.

As soon as Delia and I were in Miguel's Mercedes, I started the car and we hit the street. I explained to her about Tina.

"What are we going to do without her?" she asked.

"I'm not sure yet. Someone has to hear what she told me. I guess that's what I'm going to do."

We managed to find the downtown police station with only a few wrong turns. My clothes were still damp and uncomfortable from the rain. I didn't even want to think what my curly hair was going to look like that afternoon when I took the scarf off. There wasn't time to worry about it. I didn't plan to leave Miguel in Atlanta.

The police officer at the front desk was less than welcoming. "Have a seat over there. I'll call your name *if* someone can help you."

There were several people already waiting, but Delia and I managed to find two hard wooden chairs to sit in. Most of

the others around us waiting were soaking wet, too. Someone smelled strongly of whiskey. One man had a large cut
on his forehead, which he was holding a napkin to while
blood oozed out on his hand.

"I hope they hurry," I said.

Delia told me to relax. "It could be a while. Just take a
deep breath and think of something else. What are you planning to make for your biscuit bowls tomorrow?"

She was right. That took my mind off being in a police
station. We talked about the race and everything that had
happened. I fired off a few texts to Uncle Saul, asking what
he thought about food for tomorrow.

It was about thirty minutes later when the man at the
desk finally called my name.

"They'll see you now." He pointed. "Go through that
door and to your right."

I thanked him. He grunted and shook his head. Delia and
I hurried through the door.

The long hallway was a depressing shade of yellow green
that seemed to go on forever. I was glad when we took the first
right and came to another man behind a desk who showed us
into a room where Marsh and Helms were drinking coffee.

"What are you two doing here?" Helms asked.

"We have new information about Alex Pardini's death
that you should hear," I told her. "Where's Miguel?"

"He's cooling his heels in one of the interrogation rooms.
What kind of *new* information do you have?"

Marsh did air quotes. I hate those.

"I'd like to see Miguel." I made my voice sound like my
mother's when she was in court.

"We'd like cinnamon rolls for breakfast." Helms mocked
me. "We don't always get what we want, Zoe. New information first."

I sat down at the table with them and poured out everything that Tina had told me. Helms and Marsh didn't look
impressed.

"If she has something to contribute, why isn't Tina Gerard with you?" Helms asked.

"She got scared. The police have already interviewed her dozens of times."

Marsh was skeptical. "Why isn't this information in any of the reports?"

"I don't know," I retorted. "But it raises enough questions about Miguel's involvement in Alex Pardini's death to warrant his release. Besides, he has alibis for the times you think he killed people. He was with a member of my food truck team since we left home. We would all gladly vouch for him."

I felt like I was channeling my mother. How else could I have sounded so much like a lawyer? It might be because I was spending so much time with one.

The detectives smirked and glanced at each other.

"Are you representing Mr. Alexander now?" Helms asked. "I didn't know you were a lawyer *and* a food truck operator."

I sat back from the table and put my hands in my lap. "You're right. I'm not a lawyer. But I'd really hate for the two of you to be looking so hard at Miguel that you miss the *real* killer. How embarrassing would that be, especially since the race will be broadcast nationwide."

I could see that made them think a bit. They excused themselves and went to talk in the corner by the drink machine. Delia, who'd stood behind me like a bodyguard, squeezed my shoulder and smiled down at me.

After a few minutes of discussion, interspersed with pointing, grunting, and arms flailing in the air, the two detectives from Charlotte came back to the table.

"Okay. We're going to look for Tina Gerard to corroborate what you've told us, Zoe. We're going to release Miguel, *for now*. If you'd like to wait up front again, he'll join you there."

I thanked them, feeling stupidly satisfied. We hadn't really won the war, just a small battle.

Delia and I walked out of the room and back down the hallway.

"They didn't have jack on him or they wouldn't have let him go so easy," she said.

"I think you're right. At least we cán get him out of here and go to Birmingham."

"Yeah. We have to think of something to blow those Our Daily Bread people out of the race. We're never gonna win following behind them all the time."

I agreed with her. "We'll have to work on it. We still have Birmingham."

"Maybe I should go shopping again. Maybe my clothes aren't right."

I didn't think it was her clothes, but I didn't say so. It was wonderful how engaged she was in helping out. I had the best team in the world.

Miguel finally walked through the door from the long hall. Delia and I jumped up and hugged him. He looked tired. His black shirt and jeans were rumpled. I hadn't noticed that morning that he had dark stubble on his face. And his hair was almost as messy as mine.

I liked the look.

"I was wondering what happened," he said. "They could've kept me a lot longer."

"Not with us coming to the rescue," I added with a smile.

"Let's get out of here." Delia's eyes narrowed as she looked at two uniformed officers near the front door. "We don't want them to change their minds."

"I agree." Miguel put an arm around each of us. "Let's get out of here while we still can."

TWENTY-ONE

On the drive to Birmingham, I filled Miguel in on what Tina had told me.

"It sounds like she's had a rough time," he said.

She's had a rough time? "All she had to do was wait and come with me to get you out," I reminded him. "That doesn't seem like such a big deal."

"I was surprised that they hadn't talked to her yet about hiring me to kill Alex." Miguel looked out the side window as we drove through rain-soaked Georgia toward Alabama.

He'd wanted me to drive, and I didn't pass up the chance. It was good to be behind the wheel of something besides the Biscuit Bowl for a change.

"She said they talked to her about killing Alex. Maybe hiring you was part of that." I passed a slower-moving truck that had been in front of us on the highway. *Whee!* This baby could fly.

"I don't know. Detectives Helms and Marsh were sloppy interrogators. I don't think they really have a clue what's going on. They knew about Tina calling me the night before we left Mobile. They knew about the money. Other than that, there wasn't anything substantial. I had an alibi for Reggie's death, the detective's hit-and-run in Charlotte, and Alex's murder. They were spinning their wheels, hoping I'd contribute something to help them."

"I know you don't want to hear this," Delia said from the backseat, "but I think Tina is setting you up, Miguel. You're too nice to see it."

I agreed with her. Even though Tina seemed sincere about Miguel's predicament, actions always speak louder than words. "If she *really* wanted to help, she would've waited a few minutes. The police wanted to hear from her, not me. She knew that."

He smiled. "Okay. I get it. You two don't have any hard feelings about Tina, do you?"

"I'd like to drag her around by the hair until she tells the truth." Delia wasn't shy about her feelings.

"I don't have anything against her. I'd like her to tell the truth. Now we have to hope the police can find her."

"It shouldn't be too hard. She's going to get her daughter," he said. "If they really want her, all they have to do is look."

The talk turned from Tina to the outcome of the Atlanta challenge. Miguel wanted all the details on what had happened. Delia gave him her declaration of war on Our Daily Bread. She had all kinds of sneaky ideas on things we could do to slow them down.

By the time we stopped for lunch at a small café off the interstate, we were all in much better moods. Delia and I headed for the ladies' room before we went to a table. My cell phone rang and I motioned for her to go on as I took the call.

It was Detective Helms. "Zoe, we've just received official confirmation from the Charlotte medical examiner's office. They're ruling Reggie Johnson's death a homicide."

"I thought they already knew that." I leaned on the large windowsill. "What does that mean to your case?"

"I don't know yet. Something's fishy. If McSwain was killed because he asked the wrong questions about what you heard, we're missing some information."

"You should try asking Tina Gerard, like I said. She may be your missing link."

"We're going to, when we can find her. I think we're all wrong about Miguel, but I can't prove anything. Not yet. Stay sharp. Who knows what else is coming your way."

"I will."

Helms sighed. "This will all make sense once we have the right pieces. But who knows where we'll find them."

- - - - - - -

I went to the ladies' room and freshened up after talking to Detective Helms. I was glad I wasn't responsible for figuring out what had happened to Reggie, Alex, and Detective McSwain. Making food was much better.

Because Miguel's reputation, and maybe more, was also on the line, I tried to imagine what had happened. How did all the deaths, Dante's hijacking, and the cut power cords fit together?

Maybe Reggie was killed to try and stop the race. Alex had been working with someone who wanted to shut down the race. McSwain got in the way of the plan. Alex was killed because he hadn't been able to stop the race.

I couldn't imagine Alex killing anyone, though. He hadn't seemed the type to me. And what would that have to do with Tina?

Maybe the race wasn't even part of it. Everything else that had happened was just to make it *appear* like it had something to do with the race.

I definitely didn't want to be a cop!

My brain was starting to hurt, and I was hungry. I left the ladies' room after a cursory glance at myself in the mirror. There wasn't much I could do to repair the damage until we got to the hotel in Birmingham. I had to hope that Miguel was tired and distracted enough not to notice what a mess I was. We were nowhere near the part of our relationship that I could think it didn't matter.

I noticed, as I found the circular booth that Miguel had chosen, that he'd placed himself in the middle so that Delia would be on one side and I would be on the other. The two of them already had coffee and sweet iced tea. I ordered the sweet tea from the waitress who went by as I sat down.

"I got a call from Detective Helms," I told them. I explained, as best I could, about Reggie. "She asked me again about the conversation I'd overheard in Charlotte between Alex and whoever he was talking to."

Miguel looked thoughtful. "It happens sometimes when the police are more motivated to figure out what happened. The race was a big deal to have in Charlotte. I'm sure they let Helms and Marsh go all this way with it because the city took a black eye from the publicity."

"They don't like it when you mess with one of their own, either," Delia added.

"I understand if Tina killed Alex and wants you to take the blame for it. She had motive for that," I told Miguel. "But why would she kill Reggie or the police detective?"

"I don't know. I don't think she killed any of them." He glanced at Delia. "I know you disagree, but I've known Tina forever. She's not that kind of person."

"After all the years you've worked as a lawyer, you still don't get that *anybody* is capable of anything?" She shook her head at him.

"No. I don't believe that. Not everyone would be willing to kill to survive," he argued.

"I can usually get an idea about people," I added. "They feel good or bad to me. Tina doesn't feel right. I don't think she's bad, but I'm not on her cheer team, either."

The waitress came back with my drink and took our food orders. We talked about the race and what we might expect in Birmingham. Miguel asked if I had a supply list ready. I

absolutely didn't. All I'd really thought about all morning
was him.

I texted Uncle Saul to see if he was in Birmingham yet.
He immediately called me back with bad news.

"We have a flat. We can't change it out here. I'm calling
a tow truck. I'll let you know what happens. See you at the
hotel."

Could anything else go wrong?

I was immediately sorry I'd asked that question. I did
what Uncle Saul always did when he was afraid that he'd
cursed himself. I rubbed salt into my hands and tossed a
few grains over my shoulder.

"What was that for?" Miguel grinned as our greasy
cheeseburgers arrived.

"To keep my own stupid thoughts from killing me. Let's
eat and get to Birmingham."

- - - - - - -

It wasn't really that far from Atlanta to Birmingham, but it
seemed to take forever. I drove like a crazy person after we
left the restaurant. The highway had dried, and a watery sun
was shining down on us.

I'd hoped to catch up with the Biscuit Bowl, but we
weren't fast enough. Ollie and Uncle Saul had a huge head
start. I wasn't sure how Crème Brûlée was going to take
being in a garage as the food truck was being serviced. I
hoped whoever had towed us in was fair. Sometimes there
was price gouging when you had no alternative.

Most of the extra money that I'd won had gone into the
deep fryer. It looked like the rest, plus some, was going into a
tire. The Sweet Magnolia Food Truck Race was starting to
sound like a losing proposition. What had I gotten myself into?

We were in Alabama, only ten minutes from Birmingham, when Uncle Saul called to let me know that they were
at the garage.

"Will the truck need a new tire?" I asked without any pleasantries.

He sighed. "I'm afraid so. But there's still some of the money you won left. That might take care of it. I'll be glad to help you out, Zoe. Don't worry."

"And how will I pay you back if I don't win the race?"

"We'll settle that later. I have some good ideas about biscuit bowls. Let's think about that while they're working, okay?"

I had no choice. I asked him about Crème Brûlée. He assured me that my cat was all right. He and Ollie were sitting out under a big magnolia tree, and Ollie had put Crème Brûlée's bed outside for him.

"We're fine. You all go on to the hotel and we'll meet you there. Try not to worry."

I finally agreed. I knew when we'd started the race that there could be complications with the older Airstream. It had already done well making it to Charlotte and back to Alabama. At least we were getting close to home.

It was hard not to worry. It was something I was really good at even though I tried not to let it show. People thought I didn't think twice about quitting my job at the bank and buying the restaurant and the food truck. But I'd worried about it for weeks before and after. I just didn't let it stop me.

I knew I was going to have to do the same thing right now. I was here to finish the race and hopefully win it. It wasn't time to go home yet. I hadn't come this far to lose everything.

The hotel in Birmingham was nice. Not as big or elegant as the one in Atlanta, but Birmingham wasn't Atlanta. I knew the downtown area wouldn't be as busy tomorrow, either. I just hoped we wouldn't have thunderstorms.

I wasn't from Birmingham, but being close to Mobile made me feel more like these were my folks. If I came up with the right food, they'd give me their hearts. I was starting to look forward to the next day—and finding a way to best Our Daily Bread.

We checked in quickly, and I ran upstairs to my room to take a shower. I wanted to be ready for Crème Brûlée and whatever bad news Uncle Saul had for me by the time they got there. I put some extra conditioner in my hair but kept the awful scarf on the bedside table. My curls needed a night of freedom.

By the time Uncle Saul called and said they'd arrived, I was ready. I went downstairs with my big tote bag for Crème Brûlée and greeted them when they pulled into one of the parking spaces designated for the food truck race. I was glad the food trucks were going to be parked outside for the night. I was tired of underground parking.

Ollie and Uncle Saul looked exhausted. I told them both to go upstairs, take a shower, and get some rest. We could always talk about how much the tire cost later. The Biscuit Bowl was where it was supposed to be. We could get ready for tomorrow's challenge after dinner.

Since I knew Ollie had taken good care of Crème Brûlée during their unscheduled stop, I took a minute to check the back of the food truck. Sometimes I'd found that doing any work on the vehicle caused havoc in the kitchen area. I thought I might as well straighten things up now before we sent Miguel out for supplies.

I was surprised and pleased to find that everything had been tied down and put away so well that nothing had shifted.

I was even more surprised to find Tina Gerard sleeping on the floor.

She woke up, startled, when I walked up to her. "Oh, Zoe. I know what this looks like. I'm sorry I couldn't go with you to see the police."

"It looks like you were trying to get out of Atlanta without anyone knowing," I said.

"That's exactly what it is. I couldn't deal with the police

again while we were there. I hope Miguel is okay. Did you have to leave him behind?"

"No. He's here, and he's fine. But I think he might have some questions for you."

- - - - - - -

Crème Brûlée wasn't happy about going into the tote. Lucky for me he wasn't much of a fighter. He gave me a few dirty looks and howled a little. He tried catching on to the side of the tote with his back legs.

"You don't want to stay out here by yourself," I reasoned with him. "We have to sneak you inside. Food will be there, and a nice soft bed. Quit fighting."

Tina laughed as I tried to get my cat in the bag. "I don't think he agrees with you."

I gave him one final shove and he plopped into the bag. "He doesn't understand. He'll be fine once I get him inside. I think we're both ready to go home."

"I'm sorry I've caused you so much trouble," she apologized as we walked toward the elevator.

"This whole race has been nothing but trouble." I pressed the up button. "Do you know if the producers did some of this stuff on purpose? Like cutting the power cords and hijacking one of the food trucks?"

"I haven't really talked to Alex in so long, I wouldn't know, Zoe."

"What about your daughter?" We walked into the elevator. "Is she somewhere safe?"

Tina nodded. "She's with my mother. I don't think anyone will bother them in Tampa."

"Good thinking."

I had to ask for Miguel's room number. Tina hid behind some plants near the elevators while I did. With so many police hanging around with the race, they could pick her up for questioning at any time.

I thought about what Delia had said about Tina on the

way to Birmingham. I felt almost as sure as she did that Tina was setting Miguel up. I also thought it would be good to keep her close so we could watch her.

Miguel was surprised and pleased to see her when we knocked on his door. He ushered us in quickly and glanced up and down the hall before he closed and locked the door.

"She was hiding in the Biscuit Bowl." I sat in a nice soft chair.

He hugged her and smiled. "I'm glad you got out of Atlanta. This gives us a chance to talk. The police are going to want to question you again about our relationship. They think you paid me to kill Alex."

Tina started crying softly. Miguel gave her some tissues and sat down.

"I thought I should keep an eye on Alex. That's why I decided to follow the food truck race. He didn't know I was there." She sniffled and blew her nose very daintily. "I was afraid he might try one of his stupid stunts. That's why I sent Rosie, our daughter, down to stay with my mother. To protect her. Everything was a scheme with Alex. I didn't want Rosie to be part of whatever he was planning."

Miguel got her a bottle of water. He smiled at me. "Can I get you something, Zoe? We can order from room service."

"No. I'm fine." I yawned. "Just tired and ready to beat Our Daily Bread. I want to go home with fifty thousand dollars."

"Sounds like a plan." He turned back to Tina, and I thought about leaving. They didn't really need me there to discuss what had happened—not more than I needed a nap anyway.

Miguel told her what the police thought had happened to Alex. "They think you wanted him dead to end the divorce problems and to get custody of Rosie. They think you hired me to do it."

Tina laughed in a bitter, non-amused way. "That's rich. Like Alex *ever* wanted Rosie. That was only to hurt me."

"Even that sounds like a possible motive to kill him," I added.

"I can't talk to them again, Miguel." She repeated what she'd said outside to me. The only difference was that she sounded a little more pathetic—and sexy. "I just *can't*. This is too much for me. I can't take anymore."

She cried. He put his arms around her. I tried to remember that they were only friends and that I wasn't jealous. At least not much.

I got to my feet. "You know, I think I'm going to go to my room. I'm surprised Crème Brûlée has stayed in the tote all this time. He needs to eat and I need to sleep. I'll see you two later. Miguel, we're working on the shopping list. If you can't do it, just let me know."

"I'll take care of it. Just send me the list." He looked up at me over Tina's head. "I'm sorry about this, Zoe. I'll see you at dinner."

"Sure." I picked up the tote and held it carefully in my arms. The weight seemed to distribute better that way and made my cat easier to carry.

I opened the door and surprised Detective Marsh, who was standing there with his hand up, ready to knock.

TWENTY-TWO

There was no time to warn Miguel and Tina. Helms was right behind Marsh as they barged into the hotel room.

"Doesn't that make a cozy picture?" Marsh asked his partner.

Helms smiled. "It surely does. I wonder if they were doing a lot of this the day they decided to kill Alex Pardini."

Miguel and Tina sprang apart. He looked guilty. She wiped her eyes and blew her nose.

"What do you want now?" Miguel demanded. "You can't prove we did anything wrong. You would be better served looking for the real killer."

"I think we're better served talking to your *girlfriend*," Marsh said. "I can't believe you'd lead poor Zoe on this way. One lady friend wasn't enough for you?"

Miguel glanced at me. I shrugged. As far as I was concerned, Marsh didn't know his head from a hole in the ground. I wasn't taking his word for anything.

"Maybe you should both come to the Birmingham police station with us," Helms suggested.

"Yeah," Marsh agreed. "Let's have a little talk, shall we?"

Miguel took a deep, frustrated breath. "Whatever you say, detectives. Come on, Tina. Let's get this over with."

Marsh led the way to the elevator. I was still standing at the doorway, waiting for Helms to leave the hotel room.

"Could I talk to you for a minute, Zoe?" She glanced at the elevator but didn't leave the room.

I closed the hotel door. Crème Brûlée had begun shifting around uncomfortably in the tote bag. "Sure. I have to get my cat to my room. We can talk there."

She raised her eyebrows. "Your *cat*? You brought your cat with you on the race?"

"Have you ever tried to get a cat sitter on short notice? My mother wouldn't take him. My father was out of town. Ollie, Delia, and my uncle are with me. That pretty much dries up my pool of cat sitters."

Helms opened the door and said something to Marsh. I wasn't close enough to hear what it was. This was probably part of a divide and conquer kind of thing. She'd find that I was too loyal to Miguel to give anything away.

By the time we reached my room, finally, Crème Brûlée was starting to meow loudly and claw at the bag. I gave my key card to Helms and she opened the door. I held the tote bag down, and Crème Brûlée jumped out with a parting hiss at me.

"Wow. He's a big fella," Helms said.

"He's a little sensitive about it." I put the empty tote on the bed and massaged my arm. I loved my cat, but he was hard to carry around. "Every time I take him to the vet, he suggests Crème Brûlée should lose weight. He's not crazy about that idea."

Helms sat on the edge of the bed as I fed my cat. "I'm surprised they've let him in all of these hotels."

I glanced up at her. "You're not the cat police, right?"

"No. Not at all. But I *am* looking for a killer, Zoe."

"I know. What can I do to help?"

"I've thought about what you said to McSwain. Now that we know your friend Reggie's death wasn't an accident, I've been trying to figure out what McSwain said to someone that got him killed."

"And have you come up with anything?"

She nodded. "The only thing that makes sense to me is that McSwain knew the other person Alex was plotting with. I don't know if that means he was a friend of McSwain's or what. I think that's why the second person had to kill Reggie."

"And Alex? Surely he wasn't plotting his own death?"

"I don't think so. I know that Tina has a lover—and I don't believe it's Miguel like Marsh does. I think Tina's lover may have killed Alex for her. And he may have killed McSwain because they knew each other."

Her cell phone buzzed, and she looked at it. "That's Marsh, complaining because he can't find me. He thinks I have to be close by all the time. I hope we get something from Tina that leads us in the right direction."

She got to her feet, and I saw her to the door.

Helms put her hand on my arm. "I don't trust Tina. Something's not right with that girl. Look out for her."

"Okay. Thanks."

I closed the door and locked it when she was gone. I talked on the phone with Uncle Saul for a few minutes about our food list for tomorrow and what we were going to do if Miguel couldn't shop.

Uncle Saul told me not to worry about it. "Chef Art and I have that under control. He had his car brought up here from Mobile for tonight. If you trust me, I'll shop and get something amazing for tomorrow."

I laughed. "Of course I trust you! Thanks for thinking of it. Please thank Chef Art for me, too."

Crème Brûlée was done eating. He was trying his best

to get on the bed. I picked him up and lay down with him, snuggling into his soft fur.

"Between the race and the murders, it's enough to drive a person crazy."

He softly meowed and bumped his head against mine. We fell asleep that way.

- - - - - - -

My cell phone woke me up about an hour later. It was my mother again, checking on me. She wanted to know all about Alex's death and my involvement.

"When is all this supposed to be over, Zoe?"

"I'm in Birmingham today. I'll be in Mobile tomorrow. One way or another, it will be over Friday."

"Well that's good news at least." She started to say something and changed her mind. Instead, she questioned, "What do you mean one way or another?"

"I mean, either I'll win or I'll lose."

"What about that poor dead man? Bless his soul. He was good-looking, wasn't he?"

"And he wanted to ruin his ex-wife's life."

"You know, I hear those kinds of things all the time. Sometimes it's not as bad as it sounds."

I looked at the time. "I have to go, Mom. I'm going to be late for dinner. I'll talk to you tomorrow."

"Okay. Be careful out there. You never know what those other food truck people are thinking."

I got up and dressed quickly. I'd brought a nice pair of white pants and a matching halter top. It looked good with my summer tan, and even my curls cooperated. I slipped my feet into matching white sandals and was ready to go.

I had to sort out Crème Brûlée before I left. It wasn't easy. He was tired of the whole experience and didn't want to cooperate. I finally coaxed him into drinking some water, and then he rolled over and ignored me.

"You're the one who'll be sorry later when you're lonely," I promised him.

Ollie, Uncle Saul, and Delia had all called me, wondering where I was. They were already downstairs. I slipped into the large room booked for dinner that night and took my place at the table as though I'd been there the whole time.

"Where have you been?" Uncle Saul asked. "I was afraid they were going to disqualify you. I hope the cameras didn't catch you coming in."

"I was only a few minutes late. Mom called. You know I had to talk to her. We're close enough that she could've driven up here."

Patrick Ferris started messing around with the microphone, which meant we were about to get started. Ollie asked me where Miguel was. I started to explain, but Chef Art shushed me.

"Is this thing on?" Patrick asked with a laugh.

There were a few snickers from the greatly reduced group sitting at the big tables.

"Good evening, foodies. It's nice to see some of you still in the race—at least until *tomorrow*. Birmingham is gonna sort out the winners from the losers before we move on to Mobile."

"Yeah. Yeah," Bobbie Shields said. "Let's get on with it. Where's dinner?"

Patrick kept his million-dollar smile in place. "I think I see dinner coming right now. I'm hungry, too. But first, I'm sure you're all dying to know what's in that pretty package in the middle of your table."

I hadn't even noticed the package until he'd said something. I had a lot on my mind. I saw the elaborately wrapped package and reached for it—too late. Chef Art grabbed it first.

"Now what do you think is in here?" He pulled at the beautiful lavender-colored ribbon.

"Like he doesn't know," Ollie muttered.

When the package was unwrapped, he read the card inside, as everyone around us was reading their cards. Waiters began serving the meal. Chef Art finally passed the card to me.

"Now that you've had a chance to see your personal information," Patrick said, "I'm going to explain what it means."

My card said: *Do it in the red.* I had no idea what that meant.

"We're gonna get cutthroat here, campers! That personal message you received is your tag for tomorrow's challenge."

"What kind of tag?" Ollie snatched the card from me.

"What does it say?" Uncle Saul asked.

"What do you mean by *tag*?" Reverend Jablonski asked from his usual table at the front.

"Tag. You'll understand better when we talk about the next part of tomorrow's challenge. Two food trucks are going home tomorrow before we head to Mobile. They won't pass go, and they won't collect fifty thousand dollars. Remember that when you figure out what your tag is all about."

That brought a round of applause from everyone at the Biscuit Bowl table, Shut Up and Eat, and Grinch's Ganache. I didn't applaud, and neither did the team at Our Daily Bread's table.

"We don't understand, Patrick," Reverend Jablonski said. "Could you be clearer?"

Patrick laughed a trifle like a bad guy in a B movie. Kind of *bwahaha.* "That's up to you, Our Daily Bread team. No one will force you to use your tag. However, a word of warning: I'm sure the *other* foodies in this room will use theirs. Especially once they hear the challenges for tomorrow."

I stared at the empty chair next to me where Miguel should've been sitting. I wasn't a bit interested in the dried-up chicken, green beans, and rice on my plate.

It was hard to get into the spirit of the race knowing that the police were questioning Miguel again. I wished there

were something I could do to help. Sitting here and playing
games wouldn't make any difference. It made me want to
give up and go home.

That's not a bit like me, but I hadn't been sleeping well
in the hotel rooms, and the stress of being part of this race,
let alone a murder investigation, was beginning to take its
toll on me.

"What about us, Zoe?" Ollie asked. "What are *we*
gonna do?"

"I don't know. I'm thinking about giving up and spending
my time helping Miguel stay out of jail instead of worrying
about whether or not we're going to get tagged in this race."

I explained to him that the police had Miguel and Tina,
while new girls in bikinis brought out the electronic board
again. The cameramen were setting up the lighting. A
makeup artist was checking Patrick's face. It all seemed so
pointless.

"But that's good news that Helms believes him, right?"
Ollie asked.

"I hope so, but she's not the only one involved."

"Zoe, there's nothing you can do for Miguel," Chef Art
said. "If you quit now, think how that will look for *me*. I
have a lot at stake. If you do your best and don't win, that's
different. No one likes a quitter."

"I'm sorry. I can't think how else to help him."

Delia hugged me. "I completely understand. You have to
do what you think is right."

"Don't listen to her," Ollie said. "We've been through a
lot to get to this point. If you give up, that means we did it
for nothing."

"He's right." Uncle Saul surprised me by agreeing.
"Miguel wouldn't want you to quit, either. He's a smart boy.
He knows how to handle this type of situation."

"Fine." Chef Art threw down his napkin. "I'll send my
lawyer over to help the two of them, Zoe, if you stay in the
race. Happy? Will you stay?"

It was a generous offer. Chef Art's lawyer could do a lot more for Miguel than I could hanging around the police station. Even though I knew Chef Art was offering to help for his own purposes, I didn't care.

"Okay. We'll go on. Thank you."

"Now what about tagging?" Ollie asked me again.

TWENTY-THREE

‑‑‑

Before I could admit that I had no idea what the tag was all about, Patrick got everything set up and was ready with tomorrow's challenge.

"These two challenges are gonna be tough." He opened the big, secret envelope and scanned its contents.

I saw the enigmatic smile on Chef Art's face and knew he had a hand in creating the challenges.

"The stakes are going up. Tomorrow, each team will have to sell two hundred dollars in product. Remember this *has* to be your main menu item. You'll have as long as you need. There is no time limit, but again, the first person to reach two hundred dollars wins."

That sounded easy enough. I should've known there was more to come.

"Now the fun part of this challenge." Patrick demonstrated how "fun" it was by laughing almost hysterically. "Everyone on the teams has to dress in *bikinis*, just like our girls up here. Ladies, take a bow."

The two young women bowed gracefully.

"One of our sponsors, By the Beach—featuring beach toys, towels, swimsuits, and other fun items—now found at more than one hundred locations across the Southeast, has donated bikinis for our teams in every shape, size, color, and style. In other words, we've got you covered! No excuses."

Daryl Barbee stood up at his table and tossed down his big hat. "I am *not* wearing a bikini tomorrow. This is a *stupid* challenge."

Everyone watched him storm out of the room. The cameras followed him, loving the controversy. His wife, Sarah, blushed and shrugged but didn't comment on her husband's temper tantrum. One of the assistants followed Daryl out of the dining room, probably for a personal interview.

Chef Art was so busy chuckling to himself that I wanted to hit him. No doubt he thought Delia wearing a bikini as she sold biscuit bowls in downtown Birmingham was a winning idea. Or he just wanted to see her in a bikini. Who knows?

"Good one!" Ollie held up his thumb.

"What's good about it?" Uncle Saul asked. "Have you ever *seen* a man wearing a bikini? What do you think we're going to look like tomorrow?"

"Who cares?" Ollie asked. "Nobody in any of the other food trucks is hot like Delia."

"There's Bobbie's daughter," I reminded him. "She couldn't skate, but I bet she'll look good in a bikini."

"Oh yeah. That's right." He frowned a moment and then lightened up. "Maybe that's where we'll use our tag."

"That's the spirit," Chef Art commended him. "Wait. Patrick has more to say."

Now that the interruption was over, Patrick continued. "Did I mention we're gonna have a little bikini beauty pageant? Everyone will get a turn on the stage. The winner of our pageant will get a one-week, all-expenses-paid cruise to the Caribbean for their team. This is from another sponsor,

All Star Cruise Lines, hailing from the port of Mobile, Alabama."

That was popular enough, even though it meant that all team members would have to participate. Ollie and Delia didn't care. Uncle Saul was a little upset, but I knew he'd come around. I'd be okay if they had the right bikini for me.

They did a spin on the board and lit everything up to show us again what our stats were. Nothing had changed. It was a little anticlimactic. The dinner began to break up, vendors heading back to their rooms.

"I'm going to get something *real* to eat! This was tasteless fare." Chef Art got to his feet. "I'm buying. Who's with me? I'm sure Birmingham has something better to offer."

"I'm in," Uncle Saul said. "I had some basil and tomato alligator stew here in Birmingham once. Best I ever had."

I couldn't believe it. "That would be like me eating a cat. What about Alabaster? How is she going to feel about you eating one of her kind?"

He shrugged. "What she doesn't know won't hurt her."

The doors to the room burst open as everyone was headed in that general direction. Dante Eldridge, from the ill-fated Stick It Here food truck, ran in.

"Wait! Stop! I found my food truck. I want another shot." He was shouting and waving his big, muscled arms.

Patrick started to speak but was pulled aside by one of the producers. After a short conversation, he picked up his microphone. "It looks as though Stick It Here will be joining us tomorrow on the street."

"How does that work?" Bobbie Shields asked. "Why does he get to come back?"

One of the men behind the scenes, who always seemed to have the last word, came forward and took the microphone from Patrick. "Dante wasn't kicked out of the race because he failed a challenge. He was a victim who has managed to get his food truck back. I think that requires us to allow him back into the race. Thank you."

Bobbie, about five-foot-five, maybe early fifties, walked up close to Dante, who was a big man, tall and muscular, probably in his thirties. "Well, you won't look too *good* in a bikini now, will you? I'm not worried. Good night!"

"*Bikini?*" Dante glanced around the room for an explanation.

"Come up here," Patrick said. "I'll get you up to speed."

The rest of us left and were guided to another big room by one of the bikini-clad girls. It seemed fitting when she opened the door and the room was filled with bikinis. There had to be every color known to man in that room. There were micro-bikinis, thongs, halter tops, string tops. I'd never seen so many bathing suits in one place.

Of course, the cameramen were there watching and recording the whole thing. Some people made use of the small closet to try their bikinis on. Others just grabbed what they knew was their size and left.

I had an idea as soon as I saw the bikinis. I called my team together, and the closest cameraman zoomed in on us.

"Everyone grab a red bikini," I said. "I don't care what kind it is. Our tag is *Do it in the red.* All of us should wear red."

Ollie did that frown that went from the tattoo on his head to his chin. "How do we know that's what we're supposed to do, Zoe? Maybe we're supposed to shoot someone in the face with ketchup or spray-paint their food red as they're trying to sell it."

"I'm sure it's the bikini colors. See? Red. Green. Yellow. Blue. It's the bikinis. We're going to get something for figuring it out." Uncle Saul picked up a red bikini with a halter top and twirled it around on his finger. "I've admired these on many shapely women over the years. I've never thought about wearing one myself."

"Whatever." Ollie shook his head. "Let's find the most revealing bikini we can for Delia. I'll start over here."

"You look for your own, big guy," she told him. "I know what works for me. I don't need your help."

After that was over, we were boring to the cameraman, who moved to where Bobbie's daughter was trying on blue string bikinis. Bobbie either didn't get the tag idea or was going to ignore it. She was looking at yellow bikinis.

With our plan in motion, I set about finding a red bikini for me.

The thing about bikinis is that they only look good on you if you have a perfect body. By perfect, I mean tall, thin, and shapely. I was only privileged to be in that last category. I got the shapely part from my mother, but tall and thin wasn't me. I didn't look bad in a nice one-piece. Bikinis scared me.

I definitely didn't want a string bikini. Not that any of the other types hid anything. Some of them were barely patches held together by almost invisible string. I quietly picked out a red halter-neck top with a modest bottom.

Ollie and Uncle Saul were having a hard time—not surprising. We found bikinis that would fit both of them. No doubt they wouldn't be particularly flattering, but that's not what the producers had in mind.

It was too bad Chef Art didn't have to wear a red bikini, too. He probably would've dropped that *brilliant* idea if that was the case.

"I'm not shaving my legs—or any other part of my body except my head—for this race," Ollie told me.

"I don't think anyone expects you to," I assured him.

"I personally plan to strangle Chef Art when this is over," Uncle Saul said. "Of all the stupid—"

The ministers from Our Daily Bread were fussing and feuding like a bunch of schoolboys. It seemed that the race had finally found their soft underbelly.

"Don't criticize yet," I said. "Chef Art might have set this up to get Delia delivering biscuit bowls in a bikini, but it might get our competitors so upset that they lose their edge, too."

Uncle Saul shrugged. "So be it. I'll be glad to get back home."

I hugged him. "Have I said how much I appreciate you being with me through all of this?"

"You don't have to say it, Zoe. I love you, and we're family. That's what family is for."

"I don't want to be part of a family that requires its members to wear a red bikini," Ollie interrupted.

I looked up at him. He was at least a foot taller than me. Sometimes it was easy to forget that this man was a tough ex-marine who was still in fighting shape. He was such a sweet person.

"You don't have to wear if it bothers you too much," I said. "You can sit this one out. No one will think less of you for it. I appreciate everything you've done."

"Like I'd do that." He hugged me, almost lifting me off the floor. "A man can gripe, can't he?"

"Yes, he can."

Delia had her bikini. We were ready to go. There was still so much going on in the bikini room that we were able to walk out unmolested by any of the camera crew.

"What?" Uncle Saul grinned. "No deep questions about what red bikinis mean to us or what our plans are for tomorrow?"

I laughed. "Not when you've got a bunch of angry ministers trying on bikinis."

"Good. I'm hungry, and I need a drink." Ollie sniffed. "I smell food coming from that way."

Chef Art still had other plans. He was waiting close by when we emerged. "Hey. We're still going out to eat some decent food, right? My limo is waiting."

Uncle Saul and Ollie glanced at each other and then high-fived.

"All right," Ollie said. "Let's go."

"I'm right behind you." Uncle Saul slapped him on the back.

"Let me run up and stash these bikinis." I was nervous about losing one of them before tomorrow. I gathered Ollie's and Uncle Saul's with mine.

"I'll just go up with you and drop mine off, if that's okay." Delia smiled with a hint of blush in her cheeks and whispered, "I don't like my clothes to touch other people's clothes."

I smiled back at her, after I pushed the elevator button, thinking she was joking. "You're serious?"

"Yes. It's a habit of mine, I guess." She shrugged. "It's a thing I learned to do when I was a kid. It's hard keeping clothes to yourself when you have five sisters."

We got in the elevator and I hugged her. I could see she was uncomfortable even discussing it. "That's okay. We all have weird things about us."

Her eyes narrowed. "Like what?"

"Oh. You mean like *my* weird thing?"

"Yeah. What do you do weird—besides sleeping with your evil cat?"

"Is that weird?" I'd never thought of sleeping with Crème Brûlée as weird. "No. I was thinking about when I quit my job to run a food truck."

"I think sleeping with the cat will do."

The elevator door chimed and opened. We went to our room and dropped off the suits. I gave Crème Brûlée a little hug and a kiss on his nose.

We went back down in the elevator. The men were waiting in the bar. I wished Miguel was there, too. How long could the police talk to him about what happened to Alex?

When we got into Chef Art's limo, I took the opportunity to ask him if he'd heard anything about Miguel.

"Zoe, I only called my lawyer while I was waiting for you and Delia. We talked about it over dinner, remember?"

"This is stupid. I don't understand why they keep interviewing him."

"Maybe because they think he killed someone?" Ollie said. "I'm not saying he did. But the police can get pretty nasty when they think you're lying to them."

We went out for drinks at a private club where everyone

knew Chef Art. We all had a little too much to drink knowing someone else was driving us around town. Uncle Saul and I talked about what he had planned for the biscuit bowls the next day. I was surprised and pleased by his choices.

Chef Art was welcomed with a big hug from his friend who owned the exclusive restaurant where we went for dinner afterward. He ordered champagne, and we all had elaborate meals with wine.

By the time we'd stopped for drinks again after dinner and then gone back to the hotel, I was a little on the wobbly side. The elevator seemed to be going in the wrong direction. Delia wasn't as affected by it. She helped me get on and off the elevator with a smile.

"You aren't used to drinking so much." She took my key card after the third time I couldn't open the door.

"Not so much." I grinned at her. "Thanks."

"Can you make it to bed by yourself? I'm going back out for a while with Ollie."

"I'll be fine. Good night, Delia. I hope our clothes *never* touch."

She laughed at me and closed the door on her way out.

I was getting undressed, but my shoes were proving difficult. Someone knocked at the door. Hoping it was Miguel, I ran for it, almost tripping over my own feet.

It wasn't Miguel. It was Macey Helms. I looked past her for Marsh, but there was no sign of him.

Great. Like I can talk straight about who killed Alex right now.

She had a strange expression on her face. At least I *thought* she did. I hoped it wasn't me, and I was imagining that she looked odd.

Before I could say anything, she held up her hand. It was covered in blood.

"Zoe, I need your help."

TWENTY-FOUR

I guided her into the hotel room and called 911.

"What happened?" I helped her take off her dark pink jacket. It was covered in blood, too.

"Someone shot me as I walked up to the hotel." Her face was very pale, eyes sunken, with dark circles around them.

"Where's Marsh?" I looked at my cell phone, called his number and the emergency services number. I hoped the paramedics wouldn't be far away. "Listen to me a minute." She put her hand on the cell phone to stop me from calling for help. "I learned something about the killer. I haven't had time to tell anyone else. You have to remember—"

Her voice started fading, and her eyes closed. Her hand dropped from the cell phone, leaving a smear of blood behind it.

"You can't die," I told her. *Weren't people supposed to stay awake?* "Stay with me, Macey. Don't lose consciousness."

Her eyes fluttered open for a moment, and her lips moved, but I couldn't hear what she was saying.

I tried to flag down a passing porter. Maybe the hotel could get someone here faster. Hotel staff passed me by like I was invisible.

"Zoe?" Miguel said on his way to the elevator. "Oh my God, what happened?"

Tina came in and sat on the bed while Miguel knelt by my side on the floor.

"She said someone shot her. I don't think she knew who it was. How long does it take for an ambulance to get here?"

I heard the elevator chime. Uniformed paramedics rushed into the room with a stretcher and other equipment. "Help her, please."

Miguel put his arm around me and we moved away from Helms. The paramedics were all over her, calling out her vitals and attaching needles and other apparatus to her. She was so helpless.

"She said she was shot," I repeated, wanting to be *some* help.

One of them briefly turned to face me. "We can see that, ma'am. Best for you all to wait outside until we can get her out of here."

"Come on," Miguel urged me, taking Tina's hand and leading her out, too.

Marsh was next off the elevator. I told him what had happened. He started to storm into the hotel room, but the paramedics pushed him out of the way and walked quickly past him.

"What happened?" Marsh asked me. "Who shot her?"

"I don't know, and I don't know why she came up here. She was trying to tell me something. I couldn't make out what she was saying."

Tears in his eyes were hastily pushed away as he pulled himself together. "What is it with you people? This race needs to end *now*."

He rushed for the next elevator to follow his partner to the hospital.

Hotel security came next, ushering me out of my room and into another room. The red bloodstain on the beige carpet stood out as I quickly gathered my things together and hid Crème Brûlée under a blanket. He was squirmy and hard to carry.

"Why did she come to see me?" I kept asking Miguel as he helped me relocate. "She said she was shot outside the hotel. Why didn't she stay outside and call for help? Or ask for help at the check-in counter. That would have made more sense."

"People do strange things during emergency situations," he explained. "It's as though whatever is on your mind supersedes what's happening to your body."

Tina was crying and following us around like a puppy.

"She's exhausted. Let me get her somewhere she can sleep," he said. "I'll be right back."

After he was gone, I looked around the new room. It was exactly like the old room, except there was no blood on the floor.

It was crazy. The whole thing seemed *crazy* to me.

Maybe Marsh was right. Maybe the race *should* be stopped. How many more bad things could happen before we got home?

I sat in a chair and held Crème Brûlée close to me until Miguel got back. He brought Uncle Saul with him. "Do you think this had something to do with the race?" Uncle Saul sat on the edge of my bed.

"I don't know." That sparkly, fun feeling I'd had after drinking too much was gone, leaving me with a raging headache. "Helms said it had something to do with the killer. I couldn't understand anything else she said."

"That poor woman." Miguel shook his head.

"We should see if Chef Art still has his limo out." I jumped up. "We could go to the hospital and find out how Helms is."

"I'm sure someone will let us know," Uncle Saul said.

"I can't sit here not knowing. I don't care if I don't sleep at all tonight—I have to know if she's okay."

"Someone will call and let us know," Miguel said. "You should get some sleep."

"I don't know if I can." I completely lost it, sobbing into Miguel's shirt. "I want to go home. I don't want anyone else to get hurt or die. This is it."

While I cried and tried to stop myself from hiccupping, Miguel and Uncle Saul came up with a plan. I was so glad they did because I wasn't drunk, but my brain wasn't functioning right, either. We went downstairs to get Miguel's car. Several of Birmingham's uniformed police officers passed us. I kept my head down, not up to answering a barrage of questions about what had happened to Helms. We managed to get out of the hotel. Miguel used his cell phone GPS to find the hospital.

When we got to the hospital, Miguel asked at the admitting desk about Helms. The nurse pointed to a place we could wait. Marsh was already there. He only looked slightly better than his partner had after she'd been shot.

He was staring at a pack of Marlboro cigarettes that hadn't been opened. "I gave these up six weeks ago. I promised Macey I'd quit. Neither of us is married anymore. No close family. She's all I have that makes my life normal."

"They won't help," Miguel said as he sat down next to me. "I smoked for a long time after my wife died. It never made me feel better. Nothing does."

It was another little piece of the puzzle that was Miguel Alexander. I was almost too tormented to even notice. I excused myself and went to the ladies' room to wash my face.

Blotchy complexion and swollen, red-rimmed eyes had taken their toll. Even my curly hair was flat. I blew my nose on some rough toilet paper and splashed cold water in my face. "Don't make me slap you, Zoe Elizabeth Chase. You know I'll do it. Pull yourself together. This behavior isn't going to help."

They were my mother's words on occasions like this one. I imagined her standing in this hospital bathroom saying similar things to herself. Somehow, that grounded me again and made me take a deep breath.

My mother was a tough, pragmatic taskmaster at times, but she was also a rock. I'd never seen her panic or lose it, as I had back there. My dad was a different story. He cried at movies and after listening to his favorite jazz songs.

Maybe it was the curly hair.

When I went back out to the waiting area, I was calmer and beginning to cope with the situation. My head still hurt, so I bought a Coke from a vending machine and swallowed two Tylenol. Good thing, too, because the Birmingham police had caught up with us.

They were actually very polite and apologized for bothering us. They asked a few questions but didn't stay long.

Marsh kind of vouched for us. I was surprised that he suddenly seemed to trust us. Maybe it was because Helms had come to me after being shot.

The only sticking point I seemed to have with anyone was that I hadn't been able to understand what Helms had been trying to tell me before she'd passed out. I said the same words over and over, attempting to explain the situation. The Birmingham police looked skeptical.

"She mentioned that there was a new development in Alex Pardini's death, right?" Marsh asked me.

"I think that's what she was trying to say." I sure couldn't swear to it. "We're going to have to ask her when she wakes up."

The surgeon finally came out to talk to us at around three A.M. He said Helms was stable and holding her own. She'd be unconscious for at least the rest of the night and on strong pain meds the next day.

In other words, we might not have any answers about

what had happened to her, or what her new information was that might have caused her to get shot, until we were already in Mobile for the last leg of the race.

"Don't worry," Marsh told us when the surgeon had gone. "I'm staying here with her. I won't let anything else happen to her."

It seemed as though there was nothing else to do. Uncle Saul said we should go back and get some sleep. I agreed, though it was hard leaving Helms.

We were back at the hotel by three thirty A.M. Everything was so quiet. Even the manager at the night desk whispered good morning to us as we walked by.

Uncle Saul decided to go up and sleep for two hours.

Miguel and I went upstairs. He walked me to my door and we went inside. The room was mostly dark. Crème Brûlée was snoring on the chair.

"I'll see you in a couple of hours," Miguel said.

He started to walk away and I caught his hand. "Will you stay instead? I don't think I can sleep, and I don't want to be alone."

He nodded and shut the door behind him. "I can do that."

We ended up sitting up against the pillows on the bed in the dark room. I had thought we could talk; you know, exchange secrets we wouldn't have said at any other time. I leaned against his chest and heard his heart beating. I thought about him being alone and smoking after his wife and baby had died.

I closed my eyes to gather my scattered thoughts before I spoke, and the next thing I knew, the alarm on my phone was going off. It was six A.M. *Time to go on with the race.*

"I think I fell asleep for a while," Miguel whispered, a smile in his voice. "How about you?"

"I think I completely passed out, and I apologize if I was snoring louder than my cat."

"There were a few gasps and a little muttering, but no snoring," he assured me.

"That's good. I'd hate to snore the first night we spend together, you know?"

He kissed me, and we sat together silently for a few minutes.

"We have to go," he said. "After this is all over, we'll talk about us. Tonight, we'll be home again. I'll see you later, Zoe."

I didn't really see him leave, but I saw the door open and close. I dragged myself out of bed and into the shower. After the terrible night I had, I'd expected to feel much worse.

Miguel assuring me that I didn't snore helped. Seeing his face first thing was great, too. That smile was enough to chase all my blues away.

I felt lighthearted and ready to face the day. It was time to take out the bikini.

- - - - - - -

There was a large crowd waiting for us in downtown Birmingham. The TV show promotion, and the building tension to see who would win, had created fans. I saw my name on two large posters that were held in the air.

"Look! There's Zoe and Delia!" A man yelled and waved.

"Weird." Ollie shook his head. "Why was he yelling for the two of you and not *me*?"

Uncle Saul slapped his back and laughed.

Ropes were up to keep the crowds away from the food trucks in the pre-dawn darkness. Camera crews were on hand from several of the major TV networks. It seemed odd after being in Atlanta, a much larger city, that people would make such a fuss over us in Birmingham.

All the food truck vendors were wearing robes or large shirts that covered up their bikinis when we met in front of the stage where Patrick Ferris was waiting.

"Why isn't *he* wearing a bikini?" Ollie asked in a sour

voice. His super-long Crimson Tide T-shirt covered his bathing suit.

"Because he isn't part of the race." Uncle Saul's bikini was covered by an ankle-length trench coat. "He gets to wear what he wants. Anyone taking odds on him making it through the rest of the race?"

"I've got some money to put on that!" Bobbie Shields was wearing a loose-fitting flowered dress over her bikini.

Her daughter, like Delia, wore her bikini out in the open. Not surprising since she looked awesome in it. It was one of those suits with the patches in strategic places that seemed to be held together with magic.

Patrick was going through his usual spiel, reminding us all of the rules and the challenge for that day. I could tell everyone was extra nervous. This was the end of the line for two more food trucks. Only one stop to go before a winner was announced.

Dante was there, up by the front of the stage. He was wearing his black bikini with no covering. It looked good on him. He pulled it off with fantastic abs and a taut tush.

I clung to my pink robe and didn't plan to remove it until I had to.

Miguel was there in jeans and a Biscuit Bowl T-shirt. Ollie had a few words to say about the outriders not having to meet the challenge. He was mostly ignored as the time neared for us to get started on making food for the day.

There was no sign of the Our Daily Bread team. Had they given up rather than wear bikinis? It seemed like too much to ask for. I waited for them to make an appearance.

When everything pertinent had been said, the remaining food truck teams started back to get ready for the day. Chef Art had managed to get a TV crew from Mobile to come in and tape us making food.

"You all remember to wear your hats," he reminded us before making room for the cameramen.

Ollie and Uncle Saul looked at each other and sighed

before they removed their outer garments to reveal the skimpy bathing suits beneath them.

When Ollie removed his T-shirt, I heard an audible gasp from Delia.

She stared at him. "Which one of us is supposed to look better in a bikini?"

TWENTY-FIVE

My jaw dropped, too. I had never seen Ollie wearing so little. He made Dante look like he'd only started working out a few days earlier. Ollie had muscles on his muscles. He was in awesome shape.

"Man!" Uncle Saul shook his head. "You look *good*. Why were you covering up?"

"I'm wearing a *woman's* bikini." Ollie punctuated each word with a dollop of sarcasm. "Why do you think?"

"I love the dragon tattoo." Delia ran her hand up his back from the spot where the dragon's tail ended under the red bottom to the head that was arched back on his broad, muscular shoulders.

"Thanks!" He looked surprised and pleased that we were so complimentary.

I took the opportunity, while everyone was gawking at Ollie's physique, to remove my robe and quickly stash it in a bottom storage bin in the kitchen.

"*Wow!*" Miguel approved quietly, but with a lustful smile that I enjoyed.

I felt myself blush all over—and I mean *all over.* "Okay. Let's get going or we don't have a chance of having the food ready by eight. Uncle Saul, what are we making today?"

He'd chosen a simple, but sure to please, menu. His gumbo was to die for, even though we'd have to take a few shortcuts to have it ready in time. For our sweet dish, he'd chosen berries and whipped cream.

We jumped right in. Delia and I chopped precooked vegetables, sausage, and chicken while Uncle Saul started the biscuit bowls. The berries had to be thoroughly washed—that was Ollie's job.

It was hard to ignore the cameramen. It was already like being in a fish bowl. Sometimes I felt like the camera was going right in my *ear.* Could they come any closer?

I knew they were doing us a favor, traveling up from Mobile to document the race. It was still hard to work that way.

It was just as hard to keep my mind focused on what we were doing. I kept thinking about Helms, wondering how she was doing and why she'd risked her life to come up to my hotel room after she was shot.

It made me feel guilty that I couldn't understand what she'd been trying to tell me. Obviously it was something important or she wouldn't have done it.

All we could do was wait until she until she could tell everyone.

I hated waiting.

The bikini was comfortable as the kitchen heated up. I'd left the back door, and the order window, open. That brought in a fresh breeze. I didn't want to turn on the air-conditioning until the afternoon.

"Okay." Uncle Saul rubbed his hands together as he finished making the roux. "Let's get the rest of it in there."

The big pot had to rest over three of the burners on the

small hot plate. All of the vegetables and meats went into the pot, and the whole thing started to smell divine right away.

It was a good thing we were using fresh berries for the sweet biscuit bowl and not cooking those, too!

"Where does this recipe come from?" one of the cameramen asked when we got quiet.

"My grandma made it and passed it to my mother." Uncle Saul grinned as he stirred the mixture. "Now I make it. You know, a man can cook, too."

The cameraman laughed. "Some men, maybe. I can barely make coffee and toast."

"It's easy," Uncle Saul assured him. "Here. Let me hold the camera. You stir the pot until the sauce thickens."

They switched places, and the cameraman awkwardly used the big spoon to stir the mixture. "Like this?"

"Just like that," Uncle Saul told him. "I hope the camera is on."

"It's on." The other man laughed. "They might want to edit this part out."

"The berries are ready," Ollie said. "Should I put sugar on them?"

"No!" Uncle Saul didn't like that idea.

I wasn't so sure. "You know how berries are—some sweet, some not so sweet. I think a little sugar would be good on them."

"Zoe! You're putting whipped cream on them," Uncle Saul argued. "How sweet do they need to be?"

"For most people, pretty darn sweet."

He shrugged. I put a little sugar on the berries and then had Ollie gently toss them in the sweet mixture.

"People eat their food too sweet nowadays," Uncle Saul said. "We shouldn't help them."

I laughed at the idea that we were in *any* way promoting healthy eating. "We serve deep-fried biscuit bowls. I don't think a little extra sugar is going to matter. Besides, you know when people eat out, they want things they don't eat at home. Maybe they're counting calories all week except for this one *special* meal."

"Okay. You win. And I know what you mean. Do I eat too much butter when I go out? Yes, ma'am. I eat a lot of cream I wouldn't eat at home, too. I get your point."

The cameraman took back his camera as he returned the big spoon to Uncle Saul.

"It's easy, right?" Uncle Saul asked him.

"Yeah—when someone else puts it all together."

I wiped my sweaty forehead with a cool, damp towel. It wasn't bad enough that the kitchen was hot. I was also wearing a huge, heavy hat.

Chef Art was smiling at me from the open doorway. I didn't take the hat off.

"It's seven thirty," I told my team. "Time to start the biscuits."

By eight A.M., we had two trays of biscuit bowls ready to go out the door. We decided to send Ollie out with Delia again. That combination had worked well for us. "Why am I going?" Ollie asked.

"Because you look *hot*, and this way you'll know when Delia starts running out of food. You did it before. Come back and get another tray so we can keep her going," I said. "At ninety-nine cents each, we're gonna have to sell a lot of biscuit bowls."

He glanced over me in a cursory kind of way. "You look hot, too, Zoe. *You* go."

"She needs to be here making biscuits." Uncle Saul's eyes were on the camera that was recording our disagreement.

"But Delia could make biscuits," Ollie reminded him. "Zoe taught her how. Or I could make biscuits. Delia and Zoe could go out together."

"No." I finished the disagreement. "You and Delia are going. Get out of here."

Ollie wasn't happy with that verdict. "Fine. I'll go out looking like a big freak in a red bikini for everyone to see on national television."

Delia lightly slapped his hard butt. "Hey, I'm going out there, too. Believe me, you'll get as many people interested in biscuit bowls with *that* body as I will."

"We'll probably sell quite a few biscuit bowls as they walk through the crowd," I said after they were gone.

Uncle Saul nodded. "Like we did in Charlotte. We need to get more biscuits ready."

While I made new batches of biscuits and put them in the little oven, Uncle Saul fried them up into biscuit bowls. We made two trays—one sweet and one savory—for Ollie to pick up on his return trip. The hard part was staying ahead. It was very different than selling my biscuit bowls back home.

Ollie was back even sooner than we'd expected. "That crowd is like a bunch of wolves. We barely got into it before we were selling left and right." He picked up the new trays, dropped off the empties, and was gone again.

"At this rate, we'll reach that two-hundred mark before nine." Uncle Saul was ladling his thick gumbo into biscuit bowls.

"So will everyone else," I said. "If we want to beat Our Daily Bread, we better sell until the sales stop or we run out of food."

We barely had the two new trays finished when Ollie came back.

"Is the Our Daily Bread team out?" Uncle Saul asked him.

"Oh, they're out. All of them, I think. They had to get that bread ready mighty darn early."

"All of them?" I asked him.

"No." Ollie picked up the new trays. "Reverend Jablonski is standing in one place while the others are around him singing hymns. It's like watching people throw money into a hat for a guitarist on the street. But they aren't wearing bikinis. Does that mean their sales don't count?"

"I don't know. It will definitely take away from their standing. We might finally beat them."

"Miguel," I called out, knowing he was standing by the open door. "Will you go take a look and see what everyone's doing?"

"Sure."

I wasn't sure why I cared. All I should focus on was getting our food to Delia. I suppose I was curious.

"Our Daily Bread is selling bagels for a quarter," Miguel said when he returned. "I guess they're going for bulk sales."

"That's a lot of bagels." Uncle Saul whistled but didn't look up from ladling gumbo.

"What about everyone else?"

"Shut Up and Eat seems to be doing okay with Bobbie's daughter out there. Dante is doing some kind of street dancing and selling pot stickers stuck in a clay holder of some kind. Grinch's is selling cupcakes with the Birmingham logo on them." Miguel grinned. "The biggest crowd is hanging around the two attractive Biscuit Bowl people."

"Is everyone else in bikinis?" Uncle Saul wondered.

"Only Ollie and Delia, and Bobbie and her daughter," Miguel reported.

I smiled at that. "Thanks for spying. I guess we'll keep doing what we're doing."

"I think it's working," Uncle Saul said. "How close are we to the two-hundred mark?"

"Four trays. We could beat Our Daily Bread. I know it's a good crowd out there, but selling bagels for a quarter each is going to take a while."

Chef Art called a halt to the cameraman being inside the Biscuit Bowl, thank goodness.

"Good luck," the cameraman called out as he was leaving.

"You all are on track to win this one, Zoe," Chef Art said. "Let's do it."

"I'm glad they're gone." Uncle Saul took a tray of biscuits out of the oven. "And this bikini is uncomfortable. How do women wear them?"

I laughed. "You should try high heels."

"No, thanks."

Ollie came back again in less than fifteen minutes. It was light outside now, and he said the crowds were thinning. "It might slow down. I hope it slows down. I feel like a piece of meat out there. I'm going to have bruises from people pinching me."

He was gone before Uncle Saul, Miguel, and I burst out laughing.

"They might have to move out of the crowd and hit the downtown traffic," I said. "I was hoping we could sell them all right away."

"We'll do better than Our Daily Bread," Uncle Saul said.

"I hope so. They're the ones to beat."

Ollie came back for the last two trays that made our two hundred dollars in sales. "Can we stop now?"

"Keep going until we run out of food," I said. "I'll go report that we made our goal."

"We're not going to go too much further," Uncle Saul remarked. "I've only got enough gumbo for a few more bowls, and there's only about that much left in berries and whipped cream."

"Okay. Let's do what we've got." I took the last tray of biscuits out of the little oven and set them aside. "I'm going over to make sure they know that we won the challenge."

Ollie came back for the last tray as I was leaving. I'd covered my bikini again and removed my chef's hat. I walked quickly from the food truck to the cool-down tent, holding the money close to me.

But I was too late. Sales had been very good for everyone.

Shut Up and Eat had finished at the same time as Stick It Here. One of the assistants marked down when I got there. Grinch's Ganache came in after me.

I hoped the "tag" would help us out, and the fact that we'd worn our bikinis. I went back to the Biscuit Bowl to find out what the decision would be.

I explained to everyone about where we were with the challenge. Ollie threw down his chef's hat and stepped on it before stalking off. Delia went after him.

Uncle Saul and I started cleaning up. It was too hot to wear the cover-up with the bikini. I took it off and worked.

"Zoe, you look mighty fine in that bikini." Uncle Saul nodded to Miguel. "Don't she?"

"I think she looks *great*."

"Thanks, but it's hard to be a business owner in a bikini." I smiled at them both. "Not that I don't appreciate the compliments."

"I'm just saying." Uncle Saul maneuvered his gumbo pot into the tiny sink.

He winked at me when Miguel couldn't see. I knew he was trying to help me. I thought I was doing okay, finally. Miguel and I seemed to be on the right wavelength.

Ollie and Delia came back to the Biscuit Bowl, and we applauded their efforts.

"I think everyone's done," Delia said. "It looks like they're all headed for the cool-down tent."

"I'm glad we're headed home today," Ollie said, pulling his shirt over the bikini.

I checked on Crème Brûlée, and then we started across the street to the stage and the cool-down tent after everything was clean and put away. I saw Patrick Ferris helping the two bikini girls with the electronic board. Delia was right. It was time to wind up the Birmingham challenge.

Ollie was right, too. I couldn't help that jump of joy in my heart knowing we would soon be going home. My bed at the old diner wasn't much, but it was going to be good to sleep in it that night.

I heard someone calling Miguel's name coming closer from a distance. We all looked back as Tina Gerard ran up, tears and black dirt on her face and arms. The dirt seemed to be mingled with blood.

TWENTY-SIX

"Miguel! Miguel!" She was screaming his name over and over until she threw herself into his arms. "Someone tried to kill me. They tried to run me down in the hotel parking lot. I managed to get away and I called a taxi. I rode all around the city, hoping he wasn't following me. I tried to call you. Why didn't you answer?"

"My phone didn't ring," he said. "Are you okay?"

"I just got a few scratches when I fell on the concrete in the parking lot. I thought this was over. Why would someone come after *me*? I'm not part of the race."

"It may not have anything to do with the race," he said.

"Surely this proves that I wasn't part of what caused Alex's death. People are trying to kill me, too. I don't understand."

"Did you call the police?" Miguel asked.

"No. I came straight here. I didn't want to talk to them by myself. I was afraid I might say the wrong thing." She buried her head in his shirt and stood there, shaking.

Patrick was waiting for the remaining food truck teams to reach the stage. I hated to leave the dramatic scene, but we'd come this far. Miguel was going to have to call the police anyway. There wasn't much any of the rest of us could do. "Go ahead," he said over Tina's head. "I'll catch up with you."

Chef Art got out of his golf cart. "What's going on? Why aren't you all down there already?"

I told him about Tina's brush with death.

"Hog feathers! Get over there and win this challenge, Zoe Chase, or you're not the entrepreneur I thought you were."

He was right. All the remaining teams were there. The producers' assistants were counting the earnings again as the four food truck owners stood by watching.

Grinch's Ganache had demanded a recount. When all the earnings for the morning were counted, the assistants returned our money. All eyes, and TV cameras, were on Patrick as he picked up the microphone.

"Everyone did an exceptional job out there this morning. Congratulations! It looks like our winner for the Birming-ham challenge is the Biscuit Bowl. Not only did they sell two hundred dollars in delicious biscuit bowls, they also knew what to do with their red tag—which meant all team members wearing red bikinis."

Ollie, Delia, Uncle Saul, Chef Art, and I were too busy squealing and hugging to even hear what Patrick said next. We finally quieted down and listened again.

"We have a tie between Shut Up and Eat and Stick It Here. The producers have decided on a tiebreaker to deter-mine who the second food truck winner will be."

"What happened to Our Daily Bread?" Ollie asked.

"I think we missed that," I whispered.

Bobbie Shields was standing beside me. "They were dis-qualified for cheating and removed from the race."

"Why? What happened?" I couldn't believe it.

"They weren't ministers after all." She shrugged. "Someone

reported seeing Reverend Jablonski on TV doing a promo for the race. He's an escaped felon from Florida."

"Don't that beat all." Uncle Saul shook his head. "And here they've been trouncing us right along."

"Darn good bread makers," Bobbie remarked.

"We've come up with a tiebreaker," Patrick announced. "We'll need the owners of Stick It Here and Shut Up and Eat to come forward. Everyone else is free to do what they want for about thirty minutes. We'll have the beauty pageant, and the official announcement of who is going on with the race, at the stage then."

"I forgot about the beauty pageant." Ollie's expression was fierce. "I don't know, Zoe. I think I might just go on home now."

"We're going home in a little while," I said. "If you back out, we'll be disqualified, too. Please, Ollie. One last thing."

"You know I might fall for that if I didn't know we still had to do goofy stuff tomorrow in Mobile." He was frowning but finally relented. "Oh, all right. As long as no one else pinches me."

"I won't let it happen again," I promised, hugging him.

We went back out in the street and saw two police cars there with Miguel and Tina. An ambulance was pulling in, sirens blaring, as we reached them.

"Is Tina okay?" I asked Miguel.

"She's probably fine. I think she should be checked out."

"Who are you people?" an officer asked when he saw our group.

I explained about the food truck race.

He laughed. "I've heard about that on TV. Sounds funny!"

Ollie muttered to himself and shuffled toward the Biscuit Bowl to wait for the final announcement.

"Come with me, Miguel," Tina asked. "I don't want to go to the hospital *alone*."

"You'll be fine," he said. "I'll come and get you. Just take it easy, okay?"

She threw herself against him again. I was starting to feel a little doubtful that she was thinking of him *only* as a friend and attorney. Maybe I was being touchy because my relationship with Miguel was very new and she'd known him forever.

"You might have to kick that girl's scrawny behind," Delia whispered.

"Thanks." I grinned at her. "At least I'm not the *only* one seeing this."

Miguel politely saw Tina into the ambulance. The paramedics got in back with her and the vehicle left.

"Why would anyone want to hurt her anyway?" Delia asked. "I thought the police accused her and Miguel of killing Alex."

"No one said it had to make sense," Uncle Saul said. "Maybe someone wanted to kill both of them—someone besides *you*, Zoe."

I answered my phone. It was Marsh calling from the hospital. Helms still hadn't regained consciousness. Her family from Charlotte was flying in later that day to be with her.

His update was brief and to the point. I explained what he'd said to everyone.

"I don't know what to think about all of this." I put my phone back in the pocket of my robe. "Marsh and Helms are the only ones who have followed this from the beginning. The Birmingham police are baffled. If we drag it to Mobile, they won't have any answers, either."

We kind of looked at one another and shrugged. We stood around in the street as the sun rose in the blue sky. Uncle Saul said he was hungry and went to get a biscuit bowl.

The thirty-minute wait to find out what was going on in the race went by slowly, until we were finally called back to the stage. With only two food trucks going to Mobile, the group was dwindling fast.

"Last, but not least, we still have time for the beauty

pageant. Biscuit Bowl team up first. Show us your bikinis."

I took off my robe self-consciously, even though everyone had said I looked fine in my bikini. This was different, being up on a stage for everyone to gawk at.

I didn't have to worry about anyone noticing me, though; not with Uncle Saul and Ollie's onstage antics. Delia and I stood to one side as the men showed their muscles and generally acted like idiots.

"Can you believe that?" Delia asked me when Ollie lifted Uncle Saul and held him in the air.

"I knew he was strong. There's a lot more to Ollie than any of us knows."

"I think that's true, Zoe." She smiled at me. "He's such a nice person. I'm worried about hurting him. I don't have good luck with relationships."

"Maybe this time will be different for you." I waved shyly to Miguel, who waved back.

"Thank you for the show, Team Biscuit Bowl," Patrick said. "Team Shut Up and Eat, come on up."

Bobbie's daughter was stunning in her bikini. She looked shy onstage, but everyone applauded her. Bobbie defiantly shed her flowered dress when she got up there. She looked like an overweight, middle-aged woman in a blue bikini with a tattoo of a swan on her chest. Nothing else to say on that score.

We all applauded again. Bobbie and her daughter were very popular, but Ollie and Uncle Saul's craziness won the day.

"Team Biscuit Bowl wins the pageant, and a Caribbean cruise," Patrick screamed. "Congratulations!"

Shut Up and Eat's prize for winning second place in the Birmingham challenge was a new deep fryer. Bobbie and her daughter graciously thanked everyone.

Patrick was grinning. "Okay, folks! We have our finalists in the Sweet Magnolia Food Truck Race. Girls, will you light up the board?"

The electronic board had to be prodded a little, but it finally came up with the names of the two finalists.

"Biscuit Bowl is on top!" Ollie yelled and did fist pumps in the air.

"That's right!" Patrick pointed at him. "The Biscuit Bowl from Mobile, Alabama, is number one. And since Shut Up and Eat from Charleston, South Carolina, wore their bikinis, they are our runner-up. Sorry about that, Grinch's Ganache and Stick It Here. Let's give them a round of applause for jumping back into the race even though they ended up losing."

We all applauded. Some of the men clapped Dante on the back and shook hands with him. He didn't seem to be a good loser like the others had tried to be, letting his disappointment and anger show.

"Only two teams left." Patrick faced the TV camera, his voice dramatic. He might have been announcing the end of the world with the serious expression on his face. "Shut Up and Eat will go head-to-head with Mobile's own Biscuit Bowl right in their home port. The prizes are bigger, and so are tomorrow's final challenges. Don't miss a moment of the Sweet Magnolia Food Truck Race finale!"

As soon as he'd finished speaking, the assistants began taking everything apart. The trucks would move on, and the race would continue with the Biscuit Bowl in the lead.

"You know, I almost think we might win this race," I said to Chef Art.

"Zoe, we are *gonna* win tomorrow. Just you wait and see."

Everything in the Biscuit Bowl was tied down or locked up, and we were ready to go. Everyone took their turns in the cool-down tent dressing room to change out of their bikinis. What a relief!

Miguel didn't want to leave Birmingham without making sure Tina was all right. I didn't want to leave without him. We decided to go to the hospital.

"If it's all the same to you, Zoe," Uncle Saul said, "I'd

just as soon go on home and check on Alabaster—and a certain wildlife officer I've missed. I can drive the food truck and take Crème Brûlée with me, if that would make it easier. This will give me a chance to think about what we should serve tomorrow for our race-winning biscuit bowls, too. It's gotta be something amazing since we're gonna be home. Text or call me if you have any ideas."

That was fine with me. I gave him, and Crème Brûlée, a kiss.

"You be a good boy," I said to my sometimes-wayward cat. "You don't want Alabaster to eat you!"

He turned up his nose and ignored me, obviously disgusted with the whole affair. I rubbed his tummy, and he pushed at me with his soft paws.

"It's going to be good to be home," I told him as I strapped him into the truck seat. "I'll make you something really special for dinner after the race."

He wasn't impressed. Uncle Saul got into the food truck. I waved to him as he drove away from Birmingham.

Delia winked as I got into the front seat of Miguel's car with him. She and Ollie were in the backseat. I didn't know if Tina would be leaving Birmingham with us or not. If she was, she was going to have to sit in the back with Ollie and Delia. I was seriously tired of her falling all over Miguel. Where did she actually live anyway? Maybe she could go there, or to Florida with her mother.

- - - - - - -

We got to the hospital. Miguel went to see if Tina had been admitted. Ollie went with him. Delia and I went to the floor where Helms was recovering.

"It's nice of you to go and see this woman, even though she and her partner have been a pain in the butt," Delia said when we were in the elevator.

"She's been all right. She's just doing her job. I feel bad that she had something important to tell me after she was shot and I couldn't understand her. I hope she and Marsh can figure it all out."

"Like I said," Delia drawled, "mighty nice."

The elevator chimed and we got off. I started toward the nurses' station to ask about Helms. There was no sign of Marsh or anyone else waiting to see her. I supposed Marsh had to work even though she was hurt, and her family probably hadn't arrived yet.

"I'd like to see Detective Macey Helms, please."

"Are you a member of the family?" the nurse asked me.

"No, but I was with her when she was brought in."

Dark eyes in a chocolate brown face narrowed. "She isn't allowed visitors right now, except family. Sorry."

I opened my mouth to argue the point, and an alarm went off. People started running past me.

One of them was Detective Marsh. "Someone tried to get into Helms's room," he yelled. "I think he wanted to finish what he started."

TWENTY-SEVEN

"How is that possible in a hospital?" I yelled after him. "Where's security?"

"We should get out of here." Delia glanced nervously around us. "It could be dangerous, Zoe."

"No! We have to find out what happened. Didn't they have a police officer protecting her?"

The nurse at the desk heaved herself out of the chair. "We don't need anyone to protect our patients. We have the best security in the world."

"It sounds like it," I muttered before following Marsh.

"I'm going to find Miguel and Ollie," Delia said. "Watch your back, Zoe."

I walked quickly down the hall, looking for Marsh. Everyone else was running down the hall toward the exit.

The door to one room was open. I saw Marsh standing in there and went in to see what he was doing.

"Zoe." He glanced at me and then back at his partner.

"Macey's safe, thank goodness. I'd like to know what she found out that made her a target."

"Me, too."

"You couldn't understand *anything* that she was trying to tell you after she was shot?"

"She only said that she had information about what had happened. It had to be important. She almost died trying to get to me."

He shook his head. "I don't know why she didn't call *me*. I don't even know where she was when she was shot. The police couldn't find a crime scene."

"I don't know. What happened up here?"

"I had to go to the bathroom. Someone walked in, pretty as you please, and cut the lines to her IV while I was gone. A nurse saw it and started screaming. Everything went crazy after that."

"Did the nurse see the person who did it?"

"I don't know, Zoe. I stayed right here next to Macey." He scratched his head. "The last few days have been like a circus. I don't know what's going on—except that a good friend of mine is dead and someone tried to kill Macey. How that goes together is anyone's guess."

I went over and held Macey's hand. It was cool to the touch. She didn't move. They'd already replaced her IV lines. She was lucky the nurse came in when she did.

"Now what?" I asked Marsh.

"The Birmingham police said they'll keep an eye on her—at least until her family can have her moved back to Charlotte. I'm going to head back home, too. The chief says he's sending someone else out with 'fresh eyes' to take a look, whatever that means."

"But they'll lose all your experience with the case."

He shrugged. "We haven't been doing all that well with it. Frankly, I'm ready to call it a day."

I studied Macey's face, willing her to open her eyes and

tell us what she'd found. It didn't happen, and the doctor and two nurses came in to shoo us both out.

"Well, I'm going on to Mobile," I said to Marsh in the hall. "Please let me know what happens. I'd like to see Helms when she wakes up."

"I will. Thanks, Zoe."

As I turned to walk away, he said, "You know, at first I thought it was you. McSwain died right after he talked to you. You were involved with the race. It seemed possible."

"I guess you changed your mind."

"About *you*," he agreed. "Not about Miguel Alexander and his girlfriend. I'd expect a call from the police in Mobile when you get there."

That was thrilling news—nothing like having to deal with police in four different states. I wasn't expecting that as part of the food truck race.

I found Miguel with Ollie and Delia. Tina had been treated and released. She'd been waiting at the front of the hospital, trusting that Miguel would come and get her.

We bundled back into the Mercedes. Tina tried to call shotgun. I edged her out. I try to be a nice person, but that wasn't going to happen. She sat beside Ollie and Delia with great reluctance. I could tell it wasn't going to be a fun trip home. At least Mobile wasn't far away.

All I could think about was Helms, and the information she may have almost died twice for. What did McSwain's and Alex's deaths have in common? How did they relate to Reggie's death?

"It had to be the same person that Alex was talking to on the phone that first day behind his RV."

I realized that I'd spoken out loud. Everyone in the car was immediately quiet. I had no idea if there was a conversation that I'd interrupted.

"What did you say?" Ollie asked.

"I was thinking that McSwain was killed in Charlotte

because he went to talk to Alex about the phone call I'd overheard. The man who was talking to Alex was the killer."

Delia sighed and closed her compact mirror. "What does that even mean, Zoe?"

"It means that what Zoe overheard got McSwain killed," Miguel clarified.

"But you said you didn't really overhear anything that made sense," Ollie added.

"Well, it was a little disjointed. I was sure that Alex was talking about being responsible for what had happened to Reggie. He sounded like there was more to come."

"The more-to-come part came true," Ollie said. "But I don't think Alex was standing there planning his own death."

"I'm sure he wasn't. But what if all the disruptions in the race were meant to cover up Alex's death?" I looked at Miguel. "This whole thing has been a setup from the beginning."

I reminded everyone how the police had somehow been tipped off about Tina and Miguel. "She gave him money to defend her against Alex, who wanted to take everything from her."

"Which I didn't ask for," Miguel reminded Tina. "And I don't plan to keep. It was only supposed to be filing fees."

"You've always been so good to me," Tina declared. "I knew you would help me if I asked. Alex had a really good attorney, and I was too emotional to fight him. You were one of the best courtroom lawyers in our class."

"Wow," Ollie said. "I knew he was good when he got me off of that burglary charge."

"Thanks," Miguel said. "But what's your point, Zoe? How is that related to Alex being killed?"

"Okay." I got ready to explain. "Alex, and the man he was talking to that first day, *were* planning to kill Tina. They were going to use all the mayhem from the race, and Reggie's death, to disguise her murder."

"He knew I was there." Tina nodded. "It's possible he was just tired of fighting and knew I'd eventually win."

"When McSwain confronted Alex, his partner—probably a paid killer—was there and realized that McSwain was a liability. How could they do what they wanted with him hanging around waiting for something to happen?"

"Let's say that happened," Miguel said. "How did Alex end up being the one who was killed instead of Tina?"

I shrugged. "I don't know. Maybe they had a disagreement. Maybe the killer wanted more money. There was some mention of money in the RV before Alex was killed."

"Why would the killer still be coming after me?" Tina asked in a whiny voice.

"I don't know that, either. It seems like it would have been over with Alex's death."

"Maybe it was for the honor." Ollie glanced at us. "You know, he wanted to finish the job so people didn't think he couldn't pull it off."

"I've never known a professional killer," Delia said. "Is that how they are?"

Ollie cleared his throat and sat back against the seat, his head almost touching the ceiling. "I don't know. I'm just guessing. It's not like I know any professional killers—at least not right now."

"I shouldn't go to Mobile." Tina started crying again. "I'm probably doing *exactly* what the killer wants me to do. Let me out here, Miguel. I'll walk to the nearest bus stop."

"We're only a few minutes outside the city," he reasoned. "I'll take you somewhere safe. At least talk to the police in Mobile first. We might still be able to sort this whole thing out."

Tina sat forward and pressed herself against his shoulder—*again*. "You always know the right thing to do."

I gave Delia a disgusted look that she returned. Ollie laughed out loud before he clamped a big hand over his mouth.

"It's going to be fine," Miguel told Tina. "It's all going to work out."

"That may or may not be true," I muttered under my breath.

Miguel managed a quick smile at me. "What did you say, Zoe?"

"Nothing. Just thinking ahead to the last part of the race." I smiled brightly at him.

He smiled back, not a clue.

"We better start figuring this out before the killer finishes his job and gets rid of Tina," Ollie said. "Once he's gone, the police probably won't be able to find him."

Tina made a slightly strangled cry.

"If there *is* a killer on Tina's trail," Delia added, "he probably won't stop until she's dead. Bless her heart."

I smiled but kept my thoughts to myself.

It was wonderful when we finally rolled into Mobile. I love my hometown, and I was looking forward to clean clothes and staying in my own place, such as it was. Whoever it was that said, "Be it ever so humble, there's no place like home," had to know circumstances like mine.

Delia was staying with me since she had to give up her apartment after she'd lost her job. Ollie was still living at the homeless shelter two doors down. What I could pay either one of them wasn't enough to have their own places. I hoped it would get better soon, but there were no guarantees.

Miguel pulled the Mercedes smoothly into the rutted and overgrown parking lot for the old shopping center where my diner was located. He got out as we did. Tina stayed in the car.

"Back where we started from," he said with a smile.

"Almost. A little better off, I think." I couldn't resist putting my arms around him and giving him a big kiss. I knew Tina was watching from the car. That wasn't the *only* reason I did it, but it was one of them.

"That part is a lot better." His arms were around me. "What are you doing for dinner tonight?"

I sighed. "I still have to go to the race dinner and see what we have to do tomorrow."

"Yeah. That's right. I'd almost forgotten. Where are they having the dinner?"

"At Chef Art's mansion, Woodlands. He invited everyone to stay there, too. You know how he likes to show off his place."

"I'll be there. Six P.M.?"

"Yep. You could pick me up, if you don't mind. Uncle Saul has the Biscuit Bowl. I'm not sure when he's going to be back."

"I'd like that. I can't wait to see what they want you to do for the finale. Whatever it is, it probably won't be as good as seeing you in that red bikini."

I smiled, and he kissed me again.

"Hey, can I get a ride, too?" Ollie yelled from across the parking lot.

"Me, too." Delia was waiting for me to open the door to the old diner.

"He's got big ears," I told Miguel.

"I heard that," Ollie shouted.

"I'll see you tonight." Miguel laughed.

I kissed him again, with one eye on Tina's face. "I can't *wait*."

- - - - - - -

It was good to be home. The diner was a little decrepit, but it was mine. I could still look at it and see all my big dreams coming true. Someday, I planned to be as famous as Chef Art. People would come from all over the world to eat my food. The dream kept me going. If I won the fifty-thousand-dollar grand prize for the race, I'd be a step closer to that dream.

"If you win the money," Delia asked, painting her toenails, "will you still run the food truck?"

"I don't know. I suppose it would all depend on whether

or not that's enough to remodel everything here—and still have money to live on until the customers come to find me."

I wasn't crazy, despite what my mother, some friends, and my ex-boyfriend thought. Word of mouth for a good meal was essential, but so was having an advertising budget and being able to buy more food. I knew restaurants closed more frequently than any other small business. I'd worked at a bank for years. I was aware of the odds.

Still, most people didn't think I'd come this far. When I'd given up that other life of watching food shows on TV and started making real food for real people, I'd been determined to reach my goal. The food truck had already played a big part in my plan. Even with the fifty thousand dollars—only half of which would be left after taxes—I'd still have a long way to go.

We were sitting on the stools by the remodeled bar, next to the cooking area in the diner. The four booths were like traps when you sat on them. They sank down so low under the tables—it was almost impossible to get up. We were relaxing and talking about the last few days as I worked on my shopping list for the next day. I hadn't heard from Uncle Saul yet, but I knew the basics of what would be needed for the last day.

"I can't believe what's happened with Ollie and me. Delia smiled like the cat that drank the cream. "He's a little rough around the edges, but he has a good heart. And he's sexy, too. That surprised me."

"A good heart I hope you'll try not to break." The dryer buzzed and I went to get my clean clothes.

"Zoe, you can't expect me to be alone the rest of my life because someone might get hurt. Ollie's a big boy. He can handle whatever happens between us."

"I don't expect that. Really. If you care about Ollie, I'm fine with it. He's crazy about you."

"Then why do you think I'd break his heart?"

I looked at her beautiful face. "I think you want more

than an ex-marine who lives in a homeless shelter can give you."

She laughed, but her eyes were guarded. "I've worked since I was twelve. I supported my mother for years before she died. I've supported my sisters. I'd like a little comfort before I die. I don't think that's too much to ask."

I couldn't judge her. I'd been born into a life of wealth and privilege. I didn't know what it was like not to have whatever I wanted. I'd given that up for my diner, but I knew in my heart, if I needed my parents, they'd be there. Delia's life hadn't been like that.

"I just don't know if Ollie can change to be that person. I wish he could, for him as well as for you."

"You may be right," she said after a long moment. "Maybe I should stay away from him."

She went into the pantry that we'd redone for her bedroom so she could have some privacy. I heard the door close softly and realized that I might have hurt her feelings. It wasn't my intention, but sometimes words get tangled up and they don't say what you mean.

TWENTY-EIGHT

I heard a horn honk loudly outside and looked through the large plate-glass window. It was the Biscuit Bowl with Uncle Saul at the wheel. I ran outside to greet him and get my cat.

"How was your trip back?" I asked him. "Did everything stay together?"

"It was fine." He laughed. "I was afraid Alabaster might try and take a bite out of me, she was so happy I was home."

"I'm glad you and the food truck made it back." I opened the passenger door, and Crème Brûlée opened his eyes a little and meowed at me. "I'm so happy to see you, baby. I hope you had a good trip, too."

He swatted at me with his paws and turned over to go back to sleep. I picked him up and hugged him as I took him inside.

"I fed him when I got home," Uncle Saul said. "The size of that feline, he must need to eat again."

"Don't pay any attention to him," I cooed to my kitty. "The man has an alligator for a pet. What can you expect?"

I got all of Crème Brûlée's necessary items set up for him. He took a short tour of the kitchen area, ate a little food, and then went back to sleep in his own bed. Seeing him there made my day complete.

"We're going out to Chef Art's place for dinner tonight, right?" Uncle Saul asked.

"We are. If you're planning to stay in town instead of driving back, you could stay with him instead of at a hotel."

He rubbed his hands together. "Sounds great. I'll call Cole and have him take me out there. I'll see you tonight."

Cole was an old friend of Uncle Saul's from his restaurant days. He drove a taxi around the city. I'd used his service many times since giving up my Prius to buy the diner and the food truck.

"What about Bonnie?" I asked. "Was she happy to see you, too?"

He almost blushed. I smiled, surprised by his reaction.

"She missed me, I think. We're not exactly ready to take any vows, but we had a good talk. Maybe something is gonna happen. We'll see."

I hugged him. "I'm so glad. She's really nice." I thanked him again for putting up with food truck madness.

"Hold on," he said. "There's still tomorrow. Unless you're saying you don't need my help."

"Never! What do you have in mind for food?"

"I'm only thinking savory, Zoe. You take the sweet. I'll get what we need for my part."

"Great. I love mystery food."

We talked for a while after he called Cole. Delia never put in an appearance, which made me feel even worse. Who was I to mess around with other people's lives? I had a hard enough time living my own.

Once Uncle Saul was gone, I decided to tackle deep cleaning the kitchen in the Biscuit Bowl. I knew a lot of my usual chores had gone undone while I'd been away. Tomorrow, the kitchen would be sparkling when I accepted that fifty-thousand-dollar check.

There were crumbs and food where there shouldn't have been. The deep fryer wasn't too bad, since the oil was new. I cleaned out the little oven—everything would still have to be cooked in there to comply with the race rules.

The floor was awful. Ollie was bad about spilling things. I scoured and scrubbed until my fingers were sore. The kitchen finally smelled clean. I vacuumed the front seat and the back of the food truck. It was surprising what a mess Crème Brûlée had made just sleeping in the seat. At least he hadn't been sick or used anything for his litter box up there. I felt blessed.

While I was cleaning, I was thinking about Alex and Detective McSwain again. I couldn't help it. I wished I could figure out what had happened to them—and to Detective Helms.

Funny how my mind didn't wander to include Tina in those thoughts.

I realized that despite Tina being injured I still considered her to be a possible suspect—without Miguel's help, of course. She could still have set him up to take the fall for Alex's death. It made sense in a lot of ways.

There was no proof that she was involved, which was why the police kept letting her go. They wanted Miguel and Tina to both be guilty, or neither of them. I thought that was ridiculous.

I had my eye on Tina. Well, at least I'd *had* my eye on Tina. I supposed Miguel was finding her a hotel room. She wasn't really part of the race at all. I didn't think she'd stay with Chef Art.

I *hoped* she wasn't staying with Miguel.

As I was finishing up my job with the Biscuit Bowl, Mobile detective Patti Latoure rolled up in her car. I'd met her about the same time I'd met Miguel last year, after a series of unfortunate events I really wanted to forget.

"Zoe." She nodded and smiled at me. She was of medium height and build, with suspicious blue eyes and dyed blond hair tied back from her face. She was wearing dressy black pants and a white top under her black jacket.

I'd gotten to know her a little. She was friendly, and I liked her. She'd told me she planned to be a lawyer until a friend of hers had been killed when she was in college. I knew she had a husband who hated her being a cop, and they had all kinds of arguments about it. I also knew they had no kids.

"Hi! I was kind of expecting you."

She got out of her car and put her hands on her slender hips. I could see her detective's badge and her gun. "That doesn't surprise me. You've been raising a ruckus all the way here from Charlotte."

I laughed, knowing her well enough to do so. "Not me personally—the race. I haven't done anything except make biscuit bowls, serve them on roller skates and in a bikini, and find a dead man. Not much."

She smiled, too. "I guess we'll keep a special eye on the race events tomorrow. It was kind of a mess, wasn't it?"

"You could say that. Come inside and I'll fill you in. I have to work on my sweet filling for tomorrow."

She followed me in and perched on one of the stools at the counter as I poured her some sweet iced tea and made some biscuits. I explained everything about the race from Charlotte to Mobile and let her draw her own conclusions.

"That's a shame about the Dog House." She sipped tea and nibbled at a biscuit. "I loved that man's Polish sausage, even though I couldn't look at him when I bought it."

"I know what you mean. I guess the Dog House was in good shape, though. The race inspectors put us through a harder inspection than we get here."

"And you say the police are sure that his death wasn't an accident?"

I shrugged as I debated putting a little sugar into the

biscuit bowls tomorrow morning. "That's what they said. Detectives Helms and Marsh came with us from Charlotte after Reggie died and their friend, Detective McSwain, was killed."

She seemed to be thinking about it as she ate her biscuit. I hadn't fried it for her. She'd wanted it plain.

Ollie came in a few minutes later and sat beside her on a stool.

I wished they were real paying customers. But the diner wasn't set up to pass inspection for more than a few nonpaying friends, and making food for the Biscuit Bowl.

"Nothing changed at the shelter while I was gone." Ollie got some tea, too. "I didn't expect it to. It always feels like something *should* change when I go away."

Patti glanced at him as though she was trying to figure out what he was saying. "Ollie, sometimes we have to make our own changes, you know? If you want things to be different, you have to *make* them different."

Delia came out of her room and joined us. I could see she was still a little upset at what I'd said to her earlier. I was sorry I'd hurt her, but I believed that what I said was true.

"Need any help with that?" she asked in a sulky voice.

"Nope. I'm fine. I've been thinking about putting a little powdered sugar into the sweet biscuit bowl dough for tomorrow. What do you think?"

"I don't think it could hurt."

Ollie disagreed. "They're not donuts, Zoe. The middles make them sweet enough."

I shrugged, still thinking about it as I put a few samples into the deep fryer.

"I suppose neither one of you saw anything out of the ordinary during the race." Patti turned to them. "Those murders have been dumped right in our lap now."

"I wouldn't say that." Delia laughed. "I saw Ollie in a red bikini. That was out of the ordinary."

Ollie grinned and Delia kissed his cheek.

"In a good way." She smiled up at him. "I didn't know a man could look *good* in a bikini."

"How about you, Ollie?" Patti asked him.

"I didn't see anything that had to do with murder or vandalism, if that's what you're asking, Detective Latoure." Ollie's tone was slightly rehearsed. He was always careful around the police.

Patti finished her biscuit and tea before she got to her feet. "I guess I'd better get going. I hear you all start early tomorrow. Let's hope this part of the race is quiet."

I agreed with her. "See you tomorrow."

"And if any of you think of anything you didn't tell the police in any of those other cities, give me a call, huh?"

"We will," I promised for all of us.

Delia and Ollie were staring at each other as though they'd never seen each other. I took the first biscuit bowls out of the deep fryer and set them on the side to cool and drain.

"I'm going to step outside and call Miguel," I said.

Neither one of them responded.

I went out, a tiny blossom of hope inside me that my two good friends had really found each other. Ollie deserved someone special in his life again. From what little I'd been able to glean from Miguel about his past, his dead wife was his first and last romance. He'd been unwilling to trust anyone since then. I couldn't say that I blamed him.

It was the same thing for Delia, though not so dramatic. She deserved someone who loved her. They both did.

I called Miguel as I sat outside on the window ledge. I tried not to peek inside at what was going on. There was no answer. I left him a voice mail and walked around the building a few times. I didn't want to go back inside right away.

The back of the old shopping center was a deplorable mess. I'd called and written letters to the city, and to the landlord, but there had been no response. Everything—including the kitchen sink and toilet—was thrown there. No wonder we had a problem with rats and bugs.

Since I had nothing better to do, I went ahead and called both offices again. There was no answer at the landlord's number. The city clerk told me I'd have to file a special complaint form. When I told her I'd already filed that form—several times—she told me, quite cheerfully, that I'd have to wait until they could review it.

I took a few pictures of the mess in back. Next time, I could illustrate my point. Maybe I could even get the *Mobile Times* newspaper to write something about it. It was sad that we had to rely on the media to take care of problems.

I'd been outside about thirty minutes. I had to go back in and work on the biscuit bowls again before the dough went bad.

Ollie and Delia were sitting at one of the old booths. Their heads were close together, and they were whispering to each other. I wished I could take a picture of that, too.

Ignoring them, I went about seeing what was in the fridge and pantry that I could use for the sweet filling tomorrow. I had some ingredients to make the pecan pie filling I'd tried a few weeks before. The brown sugar confection had been very popular the one day that I'd made it. It was expensive, too, so I hadn't made it again.

Would some of my regular customers come to the race event tomorrow? I hoped so. Mobile had a lively, and popular, food truck community. Those customers might go somewhere else rather than wade through the race crowd, but I hoped to see a few familiar faces.

I decided to make the pecan pie filling the next day. I could use my ingredients, but I'd have to wait to make it until I was in the food truck tomorrow. Since it was so sweet, I decided to go without the extra sugar. I knew it would be a good match.

I looked at the clock above the diner door. It was almost five P.M. I didn't want to interrupt Ollie and Delia, but I needed time to get ready for dinner.

I called Miguel again—still no word from him. I hoped

he hadn't gotten caught up in something with Tina and wouldn't be able to get away. I thought he'd probably call if that were the case. I tried not to imagine what kinds of things could *come up* with Tina. The woman was a whiny pest.

But I trusted him. I didn't think he'd play around with me that way. The time we'd spent away from Mobile had been perfect for us.

At least *I'd* thought so. I hoped he did, too.

TWENTY-NINE

At five thirty, I was ready to go. *Still no word from Miguel.*

Ollie had gone back to the homeless shelter and changed clothes. He was still wearing jeans and a T-shirt, but now they were clean.

Delia had changed, too. She was wearing a short, heavenly blue dress with a sparkly silver chiffon overlay. Her hair was up. She looked like a princess.

I cleaned up pretty well, too. I went for my favorite little black dress—scoop neck and ending above my knees. My curls were perfect and glossy. I added black heels and a blue star sapphire necklace and earrings that had been a gift on my sixteenth birthday.

"Ladies!" Ollie looked us both over, but his eyes got stuck on Delia. "I guess we're going without Miguel?"

"I haven't heard from him all afternoon. Maybe he's too busy to go to dinner." I shrugged. "He might have had to get caught up with stuff at his office."

Delia and I exchanged knowing glances.

"He's not *that* kind of man," I said.

"She's *that* kind of woman," Delia warned.

"Are we taking the food truck?" Ollie asked.

"No." I'd called Uncle Saul's taxi driver friend, Cole. There was no point in bothering Miguel for a ride. We could certainly get there without him. He could join us later when he could get away.

I called Miguel one last time while we were waiting for the taxi. I left a voice mail to make sure he knew he could come late if he wanted to.

"I hope he's okay," Delia said.

"I'm sure he's fine," Ollie added.

"He probably just got busy," I said again. "There were probably all kinds of clients that missed him while he was gone. He'll come later."

I didn't want to feel miserable or pathetic—I was in the lead to win fifty thousand dollars. I was disappointed that Miguel couldn't be there tonight, but I couldn't expect him to drive me all over the city after going with me on the race.

I pasted a happy smile on my face when Cole pulled up, and the three of us got in the old Chevy taxi.

"Hey there, Zoe," Cole said. "It's good to see you. Don't tell me—you're on your way out to Chef Art's place like Saul, right?"

"That's where we're headed." I was careful to sit on the outside of the backseat so Delia and Ollie could sit next to each other. "I suppose Uncle Saul told you all about what happened while we were gone."

He nodded as he pulled out of the parking lot. "He sure did. Sounds like you all had a heck of a time. Good eating, too. I'm glad you're home. I missed those biscuit bowls of yours."

That made me feel better. It was nice to know that someone had missed me while I was gone; even nicer that someone had missed my food.

Chef Art's home was one of Mobile's best, and most

famous, antebellum mansions with stately oaks surrounding it. All the oaks had been cut down so that Confederate artillery was free to shell Federal troops. The trees there had been replanted using acorns from the originals.

Woodlands had been built in 1855. It had been restored with plenty of money and loving care so that the massive rooms, circular staircase, and crystal chandeliers were in great condition.

Chef Art regularly entertained here. I'd only been in the house one other time. I was happy to be back again.

Cole dropped us off out front in the circular drive. The place was buzzing with activity—a lot more than there should've been for two food truck teams and some producers.

Chef Art greeted us at the door, as befitted a host of the old South. He was wearing his famous white linen suit, as always. "Good to see you. I'm glad you could make it."

"What's going on?" There were hundreds of strangers walking around inside.

"I thought I'd ask a few friends over for dinner. It seemed like such a small party with just you all and the other team. We won't count the race officials and sponsors. It was short notice, or I'm sure there'd be a lot more people. Go on. Introduce yourself, Zoe. Make yourself known. That's how you get rich and famous."

I did as he suggested. I recognized some of the people from national TV food shows that I watched regularly. I loved most of them, and had spent hours planning to be one of them. It wasn't happening yet, but there was plenty of time.

Ollie and Delia found a quiet place in a corner and didn't bother introducing themselves to anyone. That was fine, and what I'd expected.

I found Uncle Saul at the canapé table. He hugged me. "You have to try these okra treats. You won't believe how they taste."

I tried one—not really an okra fan, but he was right. "What is that stuffed with?"

"I think it's sausage and some kind of filler."

I tasted it again. "Quinoa? I think that's what it is."

"Whatever it is, I like it." He grabbed another one and looked over my shoulder at the same time. "Are you here alone? Where is everyone?"

"Well, Delia and Ollie are finding each other." I nodded toward their corner. "Miguel was busy. I've taken up a lot of his time. I'm glad he could be there for the other parts of the race."

He smiled and put his arm around me. "Zoe, you sound like the people who don't win the Academy Award. 'It was just an honor to be nominated.' Come on. Cheer up. You'll see him tomorrow."

He was wearing a bright blue and pink checkered jacket over a matching vest. His dress pants were a shade close to the pink in the jacket. Uncle Saul could be a snappy dresser when he chose.

"Excuse me." A young woman wearing a small black fascinator on her blond hair joined us. "I'm Tiffany Bryant. I represent the committee putting on carnival next year. I was wondering if you'd be interested in bringing your food truck to the festivities? We're interested in having the *best* food Mobile has to offer."

I was certainly interested in being called the best food Mobile had to offer. I knew getting into the two weeks leading up to Mardi Gras was hard. There were thousands of people there every year for the events.

"Yes. I'd love to be there. Thank you for asking."

She handed me her card. "Just give me a call or text me. I'll send you an invitation. The food truck race has been so exciting, especially having someone at the head of the pack from Mobile. Good job, Zoe!"

"Thanks. It's been a lot of fun."

"Except, of course for the deaths and the other problems," she said. "What a bother those were."

Bother wasn't the word I would've used, but I wasn't

going to argue with someone recruiting for carnival. I didn't agree, either, but our quick conversation was over. She had moved on to someone else.

I saw my mother's face on dozens of campaign buttons before I saw her coming toward me. No button or poster could do justice to her perfect blond hair or dazzling, intense blue eyes. She was determined to be a judge, and I knew what that meant—look out other people running for that position!

I *knew* she'd be here. Anabelle Chase was at *all* the important social functions around the city even before she began running for office. I knew because I was always with her, until I'd turned eighteen and had refused to go. That wasn't my kind of life at all.

"Zoe!" She air-kissed my cheek. "It's so *good* to see you home and in one piece."

"Thanks, Mom. How's the campaign going?"

"I think I'll be a judge by this fall." She walked up close to me. "That dress is a *little* short for you, don't you think?"

I looked at my hemline, which seemed reasonable to me. "No. I think it looks fine."

She tried a shrimp canapé. "You might want to toss that old thing out and reinvest in something nice if you're going to big parties like this one. I'll be glad to take you shopping if you're low on cash."

"Thanks." I loved how she always said these things in ways that were meant to undermine my confidence. Sometimes they still rankled. I knew she couldn't help it. My mother was competitive with everyone.

Not that I was going to let what she said bother me tonight. This was *my* night, my success. Oddly enough, the success she was so sure I would never achieve when I started my food truck.

"So the race ends tomorrow?" Her expressive eyes swept across the room to see who was there. "You've done very well. I hope you win, honey."

Like she even knows what that means. "Thanks, Mom."

Sam, her discreet assistant, came up close to us. He had a small camera—nothing too obvious. He was a nice man, as had been the other thirty or so personal assistants I could recall. There was a certain type my mother liked to work with.

"Hi, Zoe. Congratulations on doing so well in the race!"

"Thanks, Sam."

"Maybe you two could move in closer and hold your glasses up, like you're toasting something," he suggested in a quiet tone.

"Of course." My mother was almost jolly in her quest for a judgeship. "Zoe, honey?"

I moved in close, as Sam had suggested, and we even put our arms around each other.

He took several carefully considered shots and then stood back. "Maybe you should eat something, Anabelle. I could take pictures of you eating with your daughter."

My mother moved her arm away and her eyes narrowed. "Don't be absurd. I don't want pictures of me *eating food* in the media. Let's find Chef Art. I need some pictures with him."

"See you later." I waved as she walked away.

"Bye, Zoe," Sam said as she dragged him with her. "Good luck tomorrow!"

I thanked him but he was already gone. I took a deep breath, knowing my father would be around here, too.

He wasn't running for public office, but he liked to be seen with popular people. He was the president of the Bank of Mobile, a position that had been passed down through his family.

It would've been hard to find two brothers—him and Uncle Saul—that were more different.

I looked down at my phone when it buzzed. It was finally a text from Miguel.

I read it eagerly, but the news wasn't good. Miguel said he'd decided that he wanted to be with Tina and that he wasn't going to finish the race. He was sorry, but there was no point in letting me think he cared about me when he didn't.

What?

I read it again, thinking I may have mistaken his meaning.

That was it. And he'd *texted* me to say it. Not even a phone call.

THIRTY

I walked around like a zombie in the crowded rooms until I reached the front door again. I was exhausted, on the verge of tears, and ready to leave.

"Where are you going, Zoe?" Chef Art stopped me before I could walk outside.

"Home."

"Not yet. What about dinner? You won't even know what you're supposed to do tomorrow. I promise, it's gonna be *amazing.*"

I looked at him in his tiny black string tie and burst into tears. I was never particularly good at hiding my emotions. My mother had never been able to teach me that trick, though she'd tried hard enough.

"Good heavens!" Chef Art put his arm around my shoulders, and his burly bodyguard parted the crowd before us like Moses parting the Red Sea.

He led me to a small sitting room that was done in pretty shades of blue and white. I knew from a childhood of following my mother around to antique fairs that the furnishings looked shabby, but they were all very expensive.

"Now sit down and tell me about it." He handed me a clean, white handkerchief and sat back to light the biggest cigar I had ever seen.

I told him all about me and Miguel and trashed Tina. My words weren't pleasant but at least they were G-rated.

Someone knocked at the door. The bodyguard opened it and my dad walked in. He was dressed in his old tuxedo, the one I'd seen him wear dozens of times. The look on his face made me start crying again.

He came over and put his arms around me. "What in the world is wrong, Zoe?"

I sobbed into his white shirt and gave him the details. By that time, I was all cried out.

I had been stupid to think Miguel was interested in me as something besides a client. I was even more stupid to think he and Tina were only friends after the way she'd acted with him.

Why am I so darn naive?

My father sat down and held my hand. I had always thought he was a handsome man. Now he was very distinguished with his year-round tan and close-cut hair. While my mother had always pointed out the right and wrong way to do things, my father was my heart.

There was another knock on the door. I hoped this wasn't a cameraman who wanted to film my breakdown and hear my story again. The bodyguard opened the door, and Uncle Saul came in.

"I heard you all were in here," he said. "How are you doing, Chef Art? Hello, Ted! What's going on?"

"Tina and Miguel are together." I abbreviated the tale and took out the tears.

"Sorry, Zoe." He sat down, too. "I guess I should've spent time with you working on Miguel instead of helping Ollie with Delia."

I sniffed. "Although that worked. Did you see them together?"

I certainly didn't want my uncle giving me pointers on relationships.

My father admired Chef Art's big cigar. Chef Art gave him and my uncle cigars, too. They lit them, and the smoke filled the room. The three of them started talking about something going on in Mobile politics. I was completely forgotten.

That was okay. I wanted to get out of there. I was going to stay for dinner and get the race over with. I was going to win and never think of Miguel Alexander again.

I went out of the room and removed Miguel's number from my phone. I even took him out of my contact list. That was that.

Dinner was served shortly after. Chef Art had a huge dining room table. All the food truck personnel and sponsors fit around it. The room was big enough that the cameramen had plenty of space to walk around and take videos of us during the meal.

Chef Art welcomed all of us to his home. "I guarantee the meal I'm about to feed you will be a thousand times better than the meals we had on the road."

Everyone laughed. Chef Art's bodyguards closed the doors to the dining room while the party went on in the rest of the mansion.

"Still, I've had a great time. I can't wait to see how my Biscuit Bowl team does in the morning." He nodded to Patrick Ferris who stood up at his chair.

"Hello, foodies!" He sounded exactly as he had during the race, but with no microphone. "I know you're ready for the finale tomorrow. We're down to only two of you. Teams, please stand when I call your names."

Ollie, Uncle Saul, Delia, and I got to our feet as he announced the Biscuit Bowl. Bobbie and Allison stood up when he said Shut Up and Eat. The cameras zoomed around the table to get close-ups. We all waved and smiled, even Bobbie.

"We've got a tough day planned for these two teams tomorrow. Of course we'll begin at six A.M. in the heart of Mobile. I doubt if even the Spanish moss will be out that early."

He guffawed, and the rest of us laughed with him. Fleet-footed waiters began bringing in the first course of the meal, cream of celery soup.

"But you all are used to that, aren't you?" No one responded, and he moved on. "You'll be making your signature foods again tomorrow. This time, though, we're gonna tie you down a little. Bobbie and Zoe will stay with their respective trucks while the rest of you swap teams. The Biscuit Bowl team will be working as the team for Shut Up and Eat. The team for Shut Up and Eat will be making those great biscuit bowls. How's that for excitement?"

Ollie didn't like that idea at all. "I didn't sign on for that. I'm not helping another team win the money."

"That's not fair since we have three people in our team and Bobbie only has her daughter." Uncle Saul nodded to Bobbie's daughter. "No offense, young lady."

One of the producers, the quiet one who always seemed to have the last word, whispered something to Patrick.

"I guess we're going to allow one Biscuit Bowl team member to stay with Zoe Chase because of the difference in team size," Patrick announced. "Zoe, pick your favorite team member."

That was a no-win situation for me. All the cameras focused on my face. I had to look like I had shell shock. *How could I pick one person?* No matter who I picked, the others would be hurt.

I knew they were waiting for my reaction. "This really isn't fair. I can't pick one person on my team who's my favorite. I love them all, and I think this is a stupid way to end this race."

Patrick grinned. "Remember, we told you we'd have some tricks up our sleeves. Make your choice, Zoe, or forfeit to Shut Up and Eat."

Uncle Saul whispered to me, "Don't worry about me. We'll work out the savory filling between us. Choose Ollie or Delia."

Ollie again stated his position on how wrong this was. "What if we sabotage the other team so our team wins?"

"We've thought about that, Biscuit Bowl team member. If either team loses because of poor work performance, the fifty thousand dollars will be awarded to the other team, the one that *didn't* cheat."

Delia smiled at me and put her hand on mine. "Choose Ollie. I don't think he can handle it if you don't. I'll be fine. I *know* I'm your personal favorite."

I felt like my hands were tied. I knew from the look on Bobbie's face that she wasn't happy with the terms of the race tomorrow, either. Her daughter was equally stricken. She was just a kid. She probably had no idea what to do or say.

"All right." I got to my feet as the waiters were clearing the soup bowls. I hung onto mine. Cream of celery was my favorite and I wasn't finished. They weren't taking it away until I was done. "I'll choose Ollie. Not because he's my favorite, but because I don't want him to hurt you, Patrick."

Everyone around the table snickered at that remark. They couldn't disagree after comparing the two men.

Bobbie got to her feet, too. "That's fine. I agree with Zoe that this is a really bad idea, but we'll work through it. Let's race."

Everyone applauded. Patrick looked relieved. The sponsors sat back in their chairs, glad that their plan was moving ahead. Probably happy that the whole thing was almost over, too.

"And the second impossible, grueling aspect of tomorrow's

big finale." Patrick slowed down and savored the suspense he hoped he was creating as the salad course was brought in. "Each of the teams will be given the food they'll use to create their signature products tomorrow morning at the start of the Mobile challenge. So throw away all those ideas on what you *planned* to make."

Bobbie groaned and put a hand to her forehead.

"That's right," Patrick continued. "Our sponsors, Gemini Foods, Caldwell Meats, and North Star Food Products, have devised suitable menus for both our food trucks. You'll make the foods in your trucks as you have since Charlotte—I'll bet that seems like a long time ago to all of you."

Uncle Saul patted my hand. "It's not gonna matter. You can still win this thing, Zoe."

There was a bevy of prizes for the loser of the contest tomorrow. Of course, we both had our eye on the big prize. No one wanted to be the loser.

Bobbie sat several places up from me at the long table. I wondered what she had in mind to do with the money if *she* won. We hadn't really talked despite spending a lot of time together the past few days.

I knew it wasn't a good idea to start questioning if she deserved to win more than me, I realized as I finished my soup—*delicious*—and had to hold onto my arugula and peach salad so the waiters wouldn't take that plate away.

Chef Art's food was wonderful. His service left something to be desired.

The rest of the meal went without disruption. The main course was pasta with white dill sauce, vegetables, and fish. A small salmon pâté followed. Dessert was a surprise cherries jubilee. The flaming dish was brought into the always excited *oohs* and *aahs* of the appreciative diners.

Nothing says excitement like food that's on fire. I'd have to remember that for my own restaurant.

Like the old-time Southern tradition, some of the men retired to their cigars and brandy in the library. The big difference was that the women retired to the garden behind the mansion for cocktails.

I found myself in the lighted garden seated beside Bobbie Shields. The sound of the water cascading into the beautiful, clear pool was a perfect foil for the perfumed blossoms that filled the night around us.

"You know my little girl won't mess you up tomorrow, right?" Bobbie was frank and to the point, like always. "She's not that way."

"Of course. Delia and my uncle won't do that to you, either."

She grinned up at me after a long pull from her whiskey sour. "I didn't know that tall fella was your uncle."

"Yes. He used to be in the restaurant business. I'm sure he'll do a good job for you."

She nodded and lit up a cigarette. "What about that other fella with the tattoo? Will my baby be safe with him? I suppose you'll send the two of them out to sell your biscuits."

"She'll be fine."

"What happened to your outrider? I didn't see him tonight." She grinned at me. "He's a good-looking fella. I wish he was coming with *me* tomorrow. He's my type."

"That's Miguel." I bit my lip to keep from saying something I might regret later. "He had to go back to work. He's a lawyer here in Mobile."

She whistled. "How'd you get him to hang around like that?"

"Oh, he wasn't very busy. This is his slow season."

"That's funny." She blew smoke into the air above her. "Either you're blind or crazy if you think that. I never met a lawyer who'd give up billable hours to follow a food truck race and run for supplies. That fella is sweet on you, isn't he?"

I laced my fingers together and pulled them apart again. I'd thought I was through with talking about Miguel. The universe was against me.

"He's with someone," I explained.

"Yeah. *You.* I'm telling you, he wouldn't have gone through this stupid race with you if he was taken by any other woman. You can believe it or not."

I didn't respond. I didn't want to talk about it anymore. The garden was beautiful around us. A few of the guests had decided to strip down to their underwear and get in the pool.

"What are you gonna do if you win the race tomorrow?" I asked the question I'd promised myself I wouldn't ask.

She finished her whiskey and put out her cigarette in the empty glass.

Eww.

"I'm gonna send my daughter to college. She'll be the first one in our family to ever graduate past high school. How about you?"

"I'm going to remodel my diner into a world-class restaurant that people come to from all over to eat my food."

"Sounds like we both have big dreams." She shook my hand and got to her feet. "Good luck tomorrow, Biscuit Bowl."

I laughed. "You, too, Shut Up and Eat."

I could hear her smoker's wheezing laugh for a few minutes as she walked back toward the mansion.

"Hey, Zoe!" Delia called from the pool. "Why don't you come in, too?"

"I don't think so. Thanks anyway. I have somewhere I have to be."

"Going to find Miguel?" she asked.

"You got it."

"You go, sister."

I stalked back to the mansion as I called Cole. I went in front to wait by the circle drive. Uncle Saul was out there, still smoking his big cigar. He moved over on the bench where he was sitting so I could join him.

"Leaving so soon?" he asked. "Not inclined to jump in the pool?"

"No. Not now. I'm mad, and I need closure."

He nodded. "Going to talk to Miguel?"

"Yes. He owes me an explanation. I'm all done crying. I want to know why he led me on."

"That's the spirit."

"If I pushed him into acting like he wanted to be with me when he really didn't want to, all he had to do was say something. I thought I was very careful since I knew about his dead wife. Maybe I was wrong."

"I think—"

"What do you think?" I turned to him. "Did I seem too pushy? Maybe he wasn't ready."

"Since he's dating Tina—"

"That's *exactly* what I mean. If he wants to be with her, that's fine. He shouldn't have acted like he wanted to be with *me*. At least he could've called me and not left me hanging."

"Yes."

Cole arrived a moment later. Uncle Saul held the door open for me. "Okay. Don't do anything *too* crazy. I don't want to see you get kicked out of the race."

I hugged him. "I won't. I'll see you in the morning."

THIRTY-ONE

I gave Cole the address of Miguel's office. I figured Miguel might still be there trying to get caught up with his work. *Or with Tina.*

Traffic wasn't too bad getting across town. It seemed to go even faster when I suddenly got cold feet.

"What am I going to say to him?" I asked Cole after filling him in on what had happened. "If he doesn't want to be with me, he doesn't want to be with me."

He shrugged. "Sometimes you have to hear it from the horse's mouth, I guess."

"I feel stupid. I should probably just go home."

But that didn't sit well, either. I had a powerful need to see Miguel's face and look into his eyes as he told me that he loved Tina. I had a sense about these things, or at least I always thought I did. That sense was telling me that Miguel had been genuine with me while we'd been gone.

Or were my emotions clouding my judgment?

We got to Miguel's legal office, which was located in a

run-down building in a bad part of town. The lights were still on inside. I sighed as I looked up at the building.

"Maybe this isn't such a good idea."

"You'll never know if you don't go in," he said. "You'll wonder about this moment the rest of your life. Want me to come with you?"

I smiled at Cole's words of wisdom, and his offer of help. How could I turn away now? I had to go through with it.

"Thanks. Will you wait for me here?"

"I got nowhere else to be, Zoe. You take your time."

I thought about the old days when knights and soldiers put on their armor and went off to war. That's how I felt. I wished there were some magical armor that could protect my poor heart, but it was only me and my silly desire to make Miguel tell me to my face that he didn't want to be with me.

I went inside. Miguel's office was on the second floor. I took a deep breath and went up the stairs to give myself time to decide what I'd say to him. Even by the time I got there, I wasn't sure. I hoped to be inspired when I saw his face.

The office door was open. I walked in, but there was no sign of Miguel. There were only two rooms in the office. He was gone, but his cell phone was on his desk. All the lights were on. The desk phone was off the hook. A weird voice kept telling me what to do if I wanted to make a call.

Nothing looked out of place besides that. Maybe he'd gone home.

I was about to leave when I noticed a small amount of blood on the carpet near the front of the desk. Examining it closely, I could see the blood was fresh. It was still pooling on top of the carpet fibers—still time to clean it without staining.

There was something under the desk, too. I used a pen from Miguel's desk to pull it out. It was an empty pack of Marlboro cigarettes.

Marsh! Detective Marsh had been there.

Why had he been there?

A terrible thought crossed my mind.

Was it Marsh from the beginning? Was he the one who'd killed McSwain because he'd asked questions about Alex's partner in crime? Had he been the one who'd killed Alex, too?

I took out my cell phone and used it to speed dial Patti Latoure. I was shaking with fear and hoping nothing horrible had happened to Miguel.

Patti finally answered after a few tries. "Zoe. We were just talking about you."

"*We?*" My heart was pounding, hoping Miguel was with her.

"Detective Macey Helms came down from Birmingham. She has some interesting information."

"Can it wait a few minutes?" I kind of cut her off. "Miguel Alexander may be missing. I think Detective Marsh from Charlotte might be responsible for the things that went on during the food truck race."

Patti chuckled. "Funny you should say that. Macey was telling me her story about her partner shooting her right after she saw him kissing Tina Gerard."

"Kissing Tina? She's involved in this, too?"

"It seems that way. Where are you?"

I skimmed over the reason I'd come to look for Miguel and told her what I'd found at his office. "Could you look up Miguel's home address and meet me there? Maybe you could put out an APB, or whatever you call it, for his Mercedes. I don't think it's here. Tina and Marsh may have hurt Miguel."

"Take it easy, Zoe. Calm down. I'll look up Miguel's home address—although I would've thought it was something you already had. It's possible nothing has happened to him. He might not even know those two are the real culprits."

I waited impatiently for her to find his address. My fingernails tapped on the backside of my phone. I had a bad feeling about this.

"Here's his address. It's only a few blocks from where you are," she said. "But don't meet me there. You stay where you are. I'll let you know if anything is going on over there."

Like that was going to happen.

I wrote down Miguel's address. The minute I was off the phone with Patti, I ran out of the office and into the street.

"What's going on?" Cole asked as I got back in the taxi.

"I'll tell you on the way," I answered as I dialed Uncle Saul's cell phone number.

Cole raced to the address I gave him. Miguel lived in a small apartment building that was mostly covered by hanging moss from a few large live oaks. Huge, old azalea bushes obscured the front windows.

The Mercedes wasn't there, either. There were no lights on inside.

Cole got out with me this time, grabbing a baseball bat he kept under his seat. We searched the mail slots. There were four apartments. Miguel's was on the second floor.

I tried the buzzer over and over again. Either he wasn't there or couldn't answer. Both answers were bad in my mind.

"We should try to get someone else down here to open the door," Cole said.

I reasoned with a man on the first floor who answered his buzzer. I told him that we thought Miguel could be in danger. The man, dressed only in his underwear, finally came and opened the door for us. I could hear sirens in the distance. Patti wasn't far behind us.

We ran up to the second floor. The building was a little shabby, but you could see this had been a nice place at one time. I wondered if Miguel had lived here with Caroline, or if they'd had a house that he'd sold.

Thousands of crazy thoughts raced through my mind as we reached the door to Miguel's apartment.

"I can knock it down with my bat," Cole enthusiastically volunteered.

"You might break your arm before you break it in." I held him back.

"So what do we do?"

Patti was coming up the stairs with two uniformed officers. "Zoe, didn't I tell you to *stay* where you were? What part of that didn't you understand?"

I ran and hugged her, tears in my eyes. "I'm so glad to see you. I think they did something with Miguel. I don't think he's here, either."

She hugged me back, a little stiffly, but I didn't care. I was really happy to see her.

"You're determined to get into trouble, aren't you? You have to leave the police work to the police. Let's get someone to open this door for us."

She roused the building manager. By that time, Macey Helms was up there, too. She was moving very slowly, painfully, to join us.

"Hello, Zoe." Her arm was in a sling, and she was very pale. "I hope Miguel is all right. I understand we both came to the same conclusion about Tina and my partner."

"I guess so," I answered. "It occurred to me on the way home from Birmingham that Tina could've been setting up everything to cover Alex's murder. She had a lot to gain."

She nodded and winced. "I don't think she realized that paying Miguel that money and meeting with him would throw her onto our radar. On the other hand, when Miguel looked innocent of any wrongdoing, so did she. What can I tell you? Bad guys do stupid things sometimes. I'm glad it works that way for our sake."

"How did she and Detective Marsh get involved?"

"I don't know yet. Right now, we're working on the assumption that Marsh probably killed McSwain because McSwain started looking too close. He may have killed your friend, Reggie, as a decoy for what he was about to do to Alex."

The more she talked about what Tina and Marsh were

willing to do to kill Alex, the more anxious I became about
Miguel.

The apartment was small. The officers who were searching it came back only a few minutes later. Miguel wasn't
there. There was no sign of a struggle.

Patti sent them over to take a look at the office. "I don't
want to make a big deal out of Miguel's disappearance and
find out he was out all night with a client and hasn't thought
about anything else."

Helms agreed with her. "We definitely don't want to lose
Marsh and Tina."

"I have everyone looking for the Mercedes, but if they
took Miguel's vehicle, the chances are they've ditched it.
They could already be out of Mobile."

"Can't you call the FBI or something?" I asked.

"It doesn't work like that, Zoe," Patti said. "We have to
take care of this one step at a time. We'll find Marsh and
Gerard, and we'll figure out where Miguel is. Just take a deep
breath and go on home. We'll call if we hear anything."

I thanked her again for her help. Ollie, Delia, and Uncle
Saul were there, waiting downstairs with Cole. One of the
old churches nearby was chiming midnight. The air was hot
and sultry with a little hint of rain that might have been
coming from Mobile Bay.

"Now what?" Cole put away his baseball bat.

"It's Zoe's call." Uncle Saul hugged me. "I have a feeling
we're not going home yet."

There was no doubt in my mind that I wasn't waiting at
home for news. I pieced together a plan that I thought might
work and told them what I thought we should do.

"Uncle Saul, you have a lot of friends around the city that
you could call. Ollie, let's go back to the shelter and see if
we can find anyone who will help us search. Mobile is our
home. Marsh and Tina don't know it like we do. Let's find
Miguel."

THIRTY-TWO

Uncle Saul called all of his old buddies and gave them a description of Miguel and the Mercedes. When I told Chef Art what had happened, he volunteered all of his security guards to help us search as well. They had SUVs, which was good since none of the rest of us had cars. I didn't want to drive the Biscuit Bowl all over town searching for Miguel if I didn't have to.

"This is developing into a large search party," Uncle Saul said. "Maybe the four of us should split up and go with each of the teams. We actually know what Miguel and his car look like. It might save a lot of wrong guesses."

"That's a good idea," I agreed.

"Yeah!" Ollie seconded me. "I've always wanted to ride in a big black SUV with a bunch of security guards. Do I get a gun?"

"We're only looking for someone," Delia reminded him, her hand on his chest. "We're not shooting anyone—at least not *yet*."

He pouted but went along with the plan.

I stayed with Cole in the taxi. I had the feeling that he'd know Mobile better than the security people Chef Art had employed. He'd know the areas where someone might be liable to dump a car or a person. The security guards basically knew the area Chef Art needed them to know.

At least those were my thoughts at the time.

Cole had a cell phone to keep in contact, so I gave my cell phone to Ollie, who didn't have one. Delia and Uncle Saul had their own phones. The security guards probably had phones, and radios, too, but I wanted to stay in touch with my team, not them.

"Where are we going first, Zoe?" Cole asked as everyone got into their vehicles and started their engines.

"I think we should check down by the docks. What do you think?"

He nodded. "I'm with you. Lots of places to hide bodies down there."

I let out a little squeal even thinking that Miguel might be a "body."

"Oh. Sorry. I didn't mean just bodies. Did I say that? No, people hide all sorts of stuff down that way." He shook his head and started the taxi. "Never mind. I've never been good with words."

We drove slowly through the dark city. There were some bars and nightclubs still open, but mostly Mobile wasn't a party town—except during carnival. There weren't a lot of people on the street. Traffic was light.

I wished we had a big searchlight mounted on the side of the taxi. Some of the areas were too dark to see into the nooks and crannies. Waiting until morning might have been better. But there was no guarantee that we'd be able to find Miguel alive if we waited.

I got a call from Patti, relayed by Ollie to Cole's phone. A police officer had stopped at a convenience store for a soda. He thought he might have recognized Tina and Marsh.

"He said they were driving an old blue Mustang. He had the license number. The police are following up on that," Patti told me.

"Any word on Miguel or the Mercedes?" Not to be ungrateful for the update, but I was a lot more concerned about Miguel than what happened to Tina and Marsh.

"I have dozens of officers checking the city," she replied. "We'll find him, Zoe."

"Thanks."

"Why is Ollie answering your phone?"

"He didn't have one. I tried to spread the phones out so everyone had one. Chef Art's men had their own."

"Chef Art Arrington? What does he have to do with this?"

I quickly explained that we thought we'd stand a better chance with Chef Art's security team if each group had someone who could recognize Miguel.

I thought she might be annoyed that we'd set out on our own. Instead she laughed. "Probably a good idea. But this conversation never happened, understand?"

I agreed and thanked Cole for the use of his phone. We were driving very slowly through some terrible neighborhoods once we got close to the docks.

During the day, these areas were populated with snack food vendors and antique dealers trying to make a quick buck from the cruise ship passengers getting on and off the big ships.

I had brought the Biscuit Bowl down here a few times, but the money wasn't as good here as it was by police headquarters, the courthouse, and other areas farther into the business district of the city.

"It's dark as blackstrap molasses down here." Cole squinted into the blackness. He had his window open as we cruised slowly by the warehouses and port offices.

"If you were going to dump a car"—I swallowed hard on the word *dump*—"where would you do it?"

He thought about it a few minutes before answering. "I'd

take it down near the cruise ship berths. People work down there twenty-four-seven now with the ships going in and out all the time. Who'd notice another car?"

"And a dead body?" My voice trembled as I asked.

He shrugged. "The bay. That's always been the best place to get rid of someone."

I pulled myself together and assured myself that Miguel wasn't dead. We needed to find his car, and that would lead us to him.

"Okay. Let's check out those parking areas."

Cole was right about a lot of cars being parked down there. It was impossible to simply scan the parking lots and decide if a black Mercedes was there. We had to drive slowly between the rows of vehicles and check each one.

It was taking forever, and I was getting impatient. It had already been an *hour* since we'd split up. Anything could happen in an hour.

At least there were streetlights. Their weird orange glow made everything look like something out of a horror movie. At each turn, I looked for zombies or some other supernatural creatures.

I could tell Cole was uncomfortable, too, despite his nonchalant demeanor. He slowly closed his window and peered out from behind its meager protection.

"Look there!" I pointed to a black Mercedes. "I think that could be Miguel's car!"

Cole pulled over close to it, slowly and carefully. I compared the license plate—there were no other distinguishing marks—and knew that it was the right one.

"We should call everyone," he said. "We shouldn't try to do this alone, Zoe."

"But what if he needs us before everyone else can get here?" I was already getting out of the car.

"Okay. I'll call Saul. He can call everyone else. At least wait for me."

I ran toward the Mercedes.

The car was locked. I wasn't sure how we were going to get inside it. I looked at the trunk. How many times had I seen dead bodies stuffed in trunks in the movies and on TV?

"Do you think the tire iron can open the trunk?" I asked Cole when he finally caught up.

He was glancing around the parking lot with a baleful eye. "Probably. Yes. But your Miguel won't like it if we pry it open. Best to wait for the cops."

"Give me the tire iron. I'll open it."

He argued with me for a few minutes, but it was half-hearted. He didn't want to use the tire iron on the trunk, but he really didn't care if I did it. He finally handed it to me and stood back.

Before I could use it, Cole's cell phone rang. He answered it in a low tone and then handed it to me.

It was Ollie. "If you find the car, I saw Miguel take a key out of a magnetic case once when he was representing me. It's next to the front driver's side, under the car."

I gave the tire iron, and the phone, back to Cole. I felt a little out of the loop—I didn't know Miguel's home address or that he kept a key under his car.

I had to remind myself that we were just starting our relationship. I'd learn these things as we went along. He knew so much more about me than I knew about him. It was the basic difference in our personalities. If you knew me for five minutes, you knew everything about me. Miguel was harder to know.

All these stupid things raced through my mind as I used my hand to search for the key under the car. The orange lights above us made me feel like I was in a bad science fiction movie.

The parking lot was gritty and wet under my knees. The smell of the bay was strong, mixed with the smell of the fuel they used for the ships. I was weirdly cold, even though the night was hot and humid.

Cole and I walked back to the trunk. I was reluctant to

use the key I'd found, even though I'd been willing to pry it open only a few minutes before. Part of me hoped Miguel was there. The other part of me said this could be a very bad thing.

Two black SUVs pulled up, along with a Mobile police car. The siren wasn't on, but the blue lights on top were flashing.

"Open it," Cole urged me. "If he's still alive, he might need help right away."

I nodded and popped open the trunk, holding my breath.

I could see it wasn't empty. There was a dim trunk light that faintly illuminated the space. Something was in there, wrapped in a tarp.

I reached my hand down and rolled it over. *Please don't be dead!*

It was Miguel—and Tina. Their hands and feet were duct-taped together, and there was tape on their mouths.

My heart stopped beating. I could barely breathe. I put my hand on Miguel's chest. He was alive—unconscious, but alive.

"Get me an ambulance out here!" Patti shot back to one of her uniformed officers.

I hadn't even noticed she was there.

"Step aside, Zoe. Let us get them out."

- - - - - - -

They pulled Miguel and Tina carefully out of the trunk and untaped them. Neither one of them was moving. The paramedics examined them, slowly removing the tape from their mouths.

"Looks like someone hit him on the head," the lead paramedic said. "He's out of it, but he'll probably be fine. They'll want to do some tests on him at the hospital to be sure."

"But he'll wake up, right?" I asked.

"He should. It's a good thing you found him out here. The heat tomorrow could've finished him off."

Tina was alive, too. She'd been strangled. There were terrible bruises on her throat.

They took Miguel away on a stretcher and put him in the back of the ambulance. I watched the vehicle speed away out of the parking lot and up the street until I couldn't see it anymore.

A second ambulance was pulling into the lot for Tina.

"Thank God!" Uncle Saul wrapped his arms around me. "What kind of person leaves someone in a trunk to die?"

"The kind that already murdered at least three other people," Patti said. "Marsh must've run out of bullets or we'd probably be calling the coroner now."

"Have you heard anything else about the Marsh sighting?" I asked her.

"No. I've been too busy fielding calls from dozens of people across the city who thought they'd found Miguel. I don't know whose network that was, but I'd appreciate it if they'd call them off now."

Delia and Uncle Saul both got on their phones right away. Ollie high-fived a small group of his friends from the homeless shelter who were in the parking lot with him.

"It's four A.M." Uncle Saul glanced at his watch. "I don't think there's much point in going to bed now. We'll have to be up in another hour or so."

I agreed with him, even though I yawned as I did it. "I'd like to go to the hospital until we either hear something about Miguel or we have to get the Biscuit Bowl for the race."

Ollie and Uncle Saul agreed. Delia decided to go back with Chef Art's security team and take a shower before she had to work.

"Don't worry, Zoe." Detective Helms looked exhausted in the orange light. "We're gonna find Marsh. He'll pay for what he's done."

Truly, that thought hadn't crossed my mind. I suppose it should have, but all I could think about was being there when Miguel woke up.

Uncle Saul and Ollie jumped in the taxi with me, and Cole took off. The police would be sending a crime scene

crew out to gather evidence from the Mercedes. I'd given
the key to Patti so they could work on it. I wasn't sure what
they hoped to find. It was obvious what had happened. But
I didn't want to keep her from doing her job.

We got to the hospital in record time. It looked like a
slow night for them. Orderlies jumped up when they saw us
come through the emergency entrance and then sat back
down when there was nothing to do.

I asked about Miguel at the window.

A surprisingly nice nurse told us they were still examining him. "I'll send someone out to talk to you when they're
finished. Take a seat and have some coffee. We have some
donuts, too. One of the local bakeries donates them to us."

I couldn't eat, but the coffee was good. The waiting room
was empty except for the four of us. The seats were uphol-
stered and comfortable. I could almost forget I was in a
hospital, except for the smell of antiseptic.

I think I'd gone to sleep for a few moments, leaning my
head against Uncle Saul's shoulder, when a doctor finally
came out and talked to us.

"Mr. Alexander is going to be fine. No lasting injuries
from his ordeal. He's a little dehydrated but conscious now.
If you'd like to see him for a few minutes, that would be
fine. Follow me."

Cole stayed behind, even though we'd encouraged him
to come, too. "I don't know Miguel. You go. I can shake his
hand later when he gets out of here." He helped himself to
another donut and sat down to watch TV.

Uncle Saul, Ollie, and I followed the doctor in blue scrubs
down the hallway. He opened the door to a room, and we
awkwardly went in.

There was Miguel—pale and wearing a hospital gown,
his black hair mussed. There were dark circles under his
eyes and a cut by his mouth. But he was smiling at us.

"I don't know how to thank you for what you've done."

I had decided I would be cool. I wouldn't get overemotional. Then his voice cracked as he was thanking us. That was it. I ran and threw myself at him, crying all over his hospital gown.

"It's okay, Zoe." He held my hand and smiled at me. "I'm going to be fine."

"You didn't look very *fine* in that trunk." I sobbed. "Don't *ever* do that again."

THIRTY-THREE

Ollie laughed. "I think you look pretty good for someone who let a *cop* knock him out and stuff him in the trunk of his own car."

Uncle Saul agreed. "What happened, Miguel? How did he get the drop on you?"

Miguel was a little fuzzy on the exact details, but he knew what the end result was.

"I was working at my office and looked up. There were Detective Marsh and Tina. I thought he wanted to interview us again. I got up and walked across the room to talk to him. Tina called out a warning. I glanced her way, and something hit me hard in the back of the head. I woke up here."

"I guess he didn't like that Tina tried to warn you, huh? That's why she ended up in the back of the car with you. She must have a soft spot for you." Ollie continued to joke about the incident. "What do you think Marsh hit you with?"

"I'm not sure. The police probably know."

"You're lucky he didn't shoot you," Uncle Saul said. "He must have a soft spot for you."

"I'm not sure how much better it would've been to die in the trunk of my car."

"Marsh even texted me from your phone at the party to tell me that you didn't want to see me again," I told him. "He pretended to be you and tried to convince me that you and Tina were together."

He took my hand. "I'm sorry, Zoe."

Ollie chuckled. "Yeah. You were lucky *Zoe* didn't have a gun."

"You didn't believe him, did you?" Miguel ignored Ollie.

"No. Of course not." I stared at Ollie, daring him to disagree. "That's why I came looking for you. I knew something was wrong."

I hoped Ollie would drop the subject. We talked with Miguel for a few more minutes before the nurse asked us to leave, saying that he needed to rest.

I waited until everyone else was gone, and then I hugged Miguel and carefully kissed him.

"I'm sorry I'll miss the last part of the race. I'm sure you'll win. Be careful. We still don't know what Marsh is up to."

"I will. You stay here and get well. As soon as you get out, we'll have a big celebration dinner."

He smiled. "That's great. Let's start planning to have a *real* date, just the two of us. As much as I love your friends, I'd enjoy spending some time alone with you."

I kissed him again for thinking exactly what I had been thinking. The nurse threatened to have me removed. I told Miguel good night, and the nurse watched until I had reached the elevator.

"How is Tina Gerard doing?" I asked as an afterthought, feeling a little guilty.

"She'll live." The nurse's tone was exasperated. "Go home."

Ollie and Uncle Saul were waiting with Cole at the taxi when I reached the street.

"I guess it's too late now to do much of anything." I sighed, happy to know that Miguel was all right.

Uncle Saul looked at his watch. "It's four thirty. I think we can get breakfast and pick up the Biscuit Bowl before we head over to the meeting place. It's good that we didn't have to buy supplies. The contest would've been over before it even got started."

I agreed with him.

We stopped at a fast-food place for breakfast. Not the best, but all we had time for. I bought breakfast for Cole, who'd been such a big help in finding Miguel.

Uncle Saul gave him money for gas, overruling me when I complained that I should be the one to pay for it.

"Tomorrow, after you've won all that cash, you can take us out somewhere special," he promised. "Today, you just hold on to your money."

I hugged him, and we went to get the food truck.

Cole watched us load up, waiting by his taxi in the parking lot of the old shopping center. "I hope you win today, Zoe. I'll be there to cheer you on. See you later, Saul. You, too, Ollie."

"What are we doing about Delia?" Ollie asked. "Should we go and get her?"

"Sorry. I got a text from her earlier." I'd forgotten to tell him. "She's meeting us there. One of the security men is bringing her."

Ollie wasn't thrilled about that. "I can see dating a woman like Delia is gonna be rough."

Uncle Saul laughed and clapped him on the shoulder before getting into the Biscuit Bowl. "You have no idea. Best get out now while you still can."

"No way. You know how long it's been since I dated anyone?"

"Ollie, you're not that old," Uncle Saul said. "If you won't walk away, be ready for heartbreak."

He got in beside Ollie, and I put Crème Brûlée in his lap.

"Why are you bringing the cat now?" Ollie asked.

"For good luck. He got us this far." I smiled and kissed Crème Brûlée's head.

"I don't think it was the *cat*!"

I got in the food truck and started the engine, humming to myself as we approached the downtown area where I might have been anyway on a normal Friday morning. It was good to be home.

Everyone was still getting set up when we arrived. The producer's assistant pointed to the area where we should park. The cool-down tent and stage weren't even up yet. Shut Up and Eat was parked in front of us.

I was surprised to see a few of the other food trucks that had been left behind in the race.

"I guess we'll help you get set up until they tell us to switch," Uncle Saul said, observing the situation on the street.

"Sounds like a good idea," Ollie agreed.

Antonio Stephanopoulos stopped by after I opened the back door. "Just wanted to say good luck today."

"You brought your Pizza Papa food truck all the way down here?" I couldn't believe he did that to cheer us on.

He shrugged. "They offered us another spot on the program, and a thousand dollars, to come down here for the last day. I thought, why not?"

"Thanks for stopping by. I'll see you later."

"Why would they pay the losers to come back?" Ollie asked when he was gone.

"To fill out the crowd and make the pictures better." Chef Art surprised us as he walked into the food truck. "You all play fair today, and win the race. Make sure you wear your hats, especially *you*, Zoe, when they present you with the prize money."

We all promised to wear the poufy chef hats he'd given us. I was glad it was the last day I'd have to wear it. Wearing hats made my curls cranky after a while. The hat looked like a big billowy cloud on my head that morning. Not a good look for photos, but it would have to do.

Only a few minutes later, one of the producer's assistants told us to come to the stage. Everything was set up and ready to go in the kitchen. I knew that was going to be helpful once I'd lost Uncle Saul to the other food truck.

I hoped I'd chosen the right assistant.

"Okay. I guess we're ready. Let's head over." I hugged Uncle Saul. "I'm going to miss you today."

"Cheer up," he said. "At least it's almost over."

Delia was waiting outside the food truck. She was wearing baggy jeans and an old orange sweatshirt that did absolutely nothing for her.

"You dressed down for me, didn't you?" I grinned.

"They can tell us what we have to do, but no one said anything about how we should *dress*. You'll have the cute daughter to sell product. Bobbie will either have me or Saul."

I hugged her. "Good thinking."

"My pleasure." She went to Ollie's side and held his hand as we crossed the street.

It was still a little misty outside. Not raining, at least not yet. Hopefully that wouldn't happen.

Delia's trick made me wonder if Bobbie and her daughter hadn't come up with something similar to make it harder for us that day. Just making the rule that team members couldn't openly hurt the other team's chances wasn't enough to stop some creative treachery.

The sound stage was up. Patrick Ferris was there with his microphone. Two of the assistants were struggling with the lighted board while the pretty young women, in shorts and tank tops today, waited on stage, playing with their hair.

It seemed pointless to have the board since there were only two teams. Maybe it was more for the TV viewers than for us.

I saw three other food trucks parked on the street. Grinch's Ganache was there along with Chooey's Sooey and Stick It Here. Their team members were out in front of the stage with us, which made for a bigger crowd there, too.

There was also a large crowd of people from Mobile standing outside the roped-off area, probably hoping to get on television. The cameramen were up and moving around, changing their focus as the challenge was about to start.

"Good morning, foodies!" Patrick started with his usual morning greeting.

The applause was much stronger with the other food truck teams there. The people behind the rope yelled and applauded as one of the producers prompted them.

I looked at Bobbie, who was standing next to me. I put out my hand to her. "Good luck, today. I'll take good care of your daughter."

Bobbie shook my hand. "And I'll take good care of your crew. Good luck, Zoe. May the best food truck win."

One of the cameramen who caught the last of our conversation swooped in a moment too late to record anything. "Could you do that last bit again?"

I glanced at Bobbie.

She frowned and shook her head. "I don't think so."

"These small moments are important, too." He tried to persuade us.

"I think we're about to get started," Bobbie said. "Catch us later."

He shrugged and moved away.

"So we're down to the last two food trucks in the Sweet Magnolia Food Truck Race. It looks like it's going to be a good morning in Mobile, Alabama, for one lucky food truck owner. We're all excited to see who that will be."

There was more applause and some wolf whistles. The crowd was excited and ready to go.

"As we discussed last night, the Biscuit Bowl will be giving up two team members to Shut Up and Eat. Since Shut

Up and Eat only has two team members, they will give one team member to the Biscuit Bowl. Team members—switch to your new team."

Allison came to stand between me and Ollie. Delia and Uncle Saul went with Bobbie.

"That's right," Patrick said. "It's the big switcheroo. It's not going to be easy to win the race with newbies on your team."

Everyone else applauded, but I noticed that Bobbie didn't. Neither did I. And Allison, Bobbie's daughter, was dressed down like Delia in a baggy T-shirt and jeans.

"Now for the second part of the Mobile challenge. Food is being delivered to your kitchens as we speak. You'll see your menus when you get back. These are in keeping with the food you've served throughout the race. Your primary food menu will stay the same."

"How much money do we have to make?" Bobbie asked.

"I'm glad you brought that up," Patrick answered. "Each team will have to sell one hundred and fifty of their basic menu items. That's pieces, not dollars, so there will be no tie breaking because you've equaled each other. Whoever sells that one hundred and fifty items first is the winner. Are we ready to go?"

Again there was applause and people screaming out Patrick's name as well as the names of the two food trucks.

"I can hear our name! It's louder than Shut Up and Eat," Ollie said. "We're home!"

The two girls on stage turned on the electronic board. It went completely blank (as usual) and refused to come up again.

Patrick shook his head. "Never mind. You guys get started."

THIRTY-FOUR

"Should I send her out to sell biscuit bowls?" I asked Ollie when Allison was walking in front of us.

"I don't think so. Keep your friends close and your enemies closer," he said. "I'll go out. You keep her with you, and keep her busy."

I took his advice. It was what I'd been thinking, too. We got back to the truck and looked for our menu.

I read the printed card. "Carrot, raisin, and apple compote for the sweet, and barbecue chicken for savory."

"Who eats *carrots* for something sweet?" Ollie's expression said that he didn't.

"I guess whoever buys our biscuit bowls today." I set Allison to shredding carrots. It was the only way I could imagine using them for something sweet with apples and raisins.

"I'm sure Bobbie is having the same problem," I told Ollie.

"I could check and see what Mom is doing," Allison offered.

"No. That's okay. Let's get our stuff ready. Finding out what they're doing doesn't really matter."

Ollie started stewing the apples and raisins. I started making biscuits. At least I knew how many we had to have to win. The barbecue chicken was already cooked. It just needed to be warmed before it went into the biscuit bowl. That was a plus.

"I think the carrot shredder is broken." My new crew member held up the broken article. "Mom has one. I could go borrow it."

"We'll have to do without," I told her. "There's no borrowing, remember? You have to do with what you have."

Was this going to be Allison's agenda? Was she constantly going to volunteer to go back to her own food truck and annoy me to death?

I tried to be charitable—she *was* a teenager trapped into working with strangers. Maybe she was nervous. None of us had set out to do it this way, but Uncle Saul and Delia were older. They had the maturity to deal with situations that she might not have.

"This is looking good," Ollie said of the apple and raisin mixture. "Want me to add some cinnamon?"

"Oh. Let me!" Allison grabbed the cinnamon and dropped the whole container on the floor. "I'm so sorry. I didn't mean to do that."

I wasn't sure if I believed her or not, but I had no plans to turn her in for refusing to cooperate so I could win the race that way. We could work around her.

I grabbed an extra can of cinnamon from the cabinet above my head. "Use this, Ollie."

With the first tray of biscuits in the little oven and the fryer getting hot, I made some quick white icing to drizzle over the sweet biscuit bowls. Almost anything tasted good with white icing.

"I have these carrots shredded," Allison said. "Where do you want me to put them?"

"Let me have them over here," Ollie said. "What's that red stuff all over them?"

Allison looked at her hand. "I guess I cut myself. Sorry. I'll wash off the carrots."

"I don't think so," I intervened. "We're not using carrots with blood washed off of them. Go and find me a producer's assistant so we can ask what we should do without the carrots."

She agreed and ran out of the food truck.

"That's the last we'll see of her." Ollie shook his head. "She's a devious little thing."

"We had to expect *something* from her. She's working against her mother."

"We should turn her in."

"Do you want to win like that?"

He thought about it. "Sure."

"I don't want to. We can win on our own."

I was putting in a new tray of biscuits, wondering how to deal with the problem of not using the carrots, when I felt someone else come into the food truck. With my head down, it was hard to see around Ollie.

I looked up, about to think better of Allison for coming back, but she wasn't there.

It was Detective Marsh.

"What are you doing here?" I tried to make a quick detour between getting food ready and finding him there with us.

"I think we'll find the killer here today. This is the end of the food truck race."

Ollie snorted. "Right. Miguel is conscious. We *know* what happened. You might as well turn yourself in. Otherwise we'll call Zoe's friend in the police department. She'll know what to do with you."

I wiped my hands on a towel. "Ollie's right, Marsh.

Everyone knows the truth about you. We're guessing you were paid to kill Tina. Everything else was to cover that up. You'll have to leave now. We're trying to get ready for the race."

"*The race.*" He spat back at me. "This whole race thing was a big, stupid mistake. It should have been a perfect setup. Alex was going to pay me Reggie's money plus two hundred thousand to kill his wife."

"Reggie? He was supposed to kill Tina?"

"He didn't know what he was doing. Alex didn't, either."

I was tired of hearing his confession, and wondered how we could alert the police. He pulled out a gun. "I need you to get me out of here, Zoe. No one is going to question your food truck leaving. You can come or go as you please. I can't hang around and wait for the police to catch up with me."

I carefully considered my next words. "You're wrong, you know." I put three biscuits into the deep fryer. "*Everyone* is going to question us if we leave before the challenge is done. Have you seen the police officers outside the rope in the crowd? We aren't getting out of here until it's over."

He glanced around the kitchen. "Fine. I'll be your extra team member until we can get out. Don't think about trying anything. I know how this whole thing works. Where is that other guy who was working in here? Who's selling the biscuits?"

"I'm selling the biscuits," Ollie said.

"Okay. You go wait outside until everything is ready." He jammed the gun in my side. "And don't tell *anyone* what's going on if you want Zoe to live to see her prize."

"Just take it easy," Ollie said. "There's no reason for anyone to get hurt."

"You're right. Do what I say, and no one *will* get hurt."

Ollie stared at me as though he was trying to devise a plan.

I nodded. "Go ahead. Open the window and I'll hand out the food."

"What about the other one?"

"You mean our other team member who had to go to the restroom?" I filled in quickly.

"Zoe! I hear you've lost your carrots." Chef Art walked right into the middle of our mess.

"You're the other team member?" Marsh looked at him in surprise, probably taking in the white suit that didn't look much like something anyone would cook in. "Get in here. Ollie, you get out. Keep in mind that Zoe will die before I do if you give me away."

Ollie agreed and went outside.

"What's this?" Chef Art asked. "What's going on? I don't recall this being part of the challenge. Who are you, sir?"

"I'm the new Biscuit Bowl team member." Marsh smiled, painfully shoving the gun deeper into my side. "Let's all get our aprons on and do some cooking, shall we?"

"That's not my job today. I'm a sponsor. It would look bad. You two sort out your problems. Zoe—win the race."

"You're not going *anywhere*," Marsh told him. "Didn't you hear what I told the giant? I have a gun in Zoe's side. You do what I tell you until we can leave. You got it?"

Chef Art put down his cane and took off his jacket. "I think I understand now. What do you need me to do, Zoe?"

I tried to stay calm. Panic wouldn't help. My heart was racing, and the greasy breakfast I'd eaten was threatening to come up.

"Ollie was going to fill the sweet biscuit bowls." I forced my tone to sound normal as I pulled up another basket of fried biscuit bowls and put another one down. "I'll bake biscuits and fry them. Marsh will put the barbecue into the savory biscuit bowls."

"I don't have to do anything," he told me. "I'm the one with the gun, remember?"

"Not putting out any biscuit bowls will give you away,"

I snarled. "There are television cameras, producers, and assistants crawling around here like ants on a watermelon. You made Ollie leave. I need your help to get through this."

"All right," he said. "Just don't forget that I could kill you."

Chef Art glanced at me with his white eyebrows raised. "You need to hire better team members."

We were getting the first biscuit bowls ready to go in the awkward silence. It was almost seven A.M. I was trying to think of something clever to do that could save us all—well—mostly me since the gun was on me. Nothing came to mind right away.

Ollie lifted and secured the order window from outside. "Look who I found waiting outside to see you, Zoe." His voice was only weirder than the look on his face. "Your mom and dad are here to wish you well."

"Hi, Zoe!" Daddy waved and grinned at me. "I think you're going to win this thing. It's been exciting hearing about it."

"I'm glad you're home again." My mother was dressed, as always, in an expensive suit, lavender this time, her blond hair perfectly framing her determined face.

"Hi, Mom." I smiled. "Hi, Daddy. It's good to see you. We're *very* busy."

Daddy looked surprised when he realized Chef Art was in the kitchen with me. "I had no idea you were getting help from a celebrity."

Chef Art smiled. "I want to see Zoe win the race, too."

"Do you have time for your old man to come in there and give you a quick hug for good luck?"

Daddy was taken aback when Chef Art and I both shouted "No!" at the same time.

He glanced at my mother, who shrugged and walked away.

"Okay," he said. "We'll see you later for your victory dinner."

"Okay." I waved and smiled like a trained monkey. "Bye-bye."

When they were gone, Marsh wasn't happy. "We're too exposed this way. Close the window."

"I have to get the biscuit bowls through here," Ollie said. "Read the rules. If we don't do what they say, we'll be disqualified."

"Like I care." He shrugged.

"You will," he promised. "Didn't you notice the *big* interviews they do with the food trucks that are disqualified? They want you to go off about how unfair everything is. I can show you the YouTube video from when Our Daily Bread was disqualified."

I knew there wasn't a rule about serving the food through the window, and no YouTube video. Everything would be aired with the show, whenever that would be. But it was a good play on Ollie's part. Marsh wasn't familiar with the rules. He didn't know Ollie was lying.

"Okay. Whatever it takes to get me out of here."

"Right now, it takes getting these biscuit bowls out on the street so he can sell them." I handed Ollie my cell phone, which doubled as a credit card machine, and gave him twenty dollars in cash to start with. "Good luck. Sorry I don't have anyone to run the food out to you."

"That's okay." He glared at Marsh. "Just be careful."

"We will," Chef Art promised.

We made more biscuit bowls after he was gone. It seemed he was back very quickly. With everything that had been happening, we were behind on having our food ready.

"Come on," Ollie urged. "Come on! Delia is out here hardly trying to sell anything and selling more than we are."

"We have a few *unusual* problems," I reminded him. "Let's worry about getting through this. If we lose, we lose."

"Don't even say that," Chef Art said. "We can still win this thing."

There was a knock on the back door before it opened.

"Hey, I'm from the producer. He wants to know if you're up for having a crew in here taping while you work."

Beneath the glasses—which I think she got from Chef Art's assistant—and the food truck race gear was Detective Patti Latoure. She was smiling, but I saw her sharp blue eyes zero in on the gun Marsh was holding.

THIRTY-FIVE

I knew from the look on Ollie's face that he'd gone to get her. I hoped they had a plan that didn't involve me getting shot to get Marsh out of the food truck.

"Biscuit Bowls?" Ollie said. "Are any ready yet?"

That took Marsh's attention away from Patti, who was still in the doorway pretending to wait for my answer.

"I have one tray of sweet ready." I handed it to him. As I put the tray up to the window, Marsh's hand moved with me. I didn't see any way to get out of this mess.

"What about the cameras?" Patti was as persistent as the real assistants.

"Sure. That's fine. Whatever it takes." I glanced at her. She winked when Marsh was looking away.

"I'll be right back. Don't do anything different. We want to catch you off guard, at least as far as the audience is concerned."

It seemed as though there was a kind of code in her words. I hoped so anyway. They wanted us to act normal so they could catch Marsh off guard. I held it together by focusing on what I was doing.

"You should've said no," Marsh said when Patti was gone.

"Tell her when she gets back," I said. "I don't care. I've had TV cameras all but rammed down my throat the last few days."

"It's too late now. We'll have to make it work."

I could see the fear in Marsh's eyes as he glanced around the kitchen. He had to know there was little or no chance that he was going to get out of here. I hoped we both survived his run for freedom.

Chef Art caught my eye as he handed me a filled biscuit bowl. He glanced toward a large, sharp knife that was on the edge of the cutting block beside him.

I wasn't sure what he expected me to do with it. Knives didn't stop bullets. I wasn't an expert knife person. Yes, there was a knife at hand—several, in fact. What good were they?

I shook my head in what I hoped was an imperceptible movement.

"What?" Marsh picked up on it. "Are you two plotting something? Don't forget this gun could go either way."

And that's where he made his mistake.

He swung his body with the movement of the gun toward Chef Art and completely away from me. The knife Chef Art had tried so hard to get me to notice was too far away for me to easily pick up. I would've had to lunge for it across Marsh.

Chef Art's cane was closer. I grabbed it as Marsh was swinging back toward me, the gun pointed toward the open food window. I used it to rap his gun hand as hard as I could.

In that moment of surprise, he dropped the gun and roared out his pain, putting his hand to his mouth.

"*Oww!* What are you doing, Zoe?"

I dropped to the floor and yelled for Chef Art to do the same. It took him what seemed like forever to get down there beside me. Marsh was still standing, nursing his hurt hand.

"Put the gun down, Detective Marsh." Patti stood in the open doorway with another uniformed officer.

Two more officers appeared in the food window. All of their guns were trained on Marsh.

He slowly raised his arms. "I don't have a gun. And I think Zoe broke my hand."

- - - - - - -

The uniformed officers led Marsh away. Patti took the gun from my hand and smiled at me. "You okay?"

"I'm fine. A little shook up, but I'll survive."

"Good. I'm gonna need a statement from you about this." She glanced at Chef Art and Ollie. "Both of you, too."

"But not yet," Chef Art said. "We haven't lost the race yet."

"I'll leave you to get back to work." Patti put the gun into a plastic bag. "We'll talk when this is over."

"Thanks for rescuing us," I said before I turned back to three ruined biscuit bowls in the deep fryer.

"It looked to me like you had the whole thing in hand," she said. "Good luck, Zoe."

Chef Art stayed with us in the Biscuit Bowl until a real producer's assistant came by to tell us that Shut Up and Eat had already sold their quota. Ollie put his head down on the order window. Chef Art rolled his eyes and mumbled a lot.

We stopped working and went out to the stage with Bobbie, Delia, and Uncle Saul.

Chef Art complained about the circumstances and told everyone what had happened to us. "You can't expect someone to win a race with a killer threatening their lives. I demand a redo. I *am* a sponsor."

But nothing he said made any difference. In fact, Patrick Ferris joked that he wished they'd thought of putting a stranger with a gun in each food truck for one of the challenges. He was only sorry there was no video footage of Marsh holding a gun on me.

I just realized—there was no sign of Allison. I'd been

too involved with everything else going on to notice that she never came back. I complained about that since it violated the direct words of the challenge.

"She didn't come back to me, either," Bobbie argued. "It's not like she was any help. When I catch that girl, we're gonna have words, believe me."

The sponsors and producers talked it over and decided that even though Bobbie's daughter had left, technically, I had help from Chef Art and Marsh, which could've been a violation of the challenge, too. They didn't care that Marsh had held us hostage.

In the end, the big check went to Bobbie Shields of Shut Up and Eat. She cried and wailed on stage, telling everyone about the money she was going to use to put her daughter through college.

I stood on the street with Ollie, Uncle Saul, and Delia. We were all holding hands and trying not to cry—at least I was trying not to cry.

"There's still the Caribbean cruise," Delia reminded me.

Like I could leave my business long enough to do something like that at this stage.

We'd tried as hard as we could, and made it through some difficult circumstances. I was happy for Bobbie, in a way, even though Ollie told me I was crazy.

So that was the interview I gave as the loser of the Mobile challenge.

It was embarrassing that I'd lost the challenge at home. I knew I'd hear about it for months to come. No matter. I knew Monday morning I would get up early and go out in the Biscuit Bowl to keep working toward my dream.

That was good enough for me.

- - - - - - -

Miguel was released from the hospital on Saturday morning. The police were done with his Mercedes, so I called Cole and he took me to the impound lot to pick up the car.

Crème Brûlée was difficult that morning, probably still trying to get over the trauma of the race. He didn't want to eat and kept rolling around on the bed when I tried to get him up.

That didn't stop me from spending a few extra minutes getting dressed up and coaxing my curls into doing what I wanted them to do. I wore a short white skirt and white and red striped top that looked great on me. I used a little extra eye makeup and wore a pair of white heels.

I looked at myself in the mirror at the diner and approved. I was hoping, if Miguel felt well enough, that we could have lunch out—alone together. We could always do dinner later.

It took forever to get him released from the hospital. We sat around and talked about everything that had happened.

"I know it didn't end up the way you wanted." He held my hand. "But I hope you don't regret it."

"Not at all. I'm sorry about what happened to you, but I hope you don't regret it."

He kissed me. "Not at all."

Finally, the nurse came in with his release papers. He had to endure the trip to the front door in a wheelchair, but he'd already told me that he wanted to have lunch.

My heart was fluttering in anticipation of a tiny little booth at my favorite café, Lavender Blue. The food was very good there, and I knew the manager would give us a quiet place off by ourselves.

"I like your car," I told him as he got into the passenger side. "It's older, but it's classy."

"Are you equating me with my car?" He smiled.

"No. It may only be that I'd like *any* car right now. The Biscuit Bowl can be uncooperative sometimes."

"What did you have in mind for lunch?"

"I really love Lavender Blue. Would that be okay with you?"

"Sure. It may sound corny, but as long as we're together. You know what I mean?"

I knew my face was a little pink at his words. I didn't care. Pink looked good on me. I squeezed his hand and headed across town for the café.

When we got there, there was a big sign in the window that said *Closed*. I didn't know why it was there. The café was always open on Saturday.

"I'm sorry. Something must be wrong." I knew the owner lived right upstairs. "I'm going to pop up there and see what's going on."

Miguel waited in the car. He said he wasn't sure if he could do the three flights of stairs. I got to the front door of the café and peeked inside the window. The door flew open and loud voices yelled, "Surprise!"

I took a step backward, having had all the surprises I'd wanted for a while. Miguel was out of the car and behind me, urging me inside.

I saw both of my parents there, also Ollie and Delia. Wonderful smells were coming from the kitchen as Chef Art, in his cooking whites, waved to me.

Uncle Saul came to greet me. "We thought we'd put together a little lunch for *you* since you missed the victory dinner."

I hugged him, and my friend, Lavender, who'd allowed everyone to hold the lunch in her café.

I thanked everyone for being there, and they toasted me with champagne. I toasted them back, and the party really got started.

Patti was there with Macey Helms. They were off duty and drinking with the rest of us.

"That was a brave thing you did in the food truck yesterday," Patti said. "Stupid, but brave."

"All's well that ends well," I quoted. "Did Marsh ever admit to killing Alex? He was confessing up a storm in the food truck."

"Yes," Helms said. "He tried to drag Tina into it, but I guess she was smart enough to stay away from him, except for that kiss I saw. Marsh was infatuated with her, which was why he killed Alex. He thought he could still have the money and have her, too. At least until the end when she told him to stay away from her. Then she became a liability as well."

"So she's going to testify against him," Patti said. "You broke Marsh's hand with that cane, by the way. But he's claiming police brutality."

I put *my* hand over my mouth in surprise. "I *broke* his hand? I had no idea."

"Yeah, well considering he's up for the death penalty, I guess it's not too big a deal." Helms saluted me with her champagne. "Sorry you lost the race, though, Zoe."

"Me, too." I squeezed Miguel's hand. "But that's okay. I still have the Biscuit Bowl."

They moved away, and Miguel and I circulated through the crowd. Cole was there, too. I had a chance to introduce Miguel to him, and thank Cole again for his help.

"I know this wasn't what you had in mind," Miguel said when we had a brief moment alone right before lunch was served.

"True, but we'll get to that later."

My cell phone buzzed in my handbag. Miguel excused himself to go to the restroom. I glanced at the text I'd received. It was my invitation to food truck rally during carnival festivities in February. To say I was excited about it would've been a terrible understatement.

I held up my glass again, and the room got quiet. "We're going to the Mardi Gras!"

RECIPES FROM THE BISCUIT BOWL!

- -

We're so excited about selling our biscuit bowls at carnival! We'll be working on new recipes, trying everything until then. It's going to be hard to come up with food as exciting as that event!

Here are some of the recipes from the Sweet Magnolia Food Truck Race!

Spiced Peaches

Spiced peaches were a hit for us during the food truck race. They aren't hard to make and have a cool, delicious zing!

   2 cups water
   2 cups sugar
   1 tablespoon whole allspice

1 tablespoon whole cloves
4 three-inch cinnamon sticks
10 peaches, about 2 pounds
1 small square cheesecloth

Mix water and sugar in a heavy saucepan.

Tie allspice and cloves in the cheesecloth. Add this and the cinnamon sticks to the water and sugar.

Cover and boil for 5 minutes.

Peel the peaches while the water and sugar are cooking. After the syrup is done boiling, remove cinnamon sticks and cheesecloth bag. Drop the peaches into boiling syrup, a few at a time.

Simmer peaches until tender, about 5 minutes.

Delicious with vanilla ice cream!

Barbecue Chicken

Uncle Saul doesn't like to share his recipes, but he's letting me break the rules for this.
  We'll make the barbecue sauce first.

1½ cups dark brown sugar
1¼ cups tomato sauce
½ cup red wine vinegar
1 tablespoon Worcestershire sauce
2½ teaspoons ground mustard
2 teaspoons paprika
1½ teaspoons salt
1 teaspoon black pepper

Measure and add all ingredients to a large bowl and mix well. When the sugar has dissolved, everything should be mixed. Set this aside until you're ready with the chicken.

   Shredded or pulled chicken:
   2 pounds boneless, skinless chicken
   3 cups barbecue sauce
   1 clove garlic, minced

Trim off any excess fat from the chicken. Place in a pan or slow cooker.

Combine the homemade barbecue sauce with the minced garlic and pour the sauce over the chicken. Cook until the chicken is tender and falling apart.

Remove the chicken and shred with a fork. Return the chicken to the pot and stir. The sauce will thicken up in about 10 minutes.

YUM!

White Icing

This icing is good on biscuit bowls and almost anything else!

   2 cups confectioners' sugar
   2 tablespoons softened butter
   1 teaspoon vanilla
   1 tablespoon milk

Mix the confectioners' sugar, butter, and vanilla together.

Add half the milk to start. Stir in to make a thick glaze. Add more milk by drops to reach the right consistency. You don't want it to be runny.

Spread or pour immediately over cooled pastries. The icing will form a crust and harden as it cools.

How to Make Biscuit Bowls!

I'm sharing my trade secret here for those of you who can't get to Mobile and get one from me!

  2 cups white flour
  ¼ teaspoon baking soda
  1 tablespoon baking powder
  1 teaspoon salt
  6 tablespoons butter or vegetable shortening
  1 cup buttermilk

Preheat oven to 450 degrees. Combine the dry ingredients. Cut the butter into the flour mixture until it forms coarse balls. Add the buttermilk until the mixture is slightly wet. Turn the dough out on a floured board. Gently roll or pat dough until it is about ½ inch thick. Fold the dough three more times then carefully press down to about 1 inch thick.

Here's where the normal biscuit recipe changes for biscuit bowls.

Spray vegetable shortening into a muffin tin. Use a cutter to cut circles of dough. Place these circles into the openings in the tin, pressing down the center gently. Bake for about 10 minutes until brown. The biscuit dough will rise around the circle, leaving a well in the middle for the filling.

The biscuits don't have to be deep-fried right away, but don't wait more than a few hours. The freshest biscuits will make the best biscuit bowls. If you can't use them right away, freeze them for later.

To deep-fry, simply drop the biscuits into a deep fryer set on high for 2 minutes. You want them to be crisp but not greasy. Be sure to use good-quality vegetable oil in your deep fryer.

FROM NATIONAL BESTSELLING AUTHOR

J. J. COOK

DEATH ON
Eat Street

A Biscuit Bowl Food Truck Mystery

Struggling restauranteur Zoe Chase turns an old Airstream into a food truck, and in no time she's dishing
out classic Southern food throughout Mobile, Alabama.
But when the owner of a competing food truck winds
up dead inside her rolling restaurant, Zoe needs to find
the real killer before she gets burned.

Includes recipes!

jjcook.net
facebook.com/authorsj.j.cook
facebook.com/TheCrimeSceneBooks
penguin.com

M1558T0814

That Old Flame of Mine

A Sweet Pepper Fire Brigade Mystery

Meet Stella Griffin, former Chicago fire fighter turned small-town fire chief. When Stella's dear friend Tory dies after her gingerbread-style Victorian house is set ablaze, Stella suspects arson and foul play. What she doesn't suspect is that the ghost of Eric Gamlyn, Sweet Pepper's old fire chief, is about to help her smoke out a killer.

PRAISE FOR THE SERIES

"Dark family secrets, a delicious mystery—
and a ghost. What reader could ask for more!"
—Casey Daniels

*Includes delicious hot and
sweet pepper recipes!*